Praise for

'Nicola Gill never disapp[oints...]
always satisfying'
Anstey Harris, author of *Where We Belong*

'A beautiful read full of heart and depth'
Nina Pottell, *Prima Magazine*

'I love everything Nicola writes. I'm a real fan girl! Her books are full of heart, real characters and hope and are a fantastic read – and *That's Just Perfect* is no exception!'
Olivia Beime, author of *Three Nights in Italy*

'Laughter, tears, and a whole lot of life lesions – this book has everything'
Gillian Harvey, author of *The Bordeaux Club*

'A heart-rending book that's very funny and poignant'
Victoria Dowd, author of *Murder Most Cold*

'Three generations, three brilliantly-drawn characters, three lives unravelling in different ways – Nicola Gill brings her beautifully drawn characters together with warmth and wit. Laugh out loud funny yet poignant at heart, this is feelgood fiction at its best'
Frances Quinn, author of *That Bonesetter Woman*

'*That's Just Perfect* is a gorgeous tale of mess-ups, second chances and being perfectly imperfect. So relatable, real, and uplifting. Another gem from Nicola Gill'
Jessica Ryn, author of *The Imperfect Art of Caring*

'*That's Just Perfect* has all the elements readers have come to expect from Nicola Gill's novels: warm, loveable and relatable characters facing tangible dilemmas, written with heart and humour on every page. The messaging about authenticity is beautifully executed, and the ending deeply satisfying. It's a gorgeous book which left me feeling all is well with the world'
Kate Storey, author of *The Memory Library*

'Nicola Gill has done it again. This wonderful story about Emily, her father Ed and their mutual life regrets is very funny, uplifting but also moving. Nicola places her flawed-but-lovable characters in impossible situations, and the ensuing story is always credible and a delight. A real treat of a book. Buy it'
Eleni Kyriacou, author of *The Unspeakable Acts of Zina Pavlou*

'Nicola Gill has a rare talent for skilfully conjuring wonderfully complex, relatable characters which her readers are rooting for all the way, despite, or perhaps because of, all their imperfections. I loved this book so much, and just had to know what was going to happen, so that my plan to read just one chapter became one more, then one more after that each time I picked up the book. *That's Just Perfect* is full of humour, warmth and I admit, a few happy tears at the end. A perfect holiday, weekend, or indeed, anytime, read!'
Louise Fein, author of *The London Bookshop Affair*

'A cautionary tale about the lies that can so easily fester within fractured families. Hugely readable, utterly relatable and packed with appealing characters, both major and minor'
Sue Teddern, author of *The Pre-Loved Club*

'L.O.L's and heartbreak. I love Nicola Gill's books and she's done it again! I found myself loving these flawed and very real characters. Ed is so real, and Liz's story is completely heart-breaking. You just want to get inside the pages and help her. I cried a little at the end, just before a meeting, so thanks for that Nicola Gill'
Tim Ewins, author of *Tiny Pieces of Enid*

'Absolutely bursting with feeling! Nicola has created three perfectly imperfect characters in Liz, Ed and Emily. It's a wonderfully heartfelt story that is sprinkled with Nicola's humour, and I absolutely loved it!'
Holly McCulloch, author of *The Mix Up*

'Another warm and engaging story from Nicola Gill who always manages to perfectly capture the frustrations and joys of family life. The characters are beautifully drawn – each fighting their own demons, flawed and embattled but eager to restore old relationships and build new ones. Gill handles each storyline sensitively, with trademark humour and compassion in this satisfying treat of a novel'
Nancy Peach, author of *The Mother of All Problems*

'Nicola Gill has such a talent for creating flawed yet incredibly real and likeable characters. I couldn't wait to get back to being in the company of Emily, Ed and Liz. Very

funny and often touching, *That's Just Perfect* is a must read for those wanting an injection of joy'
Charlotte Levin, author of *If I Let You Go*

Also by Nicola Gill

We Are Family
The Neighbours
Swimming for Beginners
That's Just Perfect

NICOLA GILL

IDENTITY CRISIS

First published in the UK in 2025 by Bedford Square Publishers Ltd,
London, UK

bedfordsquarepublishers.co.uk
@bedsqpublishers

© Nicola Gill, 2025

The right of Nicola Gill to be identified as the author of this work has been asserted in accordance with the Copyright, Designs and Patents Act 1988. All rights reserved. No part of this book may be reproduced, stored in or introduced into a retrieval system, or transmitted, in any form or by any means (electronic, mechanical, photocopying, recording or otherwise) without the written permission of the publishers.

Any person who does any unauthorised act in relation to this publication may be liable to criminal prosecution and civil claims for damages.
A CIP catalogue record for this book is available from the British Library.
This is a work of fiction. Names, characters, places, and incidents either are the product of the author's imagination or are used fictitiously, and any resemblance to actual persons, living or dead, businesses, companies, events or locales is entirely coincidental.

ISBN
978-1-83501-288-8 (Paperback)
978-1-83501-289-5 (eBook)

2 4 6 8 10 9 7 5 3 1

Typeset in Garamond MT Std by Palimpsest Book Production Limited,
Falkirk, Stirlingshire
Printed in Great Britain by CPI Group (UK) Ltd, Croydon CR0 4YY

The manufacturer's authorised representative in the EU for product safety is Easy Access System Europe, Mustamäe tee 50, 10621 Tallinn, Estonia
gpsr.requests@easproject.com

To Hedy-anne. For being nothing like Kerri with an 'i'.
To Debra. For being my unofficial Sales Director.
And to you both for being wonderful friends.

Chapter One

October 2023

Lots of celebrities moan it's hard being famous but I don't think they can know what hard is. Look at me now – surrounded by people who are gazing at me as if I could walk on water, laughing uproariously if I say something even vaguely funny, grateful for a couple of minutes of my time. *Hard?*

I've spent the day shooting a TV commercial around the corner from Selfridges and have decided to pop in on my way home. I'm nearly out of Charlotte Tilbury Pillow Talk lipstick – a situation that demands immediate and decisive action.

As soon as I entered the shop, I was aware of eyes upon me. Some people stared openly while others tried to look as if they were uninterested and insouciant – as if they see celebrities every day. I made my way through the perfume department, competing scents assaulting my nostrils as I made sure to keep a neutral expression pinned to my face. You can't go around grinning like a loon, especially when you're on your own, but woe betide you if your resting face tips even slightly into bitch.

Two assistants swoop as soon as I get to the brown and gold counter and another, who is doing a smoky eye on a woman in a denim jumpsuit, stops with her make-up brush hovering mid-air.

'May I help you?' says an assistant with 'invisible' braces and poker-straight blond hair.

'Don't worry, Sienna,' says her dark-haired colleague. 'I've got this.'

The two of them have an unspoken battle with their perfectly made-up eyes before the blonde concedes defeat and scuttles back behind the magic skin collection where she rearranges the display with more force than is strictly necessary.

The brunette gives me a beaming smile and asks how she can help me today. I get the impression that her help would extend to running to the food hall and grabbing me a coffee if I was to suggest that. Instead, I ask for the lipstick.

'It really suits you, the Pillow Talk,' the assistant says, blushing furiously.

'Thanks.'

There's a conflict raging behind her eyes and I imagine she's weighing up whether she should say something or whether that's unprofessional.

Her hand shakes as she rings up my purchase. 'My mum loves you,' she blurts out, as she passes me the little yellow-and-black bag she has crammed with freebies. (Side note: what an irony it is that the people who least need freebies are the ones most likely to receive them.) 'And so do I. My whole family are fans of *You've Got It*. We never miss an episode.'

I smile graciously. 'That's lovely to hear! Have a great evening.'

The assistant looks as if she might cry. 'You too.'

As I walk away, I know I'm being watched by several people in the vicinity. The woman in the denim jumpsuit with one smoky eye and one naked one is whispering to the assistant doing her make-up.

Meanwhile a woman with lots of carrier bags is being propelled towards me by the man she is with. 'We thought it was you but we weren't a hundred per cent sure,' she says, her words falling into each other before a staccato laugh of a full stop. 'My boyfriend said there was no way you would buy your own make-up, that you'd have a stylist to do that for you. But, I said, "No, she's very down to earth." I can just tell, you see.'

I laugh.

'We love *You've Got It*,' the woman gushes.

'Yeah,' adds her boyfriend who has now sidled up alongside her. 'Best talent show on TV.'

'Best show on TV,' his girlfriend corrects.

One of the assistants at a nearby make-up counter is staring at me in a manner that suggests she'll soon be asked to draw me from memory. I bet she's thinking I look older and fatter than she'd expect. I can imagine her talking to friends later: *I thought the camera was supposed to add ten pounds.*

'I actually cried when Josh was voted off the show,' the man says.

'Josh was a sweetie,' I say.

I catch the eye of a security guy by the door. I've got you, he says with a look, let me know if this all gets too much.

My posse has been joined by a group of middle-aged women with lilting Irish accents. One of them says that Josh deserved to go. Yes, he was nice but it's a talent show and he had no talent. Her favourite was Ellie. She had a gorgeous voice.

This sets off a heated disagreement. How can she say Josh had no talent? Ellie did have a gorgeous voice but she didn't have an ounce of Josh's charisma. He's got that 'it factor'.

I don't embroil myself in the debate. Experience has taught me that it's best not to say too much.

'Excuse me,' says a man in an ill-advised red jumper that makes my skin itch just looking at it. 'While this lot argue it out, please may I get your autograph?'

'Of course.' I take the pen from his shaking hands. *All the best,* I write in big loopy handwriting, *Jenna Cox x*

I hand back the piece of paper. I can see he's delighted. And so am I. It's the first time I've nailed her handwriting.

Chapter Two

May 2023

Is there anything crueller than struggling to shift post-baby weight when there is no baby? And there's a woman on the leg-curl machine who keeps staring at me. I imagine she thinks I don't fit with the gym's aesthetic – that my cheap black leggings and baggy cotton T-shirt aren't de rigueur. No doubt she'd find me slightly more acceptable if I was wearing one of the cute matching sets I have from Lululemon or Nike. But they're all tucked away in a drawer at home because they're a bit, shall we say, snug.

I focus on my leg curls and try to ignore Little Ms Sticky Beak. I was in a bad mood before I even got here. I've written a grand total of four hundred and seven words today, which is pretty pathetic given I've had no freelance work so have had eight hours to devote to my book. I used to manage more than that in a day when I worked full-time as an Advertising Creative Director and I only had my commute to write. But then I used to manage a lot of things.

The gym is doing little to improve my state of mind. Not only is my ragged breath and puce face a reminder that my fitness levels have nosedived, but this room has all the warmth and personality of an aircraft hangar. Think serried ranks of black torture machines in a grey windowless basement where an eye-pricking floral air freshener is failing to mask the smell of stale sweat. Someone obviously thought it would be a good idea to 'lift' the space with neon motivational quotes in a swirly typeface:

The only bad workout is one you didn't do.
Yesterday you said tomorrow.
A winner is just a loser who tried one more time.

Pass the sick bag.

I move to a rowing machine, glaring at a man who has just got off and failed to wipe it down despite sweating profusely over it. He doesn't even have the good grace to look embarrassed as he sees me fetch the antibacterial spray.

What did they say in the induction session about rowing technique? Remember not to hunch, engage your core, lead with your legs. I pull the handle towards my ribs or where I assume my ribs must still be.

The woman is staring at me again. Rude.

I finish on the rowing machine and head towards the treadmill. One of the many things I dislike about the gym is the noises. Heavy breathing, metal plates clanging together, PTs bellowing at people, 'Gimme one more,' 'Let's do this,' 'Believe in the possible'. And the grunting. Oh God, the grunting. Today, that's not even the most annoying noise though. Sweaty man has a disposable plastic water bottle, which he keeps slurping from with such force that it collapses in on itself before slowly and noisily crackling back into its original shape when he stops drinking (wiping his mouth with the back of his hand every time).

All four treadmills are in use. I'm actually happy to wait, not only because it gives me a chance to get my breath back but because two women who are doing plank nearby are engaged in a rather intriguing conversation. 'He told me he loves me but it was during sex so it doesn't count, right?'

'Right.'

Is that the rule? I had no idea. Not that it matters to me. No one will be declaring their love for me anytime soon during coitus or otherwise.

Stare-y woman is on an exercise bike now. She glances over constantly.

'So I haven't said it back obviously.'

'Obviously.'

A man gets off a treadmill and I get on. I couldn't help but notice how pleased my mother sounded when I told her I was going to the gym. 'That'll be lovely,' she said, all sing-song voice and children's TV presenter in tone. My friend Meg laughed when I told her. 'She just wants you to be happy.'

Happy.

I jog slowly and unenthusiastically. The woman next to me in the pink leopard print two-piece is running unfeasibly fast, her high ponytail swishing through the air. Everything about her, from her tits to her demeanour, is perky.

A personal trainer is holding up pads for a woman to punch. For a gym activity it actually looks kind of fun and the woman is punching for all she's worth. I bet she's imagining everyone who has annoyed her recently. I'd have punches for lots of people. My ex-husband and his annoying Instagram posts (#solucky #lovinglife #goodtimes); the bus driver who pulled away despite the fact he had definitely seen me running; the woman on the Tube with the little plastic strawberries dotted all over her hairband. What are you, six?

My mother told me I seem angry a lot of the time nowadays.
'No, I'm not,' I snapped.

I head for the chest press machine, only realising when I've already sat down that stare-y woman is on the neighbouring machine. Never mind, I shall ignore her.

Directly in front of me is a sign that reads: *One last push!*

It makes me think of a labour ward and I choke back tears.

'Excuse me,' stare-y woman says suddenly.

I turn my head towards her, squashing down a wave of irritation. It's bad enough being here without people talking to me. 'It's you, isn't it?'

What on earth is she on about?

'I'm such a fan.'

My heart lifts. Unless you're a big name like Marian Keyes or Stephen King, you don't get recognised as an author. It's certainly never happened to me before.

'I thought it was you but then I told myself you wouldn't be somewhere like this.'

'What?'

'You'd be somewhere much more swanky where you won't get papped.'

Papped?

'Wait until I tell my sister that I saw Jenna Cox in my gym.'

Jenna Cox? Reflexively, I glance at myself the mirror. Do I look like her? I had a meeting this morning so, for once, am sporting both make-up and clean hair, but I still don't think it's a comparison the celebrity would be flattered by. 'Umm, I'm not Jenna Cox.'

The woman's face falls. 'Really?'

'Really.'

'That's a pity. I did think you were a little... er, bigger.' She adjusts the strap of her sports bra. 'I was so excited to tell my sister I was in the gym with Jenna Cox.'

'Sorry.' I don't know why I'm apologising but the woman looks so disappointed.

'I really thought you were her.'

'So—' I'm not apologising again. I mean it's not my fault I'm me, is it?

Three weeks later, I'm scrolling for something to watch on TV when I stumble across *Faking It*.

> Step into the bizarre world of celebrity doppelgängers and find out what it's really like to make a living being someone else, from Bucks Fizz to Harrison Ford to Cheryl Cole.

I pour myself a glass of wine and press play. The owner of the lookalike agency, himself a Gary Barlow impersonator, explains he has all sorts of people on his books from Kylie to David Brent to Jesus. 'Although there's not much call for Jesus nowadays.'

The camera cuts to a tribute night in a student union where 'Taylor Swift' is performing. She's actually pretty good although that's wasted on most of the students because they're so wasted.

When that woman in the gym thought I was Jenna Cox, I admit I was flattered. I glance in the mirror, something I generally try to avoid these days, and see a woman who wears life's (many) disappointments and looks every day of her forty-one years. So, being mistaken for a glamorous celebrity was a nice ego boost. Even if, when I told my brother, he asked if she had a white stick. (Ha bloody ha, David, that's so original.) It never crossed my mind that any resemblance could be monetised and it seems an odd way to make a living, although, granted, as a novelist, I'm not one to talk. I literally make up shit for a living.

A Jamie Oliver lookalike is taking part in a photo shoot. He's nailed the body language but sounds disconcertingly posh when he opens his mouth.

'Can you cook?' the interviewer asks.

'Jamie' lets out a braying laugh. 'Not a sausage. Oops, unintentional pun.'

I go to take a sip of my wine and realise the glass is empty. On the way to the kitchen, I stop in front of the hallway mirror. Do I really look like Jenna Cox? I mean, not tonight obviously with my make-up free face but, on a good day, maybe there's a resemblance? We're both little with reddish-brown hair and green eyes.

I go back to the sofa and un-pause the TV. A gaggle of Victoria Beckhams are comparing notes about their experiences. We then meet a B-tech Ryan Gosling, a David Brent who sounds exactly like him and an ABBA tribute band who've been working together for twenty-seven years. In real life 'Agnetha' is married to 'Frida'.

Realising once again I've somehow finished my wine, I head back towards the kitchen, again pausing in front of the mirror. I google photos of Jenna and hold one up next to my face. I definitely do look a bit like her. Well, her older, uglier sister at any rate. It helps if I brush my fringe to the side and smile so widely it hurts. Jenna has a *big* smile.

Without thinking too much about what I'm doing, I fetch my make-up bag. Jenna favours winged eyeliner and a nude lip. I'm a bit out of practice but manage to do something semi-passable.

What on earth am I doing? This is what happens when you have two large glasses of wine on an empty stomach. And spend too much time on your own.

I head back to the sofa, my wine glass refilled. On *Faking It,* a voice coach is trying to teach a reluctant 'Kylie' how to sing. 'Hold your diaphragm.'

My mind flashes back to being in youth theatre when I was a teenager. I never wanted to be an actor, well, not really, but youth theatre was so much fun and transformed me from being a shy kid to someone who could talk to anyone. We had incredible teachers too – West End choreographers and directors and singers. The voice coach on the programme reminds me of Jules, one of ours. She has the same indomitable patience, the same ability to find a speck of something and turn it into a positive. 'That "luckyyyyyy" was spot on.'

I was actually okay at youth theatre, not one of the stars but pretty competent. I could project my voice, remember lines and dance in time. I was also an excellent mimic. 'You've an ear for accents,' Jules said. 'A right little parrot.'

I pull up a YouTube clip of Jenna Cox presenting *You've Got It*. 'And now let's give it up for the one and only Josh Nolan.'

'And now,' I say. 'Let's give it up for the one and only Josh Nolan.'

Rubbish. Perhaps my parroting skills are dead? And anyway, what does it matter? It's not like I'm going to get work as a lookalike. I already have a job. Two jobs if you count my sporadic freelance copywriting. My main focus is being a novelist though. *Your main focus?* scoffs my laptop from the corner of the room. *Would hate to see how you do with something you're not focused on.*

'Let's give it up for the one and only Josh Nolan,' I say. A little better. I try again elongating all the vowels.

I pad into the kitchen where I slosh some more wine into the glass. This is definitely my last one.

I go back to *Faking It*. 'Agnetha' and 'Frida' are working side by side in their suburban garden. They look quite different without the sequins and the blue eyeshadow but then, don't we all?

I drink the rest of my wine and google lookalike agencies in London. There are loads of them.

The 'Beckhams' attend a wedding, 'Tom Jones' does a sixtieth birthday party and 'Johnny Depp' moans about how most of his work has dried up. *Most?*

I open the camera app and look at myself. I suppose I could pass for Jenna Cox, especially with my fringe swept to the side.

A 'Camilla' is earnestly telling the interviewer she has worked with five different Charleses over the years. Two of them are now in 'a better place'. She does an awkward little laugh.

I snap a couple of pictures of myself and fill in the contact form of the first lookalike agency that came up. I know I'll never hear back from them, of course.

Chapter Three

April 2021

I have made it out of the house. I even remembered to take my slippers off.

It's a ridiculously perfect day outside, all sunshine and cloudless blue skies. Fury bubbles up in my throat: How dare you, world? Why are you acting like everything is fine?

My intention is to go for a walk, I am not sure where to. Dr Asen posited that I have been 'doing so much better recently' (everything is relative) and it would be 'good to get outside' if I feel able to.

People don't seem to be staring at me so I keep putting one foot in front of the other. I see a number three bus and decide on a whim I will go into town.

On the bus, I start to sweat. This was a mistake. Too much, too soon.

I catch sight of my reflection in the window and it's not a pleasing sight. My complexion is grey and porridge-y, my hair wild and unbrushed. Did I take a shower this morning? I can't remember now.

What am I even going to do in town? Have a look round Liberty? Try on some clothes in Zara. Pretend to be normal.

I stay on the bus. Almost everyone around me is staring at a phone screen and I realise that my phone is still lying on my bedside table. Good. I don't want to talk to anyone. Or read their messages: *How are you doing? Hope you're okay. Thinking of you.*

Regent Street is heaving with people. Tourists who weave across the pavements and stop dead in front of furious-looking locals who *have places to be*.

My mouth is dry and I squash down waves of nausea.

A man outside Hamleys blows a giant bubble in my direction. I try to smile but it feels more like a grimace.

I used to work five minutes away from here. It crosses my mind I could pop in and say hello but, of course, that's a stupid idea. I'm not sure my former colleagues would even recognise me. Where is the designer handbag and the no make-up make-up? What happened to the glossy bob and the easy laugh?

I will go for a coffee and a sandwich, that's what people do. Also, I can't remember the last time I ate or drank.

I stand in Pret wondering if the lighting was always this bright; this harsh. I pick things up and then put them down again, hating myself all the time. This is what you've become: a woman who can't decide between a meatball wrap or a BLT.

I stand in the queue clutching my sandwich (tuna and cucumber, a late entrant into the competition for the World's Biggest Decision).

A couple make their way slowly down the stairs, carrying a buggy between them. The man comes first, walking backwards and the woman clutches the handles of the buggy, her eyes never leaving the sleeping baby dressed in yellow polka-dot dungarees. I press my nails into my palms and breathe in through my nose and out through my mouth.

When I get to the front of the queue, an unfeasibly smiley woman says that will be £4.50 please. I go to get my purse from my pocket but it's not there. Sweat beads on my forehead as I fumble in the other pocket. I find my keys, a battered looking lip balm and an old shopping list: *milk, cucumber, tomatoes, cheese, loo rolls.* There is no purse though. I must have had a debit card to pay for the bus but now I can't find it. Did I pay for the bus? A school trip was getting on at the same time as me and it was chaos.

I'm not entirely sure what happens next. One minute, I am rummaging in my pockets and then there's this awful animalistic howling that I suddenly realise is coming from me.

The woman behind the counter isn't smiling anymore and people are moving further and further away from me. And I want to scream: I wasn't always like this. I WASN'T ALWAYS LIKE THIS.

Chapter Four

July 2023

I know more about Jenna Cox than people I've been friends with for twenty years. I've watched everything from her daily appearances on breakfast TV to all four seasons of *You've Got It*. I've read articles, watched interviews, pored over endless photographs. I know she has a sister who's a hairdresser. They grew up in Harrogate, which Jenna will 'always think of as home'. She drinks Earl Grey tea 'by the bucket' but hardly any alcohol because she's a self-confessed lightweight.

I stare at myself in the mirror. I am halfway between me and her. Her immaculately blow-dried hair, her eye make-up (thank God for YouTube tutorials), but my ratty old dressing gown and sour expression. I was shocked when I got a call from Jackie at Fake Faces. I'd completely forgotten emailing her. 'So you wanna be a lookalike?' she said. Did I? The money would come in handy, especially since book two isn't exactly going well and my freelance advertising work is sporadic. But I only contacted Fake Faces on a drunken whim.

Tonight's product launch is my first gig. 'What do I need to do?' I asked Jackie when she told me about the booking.

'Get your photo taken. Smile.'

She made it sound so easy but nerves are coursing around my body and I've been to the loo three times in the last twenty minutes.

I need to try to eat something even though the very thought makes me nauseous. I pop two slices of frozen bread into the toaster forgetting that it has taken to only toasting one side of the bread. *Get toaster fixed* has joined the long to-do list that never gets done. I bet the real Jenna doesn't have to deal with things like broken toasters. And I don't imagine she eats a couple of slices of half-cooked toast for her dinner either. Jenna will have people to do things for her, whether that's repairing domestic appliances or putting a nutritionally balanced meal in front of her. No wonder she's so relentlessly upbeat on Instagram.

I nibble on my bread/toast. For all the differences between my life and Jenna's, there are things we have in common. We're both forty-one, divorced and without kids (although Jenna is child free and I am very much childless).

The phone rings and I jump. When did I become that person? My phone used to ring all the time.

It's my mother. She asks me how I am. I tell her I'm fine and the word hangs between us in all its naked meaninglessness. I know she and Dad worry about me.

'What are you up to?' she says, her voice studiedly casual. Like when she used to pick up my brother and me from school and ask us who we'd sat with at lunch.

'Getting ready to go out.' It's not a lie.

'Lovely!' She can't keep the surprise from her voice. 'With Meg?'

Meg. The friend who has stood by me despite my best efforts. 'No.' I stare at the silver faux-leather trousers hanging on the wardrobe door. 'It's a work thing.' I don't say any more. I haven't told anyone about the lookalike work yet. I don't know why. It's not as if I'm becoming a sex worker or a Tory MP. Still, though.

'How nice.' I know Mum's mind will be in overdrive now. Imagining me having a crowd of new friends, maybe even meeting someone. Moving on, getting better. I guess that's why I don't tell her the truth.

We chat for a couple more minutes, Mum telling me about Terry and Shirley's golden wedding anniversary party and the book she's just read, which is not as good as mine (in her totally unbiased opinion) and how David called yesterday from Australia and she saw the kids on FaceTime and they've got so big.

After saying goodbye to my mum, I finish my make-up. Although it's unseasonably cool for July, I'm sweating and have to keep pausing my attempts at lining my lips to blot my face with a tissue.

I pull on the silver trousers and white shirt I bought especially for tonight. They both come from one of Jenna's favourite shops and have an extra zero on their price tags compared to anything I'd buy myself. But Jenna's look doesn't come cheap and details matter.

I try to picture myself walking into the hotel this evening. Smiling and introducing myself. Do I say. 'I'm Clare' or 'I'm Jenna'? Saliva floods my mouth. I can't do it.

You can't smile and get your photo taken? You're pathetic but you're not that pathetic.

I force myself to breathe and then slip my feet into my new high heels before standing back to look at myself in the mirror. Not bad. I mean, Jenna's mother is never going to mistake me for her but, to most people, I'd pass.

Chapter Five

I've been doing the lookalike work for nearly two months now and still haven't mentioned it to any of my friends and family. I tell myself they haven't asked, which is a nonsense, of course, but it's a lot more palatable than examining the fact I'm slightly embarrassed by my new side hustle.

Not that my 'proper' jobs are exactly a source of pride. I'm a novelist who hasn't published anything for seven long years and a freelance copywriter who does the sort of work that would have seen me wrinkling my nose in disgust when I was the creative director of a top advertising agency. Little did I know when I walked away from that job, leaving behind a corner office stuffed with awards, a company credit card and a team of thirty people that nearly eight years on, I'd still be trying and mostly failing to write my second book. I have had to go cap in hand back to the industry I loftily turned my back on to pick up whatever scraps of work it deigns to bestow on me. I write articles for pet care websites, incontinence pads and 'revolutionary' skincare products like the serum I am supposed to be writing social media posts for today.

I stare at the menacingly blank screen in front of me. To be fair, leaving my day job wasn't total hubris. My first novel topped

The Sunday Times Bestseller List five weeks in a row and outsold household names. The book was everywhere from supermarkets to independent bookshops to the tables in Waterstones. Fat lot of good that is to me now though.

I lean back in my chair, rub my aching neck and stare at the menacing blank white screen. Today's social media posts are for The Leap Agency and, although they are a regular and much needed client of mine, I particularly dislike the people there. They all seem to be about seven years old, and while this is hardly unusual in an ad agency, these ones treat me as I imagine they do the woman who picks up their dirty mugs from their desks and loads them into the dishwasher. A hired hand they'd rather not think too much about.

Get ready to reveal a brighter, younger you—

Delete.

Rosamund and Hattie, the two main account managers I work with at The Leap Agency are a particularly annoying pair. Not only are they both what my mother would refer to as 'pleased with themselves' (no accounting for tastes) but they're spectacularly lazy. Their briefs are long, confused and rambling (er, it's called a brief for a reason, guys) and they think nothing of dumping a project on me and then going AWOL when I need more information. They can't even be bothered to start a new email thread for God's sake, still using the same one they communicated with me on for the last project.

Let's get glowing!

Delete.

It was my now ex-husband Stephen who suggested I give up my creative director job. Wouldn't it be nice for me to be able to focus on my second book instead of having to keep up the insane juggling? Thanks to the advance and royalties from book one, we could manage financially. Plus, Stephen posited, the reduction in stress could only be a good thing. His sister and brother-in-law had years of trying to conceive and the second she cut down on the stress in her life, it just happened. (By that stage, we had been trying for over a year and my internet searches were a catalogue of 'how long does it take to fall pregnant', 'difficulty conceiving' and 'best IVF clinics'. Little did I know, I was worrying about the wrong problem.)

I went into the agency this morning so Rosamund and Hattie could brief me in person.

This consisted of Rosamund reading out the slides of her PowerPoint in a flat monotone and Hattie asking me three times if I was used to doing social media copy. It was all I could do to keep myself from slapping her across her smug little face and telling her that I have a portfolio of award-winning work, and social media posts are something I used to consider beneath me.

Be happier in your own skin—
Delete.

Even when Rosamund and Hattie are being nice, they irritate me. When I told them I was an author, they both simpered that was 'lovely' in the same way you might tell a three-legged dog he was a very good boy. They then told me proudly neither of them were readers. (A piece of information that wasn't exactly a shock.)

I open up the brief and reread it.

Lumiere serum is scientifically proven* to give you younger, brighter looking skin in just three weeks.

*Don't say 'scientifically proven'.

Today, when she came to pick me up from reception, Hattie did a double take before waggling her finger at me and saying, 'Ooh, someone has done their hair.' Which really hacked me off because, okay, I'll admit I don't generally make a huge effort but neither do I go around looking like Shrek.

I was sorely tempted to say I've been making good money these last couple of months because of my striking resemblance to Jenna Cox. You didn't expect that, did you, you patronising little madam?

But of course I didn't say anything to Hattie or Rosamund about the Fake Faces work. Since I haven't mentioned it to my friends and family there's no way I'm telling dumb and dumber.

I look at the blank screen.

Get ready to reveal a brighter, younger you.
Let's get glowing!
Be happier in your own skin!

They'll do.

Chapter Six

The lookalike work has been a welcome boost to my bank balance, and I'm hoping that it's about to become considerably more lucrative as I am moving from becoming a lookalike to an impersonator. Fake Faces have both on their books and there's a big distinction between them. The lookalikes are simply cashing in on what God gave them with a bit of effort in terms of styling but the celebrity impersonators or tribute acts have to 'be' their stars. Jackie was sceptical when I told her I wanted to be an impersonator. 'Most of them are actors. Or at least failed actors.' I told her I used to do youth theatre. Jackie raised her eyebrows. Well, I think that was what she was doing. Jackie has had a lot of Botox.

I did do youth theatre though. Also, I was confident that what I lacked in experience I could make up for in effort. I've always been a bit of a swot. I spent years researching my first book and I could tell you almost as much about unusually shaped uteruses and antiphospholipid syndrome as your average gynaecologist. I could apply the same sort of diligence to becoming Jenna, hopefully with a more successful outcome. I would study how she moved, how she walked and how she talked. I'd practise in front of the mirror, perfecting her speech patterns, rhythm, pitch and tone. I'd copy her body language, nail the way she cups both hands over her nose when she's really laughing.

I did exactly that and went back to Jackie who was amazed. 'Well, whaddya know? You're actually pretty good.'

Tonight's do is my first ever gig as an impersonator. I am to attend the launch party of a new high-end property developer at the recently reopened and apparently super swanky Annabel's in Berkeley Square. I will 'be' Jenna all evening and mix and mingle with the guests.

I pace around the flat doing a few of my Jenna lines. She says 'baff' not 'barth' and 'laff' not 'larrrf'. Her laugh was an absolute nightmare to get right, especially since people really know it. I reckon I can pull it off though.

A wave of panic washes over me as the cab pulls up outside the beautiful listed Georgian townhouse in one of London's grandest squares. Can I do this?

'Laff' not 'larrf', 'baff' not 'barth'.

I pay the cab driver and make sure I hold my head up high. I am Jenna Cox. A celebrity, a person of importance, a national treasure even.

My legs shake as I make my way up the grand cantilevered stone staircase. Thank God I bought a new dress for tonight, and it's one from a 'Jenna shop' not a Clare one.

'Laff' not 'larrf', 'baff' not 'barth'.

The lead party coordinator, Serena, is a willowy blonde who could manage to look expensive in a bathrobe. She tells me my task is simply to mix and mingle with the guests.

I'd question the 'simply' in that sentence but keep the smile fixed to my face. 'May I just nip to the loo first?' You know, to quietly hyperventilate and/or throw up.

With Serena out of the way, I have a chance to properly take in my surroundings and honestly it's hard not to gawp like a toddler seeing snow for the first time. This place is enormous – goodness knows how many square feet (I'll have to ask the property developers) – and spread out over four floors. I pass three different restaurants, seven bars and a cigar room and see a man whose sole job appears to be carving ice cubes into elaborate shapes for the cocktails. The decor is maximalism and then some, with heavily embroidered silk panels on the walls, themes of flora and fauna and a rococo vibe.

I normally spend my evenings alone in my flat watching forgettable reality TV and shovelling a ready meal into my mouth while telling myself that tomorrow I will definitely cook from scratch and go to the gym.

Tonight, I am Jenna though.

On the stairs, a woman of indeterminate age in a hot-pink marabou trimmed dress is having an intense conversation with a member of staff. Why is Hugo walking someone else's dog right now? The reason she likes this club is because Pickle is always welcome. It's at this point, I see a very small furry head poking out of the monogrammed handbag hanging from the crook of her arm. 'Pickle needs his walk at exactly seven o'clock. He likes his routine. His therapist says it's crucial to keep him emotionally regulated.'

How the man doesn't laugh, I have no idea. Instead, he calmly tells Pickle's mummy (and she will be his 'mummy' not his owner) that Hugo will be back soon and will walk Pickle immediately.

I continue my ascent to the ladies' room, wondering if Hugo is employed solely as a dog walker for the pampered pooches of the guests. It wouldn't surprise me. Still, I suppose I am in no position to make judgements about strange jobs. My task for the evening is to pretend to be an entirely different person.

My stomach tightens at the thought. I may look a bit like Jenna but it's another thing to *be* her.

'Laff' not 'larrf', 'baff' not 'barth'.

I open the door to the ladies' loos and am hit by a heady cloud of hairspray and competing perfumes. The room has clearly been designed for Instagram and can only be described as an explosion of pink. The vanities and sinks are pink onyx inlaid with mother of pearl and have oversized old gold swan heads for taps. Meanwhile, the ceiling is swathed in fat silk pink peonies.

A woman applying lip gloss pauses the wand mid-air and looks at me before immediately looking away. I've noticed a few people doing the same and, while it doesn't mean I can pull off impersonating Jenna, it's definitely a good start.

I shut myself in the cubicle. Even the loos are pink, for goodness sake.

After I pee, I stay where I am. Jackie has really thrown me in at the deep end with this party, and I'm more than a little overwhelmed. This would be a lot for anyone, let alone me.

I do the breathing exercises Dr Asen taught me. I'll be okay. What's the worst thing that can happen? I screw up and get fired from Fake Faces. If nothing else, I can use this extraordinary place as a setting in my novel.

Gradually, I start to get my nerves under control. I am just about to open the cubicle door when a conversation starts up outside.

'Oh my God, did you see Brad Pitt? Like just standing there in the bar sipping a cocktail and looking smokin'.'

'That's not the real Brad Pitt, silly. He's a lookalike.'

'I know,' says the other woman who clearly did not know.

'There's loads of them here tonight. I've seen the Beckhams, Cheryl Cole, Bukayo Saka...'

Jackie told me she has twelve of her artists here tonight. Apparently, the organisers were keen to create the illusion of a star-studded event and were happy to spend big bucks to achieve that. They even flew 'Beyoncé' and 'Jay Z' down from Glasgow.

'Some of them look so much like the real celebs.' The woman giggles. 'But some of them, not so much. Have you seen that Jenna Cox?'

My breath catches in my throat.

'She doesn't look like her at all. She's about three sizes bigger, for a start. And you'd think she'd have Botox on all those wrinkles.' My hand instinctively flies to my crow's feet.

The other woman cackles.

Hot tears sting the back of my eyes but I choke them back. Remind myself that I have been through much, much worse and I am still standing. I am not going to let these stupid women upset me. And I am not going to let them stop me being Jenna.

I fling open the cubicle door, holding my head high. I give the women my widest 'Jenna' smile before washing my hands and leaving the bathroom.

As I descend the stairs, I hear the gossipers giggling in my wake but I keep the smile pinned to my face as I stop to stroke Pickle who is being handed over to Hugo. I am rewarded with an enthusiastic lick. Don't worry, it says, both our nights are going to get a whole lot better.

Chapter Seven

I'm surprised at how easily I've made the transition from lookalike to impersonator. The truth is when I told Jackie I reckoned I could do it because of my 'experience', I was trying to convince myself as much as I was her. Let's face it, a few years in youth theatre as a teenager doesn't immediately mark you out as a star.

But, while I don't think Margot Robbie need worry I'm coming after her roles, Jackie tells me she gets lots of good feedback about me. Alan and Ruth Cohen were thrilled with my appearance at their son's bar mitzvah. I was utterly charming and professional. Ruth's grandma still won't believe I'm not the real Jenna.

I pull a deep red velvet cocktail dress out of my wardrobe. It was expensive but it's very Jenna and just the thing for tonight's charity auction.

It's a little embarrassing to admit how much the Cohens praise meant to me. It's been a while since I've felt I am good at anything. I couldn't keep a baby or my husband, my career is a shadow of what it once was, and I've failed to write a publishable book in seven long years.

I look at my bookshelves where there are six copies of my book. (In case you're thinking I'm a monster, I didn't go out and buy these, I was sent author copies.) I don't have to pick up a book now to know the quotes on the front cover. The *Guardian* described it as, 'A feat of a debut' while *The Times* called it, 'Dazzlingly funny and deeply moving' and the *Mail*, 'Funny, sharp and downright wonderful.'

I think about the book I'm writing now and how someone might describe that. Not funny, not sharp and downright dismal.

Don't do this to yourself. Focus on tonight. Turn yourself into Jenna. Smiley, happy Jenna. The dress helps. As soon as I pull it on, I find myself holding my head a little higher.

I order an Uber.

I don't even get that nervous before a gig anymore – in fact, if anything, I'm more confident as Jenna than myself. (Not hard, to be fair.)

My Uber cancels on me. I order another one. Minutes later that cancels. What on earth is going on? It must be something to do with the apocalyptic rain. Everyone wants cabs when it starts raining.

I break into a sweat, which is absolutely not what I want in a dress I dropped nearly two hundred quid on.

Ten minutes later I am still Uber-less and feel a visceral sense of panic. I cannot be late for this evening. Jackie has never been anything but nice to me but she is not a woman you want to annoy and 'be on time' is one of her ten holy commandments.

I'll get the bus. It takes me practically to the hotel where the charity auction is. The app tells me there's one in six minutes and I can easily be at the bus stop by then, even in these shoes. And, yes, it's raining and I'm sporting a Jenna blow-dry that absolutely mustn't frizz, but I can take an umbrella.

I stand under the bus shelter shivering. As if the biblical rain isn't enough to contend with, it's turned cold too. I don't have any Jenna coats yet and my thin jacket is no match for the chill in the air. I don't have to wait long though.

The bus pulls up and I tap my card against the reader. The bus driver stares at me and it takes me a second to realise I'm dressed as Jenna. In my haste to get to the gig, I totally forgot about that. Oh, well. I give him a sort of half-smile and shuffle upstairs with my head down.

It's not long before I realise I've been spotted by someone else though. Two middle-aged women a couple of rows back can't take their eyes off me and I can hear them talking in loud whispers. Eventually one of them can take it no longer. 'Hello,' she says appearing beside me. 'My friend and I were wondering if it was you. She said there was no way you'd take the bus but I told her you're very down to earth.'

I look at her wondering if I should tell her the truth? We'd probably have a laugh about it. But then again I could just think of this as a dress rehearsal for the event. Method acting, if you like.

I give her my best Jenna smile. 'Of course I take the bus.'

Chapter Eight

Since that time on the bus, I've been mistaken for Jenna in real life on a number of occasions and have always gone along with it.

It's not something I deliberately court. I never Jenna-ise myself to go out in the real world, except when I'm doing a job for Fake Faces. I haven't used my faux celebrity to bag a table at Nobu or to gatecrash a red-carpet event. But I don't hide myself away before a gig or rush to 'de-Jenna' straight afterwards. And when people spot 'me', I smile and chat. I used to be nervous about signing autographs but, since that time in Selfridges last month, I've got Jenna's handwriting off pat.

Not only am I convinced that none of this is doing any harm, but I believe the opposite to be true. It makes people's day to meet 'Jenna'. Their features animate, smiles spring and they stand a little taller. I know the minute they walk away from me, they'll be on the phone to their husband or sister or best friend. I've given them a story to be trotted out time and time again. *Yeah, in the middle of Sainsbury's, would you believe... ever so friendly... exactly like she is on the telly.*

I met a guy who was on the way to a job interview and said seeing his favourite TV personality must surely be a lucky omen.

There was the woman I chatted to for ages on Oxford Street. She was in the throes of a messy divorce (I can relate) and told me our meeting had cheered her right up. And who can forget Dean, the eighteen year old who had recently lost his mum to motor neurone disease and shared his cherished memories of the two of them snuggled up on the sofa watching *You've Got It*? It would mean the world to his mum to know he'd met Jenna, he said, his eyes shiny with tears he was only just holding at bay.

Look, I'm not going to pretend it's purely altruistic. The world treats celebrities better than the rest of us and you can have lots of thoughts about that, like maybe it's doctors and teachers we should be fawning over instead of people who get paid a lot of money playing dress up, but I don't make the rules. When I'm Jenna, cabs who don't have their lights on stop anyway, and people give me free coffees and make-up and generally act as if they're thrilled to just be in my orbit. I guess what I'm admitting here is that being Jenna makes me feel special and it's a bloody long time since I've felt that.

Perhaps more confusingly, being Jenna also makes me feel more like myself than I have in years. I smile more easily, laugh often and notice blue skies, the heady smell of hyacinths and the sound of birdsong. Being Jenna gives me respite from being broken and bitter and bone-achingly sad. And, maybe it's because I've had to study it and work on it so consciously, but Jenna's identity feels easier and more uncomplicated than mine. For me, the last few years have been defined by what I'm not. I'm not a mother. I'm not a wife. I'm not an author. I'm not a creative director.

I'm not.

Even when I do go back to being Clare, my Jenna jaunts create a lasting halo effect on my real life. Jenna is all about big smiles and lots of laughter. She doesn't snap or scowl or frown so deeply it's a wonder her face doesn't fold in on itself. Now, I've always been very dismissive of the whole 'fake it 'til you make it' school of happiness, thinking it about as useful as 'take a bath' or 'go for a walk'. Isn't it the sort of advice trotted out on Instagram by people who have no idea of what it means to be *properly* unhappy? The sort of hollowed-out kind of unhappy that makes you forget how to breathe or even want to. So it's somewhat discombobulating to me to discover that being fake happy as Jenna does seem to leave a sort of endorphin hangover. It's as if some of her relentless positivity rubs off on me so that when my mother says *again* wouldn't I like to meet someone new, or I see another social media post about a rainbow baby, or Hattie and Rosamund talk to me as if I'm senile ('So, half-fat butter has half the fat'), I sort of have this invisible shield.

I can honestly say that my whole life is better since I've started being Jenna. Tangibly, of course, in terms of the boost to my sorry-looking bank balance but also because I'm happier. The work has added some much-needed glamour and glitz and fun into my life, but more importantly still, long after I take off the nice clothes, peel off the false eyelashes and ditch the laugh loved by millions, there's still a little fairy dust. And that, combined with knowing you've made the day of someone like Dean, is a pretty powerful combination.

Chapter Nine

Tonight's gig is the first I'll have done with another impersonator. I'm working with Malcolm Smith who has spent the last eight years being Jonny Turner, Jenna's co-host on *You've Got It*.

'There's a room where you can leave your jacket and bag,' Felicity the event planner says. 'Malcolm is already here.'

I follow her down a long corridor, my heels sinking into the plush red carpet. The hotel is a lot grander than I expected and I feel a flutter of nerves. At least I'll have Malcolm by my side. Jackie says he's been in the business for years and there's nothing he doesn't know. She says she gets lots of requests for double acts and this could open up all kinds of exciting new opportunities for me.

Felicity walks extremely fast, although to be fair she does have the advantage of flat shoes. She's talking away about the schedule for the evening but I'm finding it as hard to keep up with as I am with her strides.

She throws open the door to a meeting room that's dominated by a huge faux wood conference table. Sat at the far end is a small, disconcertingly orange man with shoulder-length dark hair and bright blue eyes. He's wearing a sharply cut navy suit with magenta lining.

'You two already know each other, right?' Felicity says.

'We do not,' Malcolm drawls.

'Clare,' I say, extending my hand.

Malcolm looks me up and down and then stares at my hand as if I have just smeared it with dog poo. 'Jonny.'

Ah, right. We're already using our celebrity names. Although given Jonny is known for being Mr Nice Guy, it seems we're not yet in character.

Felicity says she'll leave us to it and there's water and tea and anything we might need on the side. The guests are arriving in twenty minutes or so. She'll bring us out before that so we can mingle over drinks.

'So,' Malcolm says when Felicity disappears. 'I gather from Jackie you're a newbie?'

'No. Well, sort of. I've been working as an impersonator for a few weeks now but this is the first gig I've done with someone else.'

'Well, aren't I honoured?' Malcolm says. 'To be your first.'

'I know you're an old hand.'

'Not so much of the old. But, yes, I've been doing this for years.'

I nod. 'So you must know Jonny really well.'

Malcolm's mouth bunches. 'I meant being a *performer*. I've got twenty-five years of experience. I've been in Hollywood movies and West End shows. This isn't a hobby for me, it's my career.'

Was that a snipe? I force a smile, grab a bottle of water and glug some back. 'Jackie says Kara Kendall is normally your Jenna?'

Malcolm smiles. 'Yes, dear, dear Kara. We've worked together for years and years. She's such a pro.'

Okay, it definitely was a snipe before. And this man hates me. I think of the famous rapport between Jenna and Jonny, how they always finish each other's sentences and reduce each other to fits of the giggles with a look. 'Jonny is one of the most special people in my life,' Jenna gushed in a recent interview, 'I'd trust him with my life.'

'Kara's husband has got this job in New York,' Malcolm says. 'So she has had to uproot her whole life and trot across the pond with him. It's awful.'

I'm pretty sure he means for him.

'Jenna has very distinctive mannerisms,' Malcolm says.

I nod.

'And there's a unique cadence to her voice.'

Does he not think I've studied her? Or know that I've had lots of good feedback?

'If in doubt, it's probably best for you to say as little as possible – leave most of the talking to me.'

'Umm—'

Malcolm stands up, pushes his fingers into his cheeks and blows out so his lips vibrate. 'Vocal exercises,' he says when he stops. 'Tell me you do vocal exercises? *Everyone* does them before going on stage.'

'Of course,' I put down my water bottle and place my fingers on my cheeks hoping against hope I can somehow remember what I just saw and replicate it. 'Of course.'

After the inauspicious start, I think tonight is going okay. 'Jonny' and 'Jenna' are mixing and mingling and, apart from the time I said 'no thanks' to a canapé in a voice that was a bit more Clare than Jenna, I think I've done a reasonable job.

Malcolm certainly never misses an opportunity to let me know if he thinks I'm not getting it right, either by shooting me a look that could curdle cream (which he wipes off his face before anyone else can see), or by hissing something in my ear. We hadn't got into the great hall before he told me to watch my posture and he's forever tapping his finger to the side of his mouth to remind me to smile.

A waiter comes by with a silver tray of full champagne flutes and I gaze longingly at them. I'd do pretty much anything for something to take the edge off my nerves right now but don't dare touch a drop of alcohol, not only because Jenna always goes on about how little she drinks but also because there's the risk a drink might make me forget myself – or I suppose remember myself and forget Jenna. I help myself to a glass of water and gulp it down before realising that Malcolm is giving me a look. I'm pretty sure it's supposed to indicate that Jenna would not glug her water like a trucker in a heatwave.

'So who's your favourite contestant you've ever had on *You've Got It*, Jenna?' The question comes from a sweaty middle-aged man with a rather pubic beard, and it's not immediately clear to me whether he actually believes I am Jenna or he's just playing along with the whole thing for the fun of it.

'Mine was definitely Ellie,' Malcolm says, before I have a chance to answer.

'Ellie was good,' I say. 'But I do have a soft spot for Josh.'

The people around us all pitch in to say who they liked best and I let the conversation swirl around me. I can't believe I actually thought Malcolm was going to be my friend. With the benefit of hindsight I realise I should have known he might be a little tricky. When Jackie first told me about this booking, I suggested Malcolm and I meet beforehand and Jackie said she thought that was an excellent idea but then, a few hours later, she phoned me back to say that Malcolm was very over-scheduled right now so would see me on the night. 'Malcolm is lovely,' she said. It's only now I realise this was followed by an unspoken 'but'.

'My kids are crazy about *You've Got It*,' says a woman in a red sequin dress. 'My only worry is that it will make them want to go into showbusiness.'

Malcolm laughs. 'There are worse things.'

'I suppose,' the woman says, sucking in her carmine lips. 'But I worry about the desire to be famous for the sake of being famous.'

Malcolm gives her his most beaming Jonny smile. 'Yes indeed.'

'And also—'

The woman is interrupted by the arrival of Felicity who tells us it's time for us to draw the raffle. Malcolm and I follow her towards the stage where we take it in turns to announce who has won what. When we give away a jeroboam of champagne I deliver my line, 'Ooh that's a big one,' and, as scripted, both Jonny and Jenna get the giggles. I remember to cup both hands over my mouth and nose and am pleased with the laugh which somehow I control enough to sound like Jenna's and not mine, while still making it sound uncontrollable.

'Not terrible,' Malcolm whispers in my ear as we leave the stage.

I reckon I can take that as a compliment.

'Clapham is completely out of my way,' Malcolm says.

Clapham is most definitely not out of the way if you're driving from central London to Herne Hill, but at least if I don't share a cab with Malcolm I won't have to listen to him drone on about how he has done shoots all over the world, been to the Oscars three times and is a fully trained stunt double. Nor will he be able to give me any more notes on what I can do better next time. I'm in no mood to challenge Malcolm about the route either, especially as poor Felicity, who confided to me in the toilets earlier that she is 'deep in the throes of the peri-menopause', looks as if she's about to burst into tears. 'I'll order another cab then,' she says now, her voice small.

'No need,' I say. 'I'll pick one up outside.'

'Yup,' Malcolm says. 'Should be no problem at all.'

Loathsome little man. I hope there are lots of other Jonny lookalikes on Jackie's books. And that I never have to see this one again.

Chapter Ten

Bloody Malcolm. It's not my fault I'm not Kara. I'm being paid to impersonate Jenna not Kara sodding Kendall. And I did okay tonight. Even he had to grudgingly admit that.

The hotel is on one of those quiet and mannered Mayfair streets of handsome red-brick buildings where a two-bedroom apartment costs twice what you'd pay for a family home that's a mere ten-minute car journey away. The sort of street where staff outnumber residents by about four to one and day nannies hand over, not to parents, but to night nannies.

I shiver in my thin jacket, which is no match for the late October chill. The temperature seems to have dropped by several degrees since I arrived here full of excitement about meeting Malcolm (pah!). God, he was awful with that whole Clapham being totally out of his way thing. How mean can you get?

Despite what I told him, I had no intention of getting a taxi at my expense and planned to hop on the bus. Now I'm out here in the cold, I decide I'll walk in the direction of the bus stop but hail down a passing cab if I see one on the way.

I turn on to Oxford Street which, with its plethora of neon signed 'candy' stores and tuk-tuks blasting out music as they hunt for unsuspecting tourists to charge a small fortune for the shortest of rides, feels like a different city or, frankly, world.

'Oh my goodness!' The man appears out of nowhere. 'I cannot believe it's you!'

Great. I may normally be quite happy to be mistaken for Jenna but right now I'm cold, tired and desperate to be home. It's all bloody Malcolm's fault. I wouldn't be out here on the street if I was in the cab with him like I was supposed to be.

The man is gazing at me expectantly.

'Hi,' I say in my Jenna voice.

'The kids are going to be so excited when I tell them I saw you! I'm a teacher, you see. We're putting on a talent show. We've been inspired by *You've Got It*.' He laughs nervously. 'The kids absolutely love it. So do I actually. Never miss an episode. And you're our favourite person on it – me and the kids – because you're never mean to people. It's awful when Henry lays into people, isn't it? I mean, I know some would say you've got to have one mean judge and it makes good TV, but I don't like it. Everyone who goes on the show is doing their best, aren't they? It's so brave. I know I wouldn't...'

I'm desperate to get away but this man doesn't pause or even seem to take discernible breaths. I gaze longingly towards a passing cab, its bright yellow light an invitation that's hard to resist.

'Lovely to meet you,' I say, eventually managing to get a word in. 'But I'd better get going.'

'Of course, of course. The talent show we're doing is to raise money. One of the kids in the class has cancer, you see. It's terribly sad.'

'Oh, that's awful.'

He nods so hard I fear his head may fall off. 'We're hoping to raise enough money to send him and his family to Disneyland. To cheer them up a bit.'

'That's nice.' It's a tragic story but it doesn't change the fact I'm shattered, borderline hypothermic and my feet are screaming in these ridiculous heels.

The man claps his hands together. 'I've just had the craziest idea! I don't suppose you'd come and judge our talent competition? I know it's a cheeky request but I know it would make a huge difference to the amount of money we raise. Plus it would mean the world to the kids, Alex especially. He's the boy with cancer.'

'Erm… well…'

'It's on December the fourteenth.'

My brain cartwheels. 'Ah, unfortunately I'm, er, filming on that day.'

The man smiles. 'I hope you don't mind me asking but if you don't ask, you don't get, right?'

'Of course, I don't mind you asking.' I turn to walk away. 'Lovely to meet you and best of luck with the talent show. I hope it goes brilliantly and you raise lots of money.' I open my purse and hand him a twenty-pound note. 'It's not much but it's all the cash I've got on me.'

'Aww, you are lovely. But then I already knew that! I can't wait to tell the kids I saw you. They will not believe it. Just walking along the street too. I only came this far up Oxford Street because Google Maps sent me down a cul-de-sac and now I can't find my way to the Tube.'

'Right, well, bye then.'

'Wait,' he says, rummaging around in his capacious rucksack. 'Can I just get a photo with you?'

The first time someone asked me for a photo, I felt sick with panic but then I remembered a rather nauseating Instagram post from Jenna which I trotted out almost verbatim and have used ever since. 'I'm afraid I never do photos. I prefer to have proper face-to-face interactions with fans. Really be in the moment.'

'Of course, of course.'

Almost everyone is understanding like this. I have no idea why. Surely you can be 'in the moment' and pose for a bloody photo? But famous people get away with all sorts.

'May I get your autograph then? For Alex?' He rummages in his bag and produces a bright orange notebook. He rips out a page and hands it to me along with a pen and the notebook to lean on.

I pause feeling morally queasy about deceiving a kid with cancer but then I think about Dean, the young man who lost his mum to motor neurone disease and was so cheered by an interaction with 'Jenna'. *To Alex*, I write, *all the best, Jenna Cox x*

'Thank you so much,' he says. 'It's been so lovely to meet you.'

I treat him to my biggest, brightest smile. 'You too.' I walk away, my mind turning to sinking gratefully into the back of a cab and how I cannot wait to be back in my warm flat, kick off these stupid shoes, take off the ton of slap I'm wearing and forget about this whole crazy evening.

'Wait,' comes a voice behind me. 'I've just had the most brilliant idea. I know you can't come to the show because you're filming but you could come to one of the rehearsals—'

'Well,' I say, sweat prickling my armpits. 'I'd love to but my schedule is qu—'

'The kids would love to meet you. Alex especially. It would mean the world to him.'

The kid with cancer. I mean, how can I say no?

Chapter Eleven

In the days that follow promising that teacher I'd go to a rehearsal, I'm hit by a sort of visceral panic.

This feels different somehow. It's one thing to let people I happen to bump into in the street think I'm Jenna, but quite another to dress up as her specially and deliberately set out to deceive a bunch of schoolchildren. One of whom has cancer.

I flip-flop between thinking I have to find a way out of this and that maybe the visit will actually give this unfortunate child a little boost, and goodness knows he deserves that.

One thing is for sure, I'm spending almost every waking moment agonising about this and finding it nigh on impossible to concentrate on anything from writing my book (although no change there if I'm honest) to doing my freelance advertising work.

The latter is especially problematic as I'm on a tight deadline to deliver two pet care articles by next Thursday. The work comes to me via Russell, who is a client I've worked with since we were both starting out. He's now the Chief Marketing Officer of a premium organic pet food company and has ambitions to create a website that's a go-to resource for pet parents. (Normally I'd baulk at the term 'pet parents' over 'pet owners' but since it's Russell, and since he pays me a hefty day rate, I suck it up.)

Identity Crisis

When I first started putting feelers out for freelance work, it was six years since I'd left my high profile creative director job and shortly after what I annoy my mother by referring to as my 'mental period'. (I say 'shortly after' but, as anyone who has been through something like that will know, recovery is far from linear. My meltdown in Pret happened when I thought I was better, for example, and even now I know better than to take being okay for granted.) Most of my contacts didn't have any work to give me (funny when I knew they were advertising on LinkedIn) or even return my calls or emails. Russell, on the other hand, seemed happy to pick up the proverbial bargepole and said Precious Petz would always have work for me.

So I owe him. And really ought to be concentrating on writing 'Building a relationship with your vet' right now, instead of sitting here sweating about whether I can go through with this school visit. (The only thing I know for certain is that if I decide not to go, I'll phone the school office and make up some excuse rather than doing a 'no show'. I may have somehow landed far away from the person I wanted to be but I still have some sense of decency.)

> The ideal time to get to know your vet is not when your pet is poorly, but when they're in tip-top shape. After all, the last thing you need when your furry friend is under the weather is the additional stress of trying to find a good vet in your area.

I lean back in my chair and sigh. All this business with the school only happened because of horrible Malcolm. If I'd been in the cab with him the other night, I wouldn't be in this mess.

The teacher will surely have told the sick child and his classmates about 'Jenna's' visit by now so if I don't go, they're going to be disappointed.

Can I pull off making them believe I really am Jenna though? It's not like they're babies, for goodness' sake, they're eleven. But then I fooled their teacher, didn't I? And several other people over the last few months.

Think about your article.

Start by asking other pet parents in your area which vet they use and whether they'd recommend them. And it's not just about their opinion. Do they think their furry friend likes the practice? It might be too much to expect puppy love but your pet shouldn't be frightened of the vet.

My heart races inside my chest. I can't get the school thing out of mind. Or shake the feeling that I'm damned if I do and damned if I don't.

One of the peculiar things a career in advertising bestows on you is little pockets of knowledge about strange things. I know, for example, that the reason you once used to see white dog poo but never do now is because manufacturers used to put chalk in dog food, but that's since been made illegal. I know there's a certain branded cornflake that is made differently to own brand cornflakes, each one of the former being made from a whole corn kernel but the latter being created from reconstituted corn. I know that no non-prescription product you put on your skin is going to erase deep wrinkles.

I think it would be fair to say none of this knowledge is particularly useful. And it certainly hasn't furnished me with any idea of how to deal with the situation I currently find myself in.

Chapter Twelve

I'm not sure pretending to be a completely different human is what mental health professionals have in mind when they talk of 'getting out of your own head', but I can confirm it to be effective.

I am doing a (thankfully solo) impersonator gig and have managed to go a full hour without stressing about whether I should or shouldn't go to Hatfield Academy on Wednesday.

The gig is a launch for VOdz, 'a new vodka for a new kind of vodka drinker'. It's being held at an old dressmaking warehouse in Shoreditch and, judging by some of the conversations I've had, many of the attendees have sampled a little too much of the product.

Case in point are Felix and Edmund who both seem to be struggling to form any sort of a coherent sentence.

'So,' Felix says, jabbing a finger in my direction and shouting over the loud dance track being pumped out by a DJ on a raised platform a few feet away from us. 'Are you have… having… a, er, good time?'

'It's a right laff,' I say, flashing him a Jenna smile.

Felix chuckles. 'You don't mind mixing with us plebs?'

Two thoughts occur to me simultaneously. Firstly, neither Felix nor Edmund think of themselves as plebs. Everything about them, from their signet rings to their glossy, floppy hair, to their innate, and rather mysterious, self-confidence screams privilege. Secondly, they do know I'm an impersonator, right?

I turn up my Jenna beam. 'I'm delighted to be here. Such an amazing venue too.' I gesture towards the giant central bar and ice bar which is set behind a bank of naked mannequins suspended in giant blocks of ice.

'Yeah,' Felix says. 'And great voddie too.'

'Delicious,' I say, surreptitiously glancing at my watch and wondering if it's time to move on. When I first arrived, Noah, the aggressively earnest event coordinator, told me that there was fifty-five minutes of meet and greet and I was to spend an equal amount of time in each of the three zones: Winter Wonderland, Prohibition and Neon Dreams. He said this with such an air of gravity, I wondered if he might like me to set a timer for 18.3 minutes in each.

'If you'll excuse me, I must mingle.'

Neon Dreams has the edge on Prohibition if you ask me but that could be because of the absence of Felix and Edmund. I get chatting to a couple of middle-aged women about how difficult it is to hear over the sound of the music and how they can't manage to wear heels anymore and how did they ever.

We're interrupted by the arrival of a wild-eyed Noah who, despite being all of about twelve, looks as if he might be about to have a heart attack. 'Justin wants to move the speeches *forward*. He wants to do them *now*.'

It's tempting to wind up Noah further – what, when I've only spent 4.2 minutes in Neon Dreams? – but I'm not quite that cruel.

I follow him across the room passing fire eaters and trapeze artists and old-fashioned cigarette girls handing out vodka shots.

'You'll stick to the agreed speech?' Noah says.

IDENTITY CRISIS

A prickle of irritation rises. They sent over the speech via Jackie yesterday and I could immediately see room for improvement. Yes, it's just me, well Jenna, introducing Justin the CEO and talking a little about VOdz, but it could be sharper and funnier. I spent the next hour rewriting it before sending it back to Jackie, smug in the knowledge that the client would be delighted. How lucky were they that their Jenna impersonator was also a professional copywriter and a published author? In my other life, I'd be paid good money for what I'd just given them for free. Ten minutes later, Jackie called. The client would like to stick to the original script. It had already been approved by the board and Justin himself. 'Of course,' I say to Noah now, forcing a smile.

And so it is that I take to the stage and give the lacklustre speech with none of the little jokes or Jenna-isms that would have made it sparkle. I can't even use my line: *Justin, you've got it!* Their loss.

After Justin's speech, which is even more boring than mine, Noah ushers me into the VIP section. 'This is Justin's wife, Heather,' he says in a reverential tone.

'Hi.'

Heather laughs as if I've said something hysterical. 'Hi, *Jenna*.'

'Are you having a nice evening?'

'Fabtastic.' She giggles. 'I mean fantastic.' She takes a sip of her vodka, missing her mouth and a little dribbles down her chin. 'So, I've got a bone to pick with you.' She wipes her hand across her mouth, smudging lipstick across her face. 'Yeah, I was reading an interview with you in one of the magazines. While I was getting my hair done.'

Wait, an interview with me? This woman does know I'm not Jenna, right? Since I've started this work, I've come to realise that lots of people want to pretend you are the actual celebrity. They do this in a 'wink wink' knowing kind of way, which doesn't make it any less weird but at least gives me some signal they're in full possession of their faculties. Despite my fleeting moment of doubt, I'm pretty sure that's what Edmund and Felix were doing earlier, for example. But mentioning an interview Jenna did seems different somehow. Should I step in to correct Heather? I settle for a noncommittal 'hmm'.

'Yeah,' Heather says. 'You were banging on about being child free. About how great it is and how you hate people questioning your choices.'

This definitely feels like more than 'going along with the charade'. I guess she might be trying to make me break character. Some people like to do that – as if I'm a stony-faced Queen's Guard they're trying to make smile. 'Umm—'

'Selfish. Selfish, selfish, selfish. The world needs babies.'

Why this? Why couldn't this fruit-loop of a woman take 'Jenna' to task about something else? Anything else. 'Umm—'

Heather slugs back her vodka and grabs another shot from a passing waiter. 'See, I think people who don't have children are selfish. What would happen to the world if no one had babies?'

'Well, there are actually quite a few people on the planet. Probably too many if anything.' Would Jenna say something like this or is it too contentious for her? I'm not even sure I care right now.

It is the wrong thing to say though, because it sets Heather off on an absolute rant with her myriad reasons of how I am being 'ridiculous', and how she knows I'll regret my choices and I won't have anyone to look after me when I'm old and have I thought about that?

Heat rises through my chest and I have to swallow back tears, keep the smile pinned to my face and remember that I am Jenna tonight and not Clare. Jenna who is happy to be child*free*.

Finally, after what seems like an eternity, Heather grinds to a halt and puts her hand on my arm. 'Sorry, babe. I actually like you. Y'know, despite our different views. I watch you every day on *Good Morning with Jenna.*'

She really does think I'm Jenna.

It's over an hour since I left the VOdz launch and I still can't quite process Heather and that weird conversation.

Setting aside her stupid views (I may have been desperate for kids but people's absolute right to decide they don't want them, and not have to defend that to anyone, is a hill I'm prepared to die on), it seems unfathomable that in that moment she appeared convinced I was Jenna.

I peel off my false eyelashes and suddenly feel bald of eye. It's odd, I've barely worn much make-up in years but, since I've started regularly Jenna-ing up, I feel frumpy when I'm bare-faced.

Heather was clearly plastered, of course, but it still doesn't make sense to me. Surely, she noticed her husband's stagey wink when he thanked 'Jenna' for the introduction.

I guess I could take it as a compliment. Horrible Malcolm may not be able to say anything nicer than I'm 'not terrible' but I fooled Heather. And she's far from the only one. Which means maybe I will be able to pass myself off as Jenna if I do turn up to Hatfield Academy tomorrow. Not being outed only solves one of my problems on that front, of course, but I guess it's better than nothing.

Chapter Thirteen

The only way I can get through this is to think of it as another job for Fake Faces. No big deal.

My brain hasn't done a very good job of communicating this to my body though. I am clammy all over, my heart is racing and I feel as if I may actually vomit.

Across from me on the bus is a man who looks a bit like horrible Malcolm. The lookalike of the lookalike. He is watching a very loud video without headphones and I have to muster all my self-control not to rip the device out of his hands and send it skittering out of the window.

What if the kids know I'm not Jenna? How humiliating would it be to be outed?

I try to calm my raggedy breath. *It's just another job for Fake Faces.*

The bus stop looms all too quickly. *You can do this*, I tell myself. *Just meet this poor unfortunate kid and get yourself out of there.* I picture myself at home sitting in front of my computer trying to write my new book or, more pressingly still, my pet care articles. You know things are bad when that's what you're looking forward to.

The school is a huge, red-brick Victorian monolith. I stand outside breathing in through my nose and out through my mouth. I glance down at my outfit. Casual but Jenna casual. Expensive jeans, a cashmere sweater and the kind of jewellery favoured by women who think nothing of wearing diamonds on the yoga mat. The jewellery is fake but the clothes are the real deal. The programme I watched about lookalikes featured a 'Meghan Markle' who talked with great pride of buying everything in charity shops and Primark and then making it look high end, but I don't have that kind of confidence or skill.

It's a good thing I'm doing today, I tell myself, even if it doesn't feel that way. I'm bringing a little bit of joy to a kid who deserves a break in life and, yes, you could argue it's deceitful but life is full of 'good' lies. We teach children to believe in Father Christmas and the Tooth Fairy. We tell people they look great when they don't. Pretend things are interesting when we're bored senseless.

The teacher comes to reception to pick me up. He reaches out his hand to shake mine and says it wasn't until he was on the Tube the other night that he realised he hadn't told me his name. It's Sam. I nearly say 'Clare' but stop myself just in time.

It completely passed me by the other night but Sam is good looking, strikingly so. With shorter hair, he'd be a great Ryan Reynolds lookalike. I observe this with zero pull of attraction – these days a handsome guy is something I enjoy as I would a beautiful painting or a vase. However much my mother might hint, I am done with romantic love.

Sam is exuding restless excitement. He tells me the children are beside themselves to meet me, that they can't believe I've really come to their school to see their rehearsal. Alex hasn't arrived yet but will be here any minute. He can't wait for that to happen. It breaks his heart to think what Alex has been through.

As I follow him along the corridor, I panic I'm going to forget myself for a minute. Laugh like me or say bath with an 'r' in it. I dig my nails into my palms. *It's just another job for Fake Faces.*

Sam swings open the door to a big light-filled room with a stage at one end. Kids are dotted about and, as we walk in, some of them come towards us and some hang back. Sam is practically bouncing. 'Seven J, I'm very pleased to introduce you to the one and only Jenna Cox.'

A few of the kids start clapping and I feel a flush rise through my cheeks. I remind myself I haven't got into this on purpose, any of it. I've done lots of things in my life I'm not proud of but I never set out to pretend to be Jenna in real life and if stupid Malcolm hadn't refused to let me share a cab with him, I wouldn't be here now.

'Who's your favourite person who's ever been on *You've Got It?*' a boy with red hair wants to know. 'Mine's Isaac.'

'Are you and Jonny best friends?' asks a girl with cornrows.

'Do you like cats?' says a girl with braces.

Sam cuts in. 'One at a time please Seven J.'

The girl with the braces edges closer and closer until her fingertips are grazing my sleeve.

'When will Alex be here?' I ask. As soon as I've seen him I can get out of here.

'Soon,' Sam says. 'I know he can't wait to meet you. How about we start the rehearsal while we wait?'

I take a seat on a hard plastic chair. The first act is a trio of girls who seem to be performing something between a dance and a gymnastics routine. A couple of boys sitting on the sidelines snigger and Sam glares at them. To be honest, I'm finding it quite hard not to laugh myself.

'Are all these kids from the same class?' I whisper to Sam as a girl, who looks about sixteen and must be six foot tall, takes to the stage. Sam nods. How can that be possible? Some of them still look like little kids but some, mostly girls, look like adults. Well, physical adults.

The girl starts singing and somewhat to my surprise, after the last act, has a lovely voice. She's so awkward though. As if she doesn't know what to do with her limbs and must sing directly to the scuffed parquet floor.

'You've got a lovely voice,' I find myself saying when she comes off stage. 'But try to look up at the audience and lose the penguin arms.' I have no idea why I'm offering up feedback but I blame my youth theatre background. 'Penguin arms' was something that was drilled into us on a daily basis.

The girl blushes and thanks the parquet before picking up her black-and-white fluffy floral tote bag that somehow seems familiar.

'So useful to have expert feedback,' Sam says. 'I try my best but I'm just an English teacher with an interest in drama.'

Guilt stabs at my guts. I'm not an expert, I'm a fraud.

The sniggering boys, who are very much in the 'little kid' camp, take to the stage just as a piece clunks into place in my brain and I remember where I've seen that fluffy tote bag. Last time I went into The Leap Agency, horrible Hattie had one she'd apparently just received in a parcel from her mum. Hattie made no secret of her ungracious dislike for the bag but it's clearly popular with the tweens and looking around this room, I can see at least six of them.

The sniggerers launch into what is apparently meant to be a rap.

'Such a talented bunch of kids, aren't they?' Sam says.

I search his face for irony but find none.

More acts come and go. This is my penance for ever letting myself be mistaken for Jenna. I'll get through this and meet Alex, then the universe and I are quits and I will never again let myself be mistaken for her in real life.

Halfway through a comedian's skit, a mousy looking woman in a chunky red cardigan pops her head around the door and beckons to Sam.

'Apparently, Alex has been taken poorly and can't come in today,' Sam whispers to me when he comes back. 'I can't believe the timing. I know he'll be so disappointed, the poor kid. Like he hasn't been through enough.'

'That's such a shame.'

Sam nods, his eyes shiny. 'Would you be able to come back to the next rehearsal? Just to meet him?'

Once again, how can I possibly say no?

Chapter Fourteen

June 2015

It's a scene of bucolic loveliness. As far as the eye can see are rolling vineyards bathed pink in the soft glow of a setting sun. The air is heavy with the scent of jasmine and the only sound comes from the crickets singing their nightly lullaby.

'How lucky did we get with this villa?' Stephen says.

'It's pretty perfect,' Meg agrees.

'Yep, especially when you're here with your favourite people,' I say.

'To be honest, I'm just pleased you're still happy to go on holiday with us,' Meg says. 'Now that you're a big-shot author and all that.'

I laugh. 'The book isn't even out yet. When I'm actually published then of course we'll stop holidaying with losers like you.'

'Will I still be allowed?' Stephen says, topping up everyone's prosecco.

I pretend to think about it. 'Maybe.'

He reaches out and squeezes my arm. 'C'mon let's eat. I'm absolutely starving.'

We pass round plates of Parma ham, salami and bresaola, fat loaves of ciabatta, a board of Italian cheeses, a bowl of glistening olives and a tomato and basil salad that's made with tomatoes that smell as tomatoes should. We only got off the plane a couple of hours ago so this is a hastily bought picnic from the local supermarket but, to my mind, you'd be hard pushed to find a better dinner.

'So tell me more about the book deal,' Adam says, cutting off a wedge of Taleggio.

'Meg told me we're all super proud of you but she didn't tell me the details.'

Before I can answer, Stephen jumps in. 'She had six publishers fighting over her. The book sold at auction. It's going to be massive—'

'Well,' I say.

'It's going to be massive,' Stephen and Meg say in unison.

'I think as my husband and my best friend you two might be a little biased,' I say, laughing.

'I don't know,' Adam says. 'If six publishers wanted it, your book must be something pretty special.'

'It is,' Meg says. I look across the table thinking of all the different versions of her I've known since the two of us met in reception class. The little girl who collected stones to paint faces on and name them, the teenager who cut her own hair and dyed it purple, the woman who was my maid of honour when Stephen and I got married last year. The person who has been by my side for everything.

'Can you set your next book in an idyllic Tuscan villa?' Adam asks. 'And then have to go on lots of research trips with your friends.'

'Of course,' I say. 'And obviously there will always be a private pool. For research purposes.'

'I cannot wait to get in that pool tomorrow morning,' Stephen says.

'I'm not sure I want to wait until then,' Meg says.

There are murmurs of agreement all round and, within minutes of finishing eating, defying the advice of mothers everywhere, we're all in the water.

It's glorious, cool enough to be refreshing but warm enough not to make you gasp when you dive in. I swim towards the shallow end. Stephen catches up with me, puts his arms around me and kisses me deeply. 'Happy?'

'Very.'

'Me too.'

We've been together for three years. I was about to delete all the dating apps when we met and had all but given up on finding someone I wanted to spend the rest of my life with. Hell, what am I talking about? I'd all but given up on finding someone I wanted to spend the rest of the evening with.

Stephen gives me that lopsided smile of his that makes my tummy flip. 'Let's make a baby.'

I laugh. We've talked about having kids but it's always been something for the future.

'What now?'

'Not *now* now,' he says, grinning. 'But yes.'

'Okay,' I say, my heart feeling too big for my chest suddenly because I am so ridiculously, stupidly happy. 'Let's chuck out the condoms.'

We think it's going to be that easy.

Chapter Fifteen

November 2023

The day after my visit to Hatfield Academy, I am skittish and unsettled. I wish I didn't have to go back there. I was so relieved not to have been exposed and now I've got to do it all over again.

I stare at the blank page of my notepad. Today is supposed to be a big writing day. I have no freelance work to do and, while that's bad news for my bank balance, it should be good news for my novel.

Unfortunately my brain hasn't got the memo and didn't seem to have got out of bed with the rest of me. Which means instead of writing my book, I'm looking at Jenna's Instagram. This is an obsessive new habit of mine. Today's story is Jenna working out with her 'gorgeous' personal trainer and 'great pal' Mikey. 'Mikey is really putting me through my paces today,' Jenna says, grinning to camera. Mikey, who is holding down Jenna's feet as she does sit-ups, gives a wolfish smile and instructs Jenna to show him what she's got.

In advertising, when you start working on a new brand, you brainstorm what it is that makes it unique. People who'll like this product watch such and such a programme on TV, they read newspaper x and love holidays doing y. Words this product calls to mind are blah, blah and blah.

Jenna's brand is relentless positivity. People who like this product like uplifting TV, they don't read newspapers (too depressing!) and love any kind of holibobs. Words this product calls to mind are happy, sunny and optimistic.

My brand, on the other hand, is very different. It's epitomised by this flat. The walls are a nondescript beige colour that was chosen by the previous owners and, despite being here over two years, I have yet to hang a single picture. The spare room is still full of boxes I need to unpack. Treasures from my marital home I apparently don't treasure anymore.

My mind casts back to Stephen and me picking up the keys for 32 Latcham Street. Two kids who could not wait to play house. In the months that followed, we pored over fabric swatches and paint samples with the same sort of obsessiveness you might expect from someone searching for a cure for cancer. We raced home from work excited to strip floors and spent hours at car boot sales looking for things I'd then spend days arranging and rearranging on shelves to look artfully casual.

I wonder what sort of place the real Jenna lives in. I can't see much of it in her posts. I expect she had an interior designer to make it perfect for her. A posh woman with a rich husband who tells Jenna she's a joy to work with and has amazing taste.

I don't think Mikey is really putting Jenna through her paces. She doesn't look sweaty and there is no puce face to clash with her cute lemon-yellow workout gear.

I scroll through more posts. There's a breathlessly excited one about her new clothing line with Asda. She just knows we're all going to find so many pieces in there to love, whether it's the fabulous co-ord that will take you from office to dance floor, the perfect white shirt or the little red dress you'll wonder how you lived without. The latter seems a bit hyperbolic but I do save the link as it looks like a good dress for gigs.

There's a post where Jenna waxes lyrical about her mum.

> Happiest of birthdays to my gorgeous mama! You're my best friend, my inspiration and my guiding light. Love you to the moon and back.

Jeez, is it me or is it a bit vomit-inducing for a woman in her forties to call her mum 'mama'? It reminds me of those baby dolls with a cord you pull out of its stomach to make it speak. 'Ma-ma, ma-ma.'

This flat has always felt like a place where I live rather than a home. I was never excited about it. I only looked at it once before putting in an offer. I think the estate agent thought I was mad. (He was right, although being cavalier about property buying was the least of it.)

What he didn't understand is that I was desperate to move. I had spent the previous year alone and broken in what had once been my dream home. Stephen had told me he was leaving two weeks before lockdown and, although I can't blame him for the timing because none of us knew what was to come, it did rub a little extra salt into the wound. I know a lot of people were alone during the pandemic but, my God, my aloneness seemed to come with a capital A. Rattling around that house feeling as empty as Stephen's wardrobe, crying every time I saw a freezer bag labelled in his terrible handwriting, keeping the door to the nursery firmly locked.

I keep scrolling. Then come across a post extolling the benefits of collagen shots, another of Jenna on the red carpet and one of Jenna with three other women, their faces all pressed together and the caption: *Beautiful lunch with my beautiful girls!*

I close Instagram and chuck my phone down on the side. Why am I wasting so much time obsessing about Jenna? This isn't just about work-related research anymore. It's an obsessive and unhealthy fascination and, even though I know, of course I do, that Jenna's life won't be nearly so perfect as she makes it look on social media, it still somehow makes me feel shit about mine.

Chapter Sixteen

I'm getting ready for a meeting with Rosamund, Hattie and the new Creative Director of The Leap Agency, Toby Balfour.

These days I'm not interested enough in the world of advertising to bother with the industry magazines I used to devour, but when Hattie told me of Toby's appointment, I did read some of the announcements. Toby was exactly what I expected. A young, handsome guy who has worked on several of the most lauded campaigns of the last few years. He looks screamingly posh too – the sort of man who calls his friends by their surnames, goes to the country for the weekend and talks with misty-eyed affection about Nanny.

I survey my reflection in the mirror, decide the green silk shirt dress looks way too 'try hard' and toss it on to the pile that has accumulated on my bed.

Rosamund and Hattie are beside themselves about today's meeting and are behaving as if I have an audience with the King. I must be on time because Toby has a hard stop at ten o'clock, it's probably best not to mention Darius the previous creative director and it's important that, if Toby wants to see any of my work, I only show him Google docs and *never* Word docs.

I am wildly irritated. Do Rosamund and Hattie not realise I used to be a Toby?

The answer to this, of course, is no. I am the wrong side of forty and left my creative director job seven years ago (and it may as well be a lot longer – years out of advertising equating to dog years not actual ones).

I pull on a cream jumper and immediately picture myself spilling tea down it. I wrench it back over my head and throw it on to the pile.

In other fields, experience is something that's valued. No one wants to be wheeled into an operating theatre and see a surgeon who looks as if they haven't hit puberty; your stomach would surely clench if you were on a plane and the pilot announced it was his or her maiden flight; and high court judges aren't told their many years of knowledge are irrelevant because what do they know about TikTok.

In advertising, it's slightly different because, yes, experience is all very well, but not when it's an unwelcome trade-off to being – whisper it – old. That's only really allowed if you've got your name above the door, and even then you should probably think about stepping down gracefully by fifty-five at the latest.

For creatives, there's another kicker too. You and your portfolio have to seem current. Show people a campaign the industry bestowed with multiple awards ten years ago and all they see is a campaign from ten years ago. What have you done this year?

Maybe I can wear something I've bought for my Fake Faces work? My 'Jenna' wardrobe is much more upmarket than my own. Mind you, if I thought the silk shirt dress was too much…

Hattie and Rosamund are clearly shocked that Toby wants to meet me and, although it pains me to admit it, I'm surprised too. I do the grunt work that creative directors normally don't concern themselves with too much, the sort of stuff too menial for their full-time staff. I suspect today's meeting is about the impression Toby wants to create to those above him. He wants to be able to tell the board he has personally met with every creative working on every account – when he said at interview he wanted to roll up his sleeves and get his hands dirty, he really meant that.

The stated reason for the meeting is that Toby has a 'few thoughts' on my Lumiere copy. I'm hoping these will be minor tweaks – the sort of things that make very little actual difference but mean Toby can say he's had input. Whatever the conversation holds, it would be a lot less unpalatable if the world's two most annoying account managers weren't involved in it, and I allow myself a brief fantasy of Toby telling the pair of them that we don't need 'suits' at this meeting and we'll just talk 'creative to creative'.

He won't do that, screams a voice in my head. *He barely thinks of you as a creative*. To him I'm a hack, a sell-out, a has-been. Worse than that, I'm the ghost of Christmas future – where he could end up if he doesn't crack the next few briefs (it won't occur to him I left advertising of my own volition). This might be mitigated by me being a novelist but because I haven't had a book out for seven years, I've fallen foul of the 'current' commandment.

I glance at my watch, see it's time to leave and decide I will keep it simple with jeans and a sweatshirt. I need to chill out about today. Contrary to how the gruesome twosome are behaving, Toby is just a human being. He might even be nice.

The introductions go off without a hitch. But then, as we wait for Toby to deposit his large red skateboard at the cloakroom of the Soho Club, he delivers one of my least favourite questions in the world. 'So,' (it nearly always starts with that wholly redundant 'so') 'how was your weekend?'

'Lovely,' I say, forcing a smile.

Rosamund momentarily removes her gaze from Toby's chiselled jawline and gives me a look that's steeped in pity. And that's what does it really.

'I went to this incredible party at an old dressmaking warehouse in Shoreditch.' After a full forty-eight hours without using it, my voice still sounds unfamiliar to me.

'The Yard?' Toby says. 'Love that place.'

'*Did you?*' Rosamund says.

Irritation fizzes through my veins. I did go to a party at The Yard. And okay, it wasn't this weekend, it was the VOdz launch and okay, I went as Jenna and not me, but Rosamund needn't look quite so shocked.

Hattie bursts through the door looking pink-faced and agitated. She is so sorry she is late. The Tube was a total nightmare. Some passenger incident at Victoria.

'No stress,' Toby says, giving her a smooth smile. He takes his cloakroom ticket from the fresh-faced attendant and thanks him effusively. 'Shall we head upstairs?'

Toby is even better looking in real life than in his photos and this, combined with his easy charm and ridiculous poshness, seems like catnip to Rosamund and Hattie (and, to be fair, probably many others).

We take our seats in the lounge which looks much as I imagine Toby's parents' drawing room might do, albeit without any elderly black Labradors farting on the sofa. There's an abundance of dark wood, big squashy sofas, groaning bookshelves and eclectic artwork. Sunlight pours through the huge shuttered windows.

A man who looks similar to Sam the teacher is on a zoom call at the table next to us. I still can't believe I have to go back to

Hatfield Academy in two days' time. Whatever Toby's feedback is on my work today, it can't be as excruciating as sitting there in that fetid school hall praying that none of the kids realise I'm not actually Jenna.

'So,' Toby says. 'Clare was just telling us all about her exciting weekend.'

An image springs into my mind of me standing over the kitchen sink licking pasta sauce off a wooden spoon.

Toby rakes his hand through his floppy fringe. 'She went to an amazing party at The Yard.'

Hattie does such a comedy double-take, I'm torn between laughing and punching her. Everything in her face says she imagines I spent the whole weekend holed up in my flat alone eating ready meals from their plastic containers. (She's right, although I did have a trip to Tesco Metro because I'd run out of washing-up liquid.) 'Yeah, love it there. They have divided the space into three zones and they all have quite a different vibe but they are all cool.' *Vibe? Cool?* Who even am I?

'Yah,' Toby says. 'My little sister India had her twenty-first there and it was mega.'

Zoom man tells the people he's talking to he'll circle back to them on that.

Toby scrabbles around in his backpack. 'Fuck's sake.'

'What?' Rosamund and Hattie chorus.

Toby shakes his head. 'Just I thought I had some headache tablets but I don't.'

'I'll nip to the chemist on Dean Street,' Rosamund says.

'Yeah,' Hattie adds. 'Or I can?'

Jesus, it's as if feminism never happened. 'Actually, I have some paracetamol.' I pull the packet out of my handbag and hand it to Toby.

'Lifesaver,' Toby says, giving me a full-beam smile. I've been trying to work out who he looks like and now I realise it's Hugh Grant in his foppish *Four Weddings* era.

The waiter comes over and asks if we'd like to order.

'I'll have a skinny latte with soy milk please,' Rosamund says.

'I'll just have water because I'm fasting,' Hattie says. 'Wait, can you have water when you're fasting? Or are you supposed to have literally nothing?'

Literally who cares? 'I'll have an Earl Grey with normal milk please.'

'English breakfast for me,' Toby says. 'Also with milk from a cow.'

The waiter scuttles away and Hattie pulls out a glittery notebook. 'Right, shall we talk Lumiere?'

'Let's wait until we've had some caffeine,' Toby says. 'What did you get up to at the weekend, Ros? Anything as glamorous as Clare?'

'Actually, I went to a party too. At Annabel's. You know it's reopened?'

The place where I did my first ever gig as an impersonator. 'I was there a few weeks ago.'

Rosamund looks confused and then irritated. 'Oh?'

'Yeah, it's massive, isn't it? Couldn't believe it's spread over four whole floors and even has a cigar room. I think they've done it really well. There are so many thoughtful little details like the slides they leave near the dance floor in case your heels have become unbearable.'

'That's cool,' Toby says.

'Yeah,' I say, taking a sip of my Earl Grey.

'I saw three people from *Made in Chelsea*,' Rosamund says.

'Yeah,' I say. 'The night I went there were all kinds of famous faces there.' Fake faces but faces nonetheless. 'The Beckhams—'

'David and Victoria?' Hattie says.

No, Robert and Denise. 'Yep. Brad Pitt, Cheryl Cole, Bukayo Saka.' For a second, I think about adding 'Jenna Cox' but decide that's a lie too far.

Rosamund looks as if she might be about to vomit on the marble coffee table.

'The loos are quite something, aren't they?' I say. 'So Instagrammable.'

'Did you put them on your Insta?' Hattie says.

For a second, I wonder if she's trying to catch me out but it's just her usual confusion at my lack of interest in social media. For Hattie and Rosamund, if something isn't on your grid, it didn't happen.

I shake my head. 'You know me, I don't really do social media.'

Toby smiles. 'Me either. Good to keep your personal life personal, right?'

'Exactly.' Especially when a large part of it is made up.

Chapter Seventeen

I left the meeting with The Leap Agency quite buoyed up. As hoped, Toby's tweaks to my copy were irksome but minor and he even went as far as to say he was delighted the agency could rely on such talented freelance resource. But what pleased me even more was Rosamund and Hattie's slack-jawed amazement that I have been to parties at both The Yard and Annabel's recently (yes, I am so pathetic, I'll take people being impressed by my fake life).

Instead of going straight home, I decided to visit a 'Jenna' boutique in Marylebone High Street. I am the only person in here apart from four very young, very gorgeous-looking assistants who look as if they might be related to Toby. I guess it's hardly surprising the shop is devoid of customers mid-morning on a Monday. People will be working. As I should be if I ever want to finish this book. Or indeed address Toby's entirely pointless feedback on Lumiere. (Sample comment, 'Should we say, "*see* a brighter, younger you" not "*reveal* a brighter, younger you?"')

The assistants exchange glances with each other and I'm immediately conscious of my high-street jeans and tea-stained sweatshirt (I was right not to wear the cream jumper).

'Can I help you?' one of them asks, flicking her glossy blond mane.

'Just browsing, thanks.'

She gives me a cool smile. 'Do let me know if we can help you with anything.'

I can't help but feel she'd like to help me out of the shop. I flick through the rails. There was a burble of chatter and laughter which stopped the minute I opened the door and now it's deathly silent. I have, to use one of my new words, ruined the vibe.

I pick up a pair of jeans and try not to gasp as I see that they cost £285. Never mind, I'm earning good money for my Fake Faces work and I could wear these jeans both when I'm Jenna and in my real life. They're an investment piece, as people who shop in these types of places would say.

The blonde assistant whispers something to one of her colleagues and the two of them giggle. I squash down the idea they're laughing at me.

I hover over a pile of neatly folded sweaters wondering if I dare disturb it. Well, of course I do. I am the customer here. I could do with a new top to wear to Hatfield Academy on Wednesday. People talk of Dutch courage but to my mind there are few better confidence boosters than a good outfit.

It's weird that I've almost forgotten how much I love clothes over the last few years. Having to dress as Jenna has reminded me that there was once a Clare who didn't just stick to ratty sweatpants and oversized sweatshirts. A Clare who used to put make-up on every day and do her hair even if she wasn't going anywhere.

I run my fingers over the buttery soft leather of a tote bag.

The blonde assistant clears her throat. I wonder if she's thinking I can't afford these things? That I am as out of place in this fancy store as a zit on a supermodel. Too old, too fat, too ordinary.

I stop and examine a maribou trimmed pink miniskirt. It's a

ridiculous garment. The sort of thing I can imagine on Hattie or Rosamund.

The shop door opens letting in a cold gust of air and a woman with big, blow-dried hair who's dressed head to toe in white. This is not someone who slops tea all over herself.

'Camilla,' the assistants chorus, flocking to greet her. How is she doing? Did she have a great time in Mauritius? They've got in that gorgeous little top she wanted and have put one aside.

I steal a better look at her. She's a normal looking woman but carries herself in a way that suggests she was born to shop in places like this.

I glance down at the ridiculously expensive jeans and pink fluffy jumper that I'm clutching in my sweaty hands. I put the jumper back on the pile.

'You don't want to try that on?' the blonde assistant says appearing instantly at my side. 'I could look and see if we have one in your size.'

'No. Er… no, thank you.' I just want to get out of here.

I sit on the Tube awash with self-hatred. Any positivity I felt as a result of impressing the Leapsters (yes, that is what they call themselves as a collective) has been wiped out by my abortive attempt at shopping.

A little boy and his mother sit opposite me. He is wearing a bright yellow sweatshirt and clutching a toy ambulance. He looks to be about three.

My Hannah would be three by now. Pain spreads through my body and I clench my fists and bite back tears. Hannah is the last of my five ghost children. They are always with me but sometimes there's a moment that makes the breath catch in my throat. I once cried for two days straight just because I saw a baby who I fancied had my nose.

The little boy is reaching across the aisle proffering the ambulance.

Please no. Please, please someone else.

'Waa waa,' he says earnestly.

'Waa waa,' I manage. 'That's the noise they make, isn't it?'

He looks at me from under his thick, dark lashes. 'Am-lance.'

'That's right.' I glance across at his mother who seems almost comically young. I want to tell her that she is so lucky that she will never know what it's like to have so much love to give but no one to give it to. That she won't be forced to shut off that love like you would the water mains when you've discovered a leak.

The little boy leaves his seat to cross the aisle. He stuffs the ambulance into my hands and looks at me expectantly.

I 'drive' the toy across my jeans. 'Waa waa.'

The little boy rewards me with a huge smile.

'Ambulances make people better.' Except when they can't.

Chapter Eighteen

So, I am back here in this drafty school hall that smells of feet and cheap deodorant. Only this time, as well as puppy dog Sam and his talent show for the not very talented, there is Alex. It's fair to say he is not how I imagined him. I didn't even know I had imagined him, to be honest but, when you hear 'kid with cancer' your mind conjures up things. A tragic figure. A poor little thing.

The real Alex is actually a bit of brat. He snapped at his mum three times in the two minutes she was here, talks to Sam like he's his PA and gave one of the other kids a look that could freeze a desert when she asked how he was feeling.

And, yes, I will surely go straight to hell for thinking unkind thoughts about a child who's so seriously ill but, let's be honest, given my new-found penchant for lying, that one already looked like a dead cert.

'Can you get me a KitKat?' Alex says to Sam now. 'My blood sugar's low.'

I have to force myself not to snap, 'Say please,' but Sam jumps to his feet.

While his teacher is off procuring his confectionary, Alex turns to me. 'The show is pants, isn't it? Not one act you want to watch.

I think I can kiss goodbye to that trip to Disneyland. This lot aren't going to raise enough to send me for a night in a Travel Inn in Birmingham.'

'I'm sure with a few more rehearsals—'

Alex rolls his eyes and gestures towards the stage where a girl called Bethany is murdering a Lizzo number. 'What? She's going to learn to sing?' He puffs out his cheeks. 'How did you meet Mr Jackson then?'

'He came up to me in the street.'

Alex laughs. 'For real? What and just asked you to come here?'

'Yeah.'

'Classic. Bet he gave you the full sob story about me, right?'

'Well—'

'I'm not having a go. Mr Jackson is all right. Y'know, for a teacher.'

From what I've seen of Alex, this is the very definition of high praise.

'He didn't manage to persuade you to come to the show, though? We'd raise loads more money if you did.'

'Unfortunately, I'm filming on that day.'

Alex nods. Is that scepticism in his eyes? Does he think I'm lying? I mean, I am obviously, but still.

Sam returns with the KitKat. 'Here we go.'

'Thanks.' Alex turns to me. 'So what's that mean judge Henry like? Is he as much of dick as he seems?'

'Alex,' Sam says.

'Umm,' I say.

'Oh, right,' Alex says. 'You won't say. Scared I'll tell the newspapers?'

I force a smile, turn my eyes to the stage where a dance troupe are performing what even the kindest might describe as a routine that's experimental.

'Very nice everyone,' Sam says. 'Jasmine, try not to step on Lucy's feet.'

Next up is another singer. Her number is Mariah Carey's 'Without You' although that's not immediately obvious from her rendition. Alex sniggers from behind his KitKat and even Sam struggles to find something to praise.

'That's a very hard song to perform.' The words are out of my mouth before I know it. 'Lots of very high notes. Maybe something like Rhianna's "Rainbow" would be a little easier?'

'That's a good suggestion,' Sam says. 'What do you think, Daisy?'

If I was Daisy I'd think, 'What does she know?' but Daisy of course thinks I'm Jenna so she gives me a big smile and says she'll try it.

Alex looks up from his iPhone 15 and nods. 'Yeah, can't be any worse.'

A comedian takes to the stage. Some of his jokes are reasonably funny (I mean, James Acaster need not worry, but in relative terms), but his voice is almost inaudible and what you can hear is rushed.

'What did you think, Jenna?'

It takes me a second to realise Sam is talking to me.

'Err…' I should never have got into giving opinions. I'm here to meet Alex and then get out of here.

Alex looks up from his phone, his pale face bathed in the sickly light. 'We couldn't hear you, Joe.'

'It was a little quiet,' I say. 'Also your delivery was a bit rushed, probably because you're nervous.' I suddenly hear Jules, one of my youth theatre teachers: Take. Your. Time.

'I liked your joke about the llamas.'

Joe beams at me. 'Thanks.'

I feel a bubble of something warm deep within my chest. It's been a long time since I've said something that has made someone smile like that. A very long time. I'm not horrible to people, at least I hope I'm not, but I'm not exactly a spreader of joy, mainly I suppose because I have none to spread.

'It's great to get expert advice,' Sam says.

The warm bubble bursts. But actually the advice I gave Joe may help him and Daisy does have a (slightly) better chance if she doesn't pick a track that would cast fear into the hearts of many a professional.

My phone pings with a message from Jackie: *Insurance Awards, Watford, Next Thurs?* Jackie is a woman who is too busy for verbs.

More acts come and go and each time, I offer up my thoughts. Alex chips in too, although he's definitely inclined to forget the 'constructive' in constructive criticism. I suppose it's some sort of counterbalance to Sam who tells everyone they're brilliant.

I promised to be here for an hour and, as the hands on the clock finally start to move towards that time, I allow myself to imagine being back in the safety of my flat. I will take off these uncomfortable shoes and too tight jeans, peel off my false lashes and breathe a sigh of relief at having got through this crazy situation I've somehow got myself into. I've learned my lesson and will never again allow myself to be mistaken for Jenna in real life, instead immediately telling anyone who makes that mistake I'm just a lookalike.

I glance across at Alex. Think about the first time I met Sam and him telling me it would mean the world to the kid to meet Jenna. I'm one of the few people in the room Alex has been polite to but there certainly hasn't been any sign of unbridled joy. I hope it's brought him some pleasure though. Bratty he may be but cancer at eleven years old is a tough break by anyone's standards.

The rehearsal draws to a close and Alex brandishes his iPhone in my direction and says it's time to get a selfie to sell on eBay.

'Haha,' I say, moving out of range of the camera. 'I actually prefer to really be in the moment with my fans. Experience it fully.'

Alex's brow furrows. 'Can't you do both?'

'Ms Cox doesn't do photos with fans,' Sam says. 'She explained it all on her Instagram.'

We're interrupted by Joe the comedian. 'Thanks for coming to our rehearsal. And for the tips. I'll go a bit slower and speak up.'

'She doesn't care,' Alex says. 'She's only here because Mr Jackson guilt-tripped her about me.'

'I know,' Joe says, staring at the scuffed wooden floor.

'I do think going slower and being a bit louder will help,' I say. 'And I meant it when I said I love your joke about llamas.'

Joe looks up. 'Really?'

'Really.'

'Yeah, the show still sucks though, doesn't it?' Alex says.

I scowl at him before realising that a) I shouldn't be scowling at a kid who has cancer and b) dirty looks aren't very Jenna.

Alex is undeterred. 'The show is going to be embarrassing so we might as well just accept that now. I need to know I won't be on a plane to the States anytime soon and you lot need to know you're not going to be any good.'

'Don't say that,' Sam says. 'We've still got five weeks of rehearsals. Plenty of time to sell lots of tickets and plenty of time to work on the performances.'

'That's true,' I say, looking at Joe's crestfallen face.

'What do you care?' Alex says.

'*Alex*,' Sam admonishes.

'I'd like the show to be a success,' I say. 'And I'd like you to be able to go to Disneyland.' Although God help the Mickey Mouse who tries to bring a smile to your face.

Alex shakes his head. 'I bet when you walk out of this place today, you don't give us a second thought. You're not even coming to the show. Even though you just turning up would mean we could sell loads of tickets.'

I look around the room. All eyes are fixed on me and there's deathly silence suddenly.

'I can't come to the show, I'm filming that day.'

'I did tell you that,' Sam says.

'But I am going to come to all the remaining rehearsals. Help make this show the best it can be.'

Afterwards, I will ask myself over and over why I said this. Maybe it was the look of hope in some of the eyes upon me or maybe it was the look of contempt in Alex's. I couldn't tell you. What I do know is I made a promise. It was unplanned and unwise and unhelpful. But it was a promise nonetheless.

Chapter Nineteen

By the time I get home, the enormity of what I've done has fully hit me. I may have managed to get away with pretending to be Jenna a couple of times, but that doesn't mean I won't be rumbled in the future. What if I make a slip that exposes me for the fake I really am? What if Jenna posts something on her Instagram about being on holiday in the Maldives on a day 'she' has been at one of the rehearsals? And even if I can somehow get away with it, that doesn't make what I'm doing less morally questionable. (Yeah, I can tell myself I'm helping Alex and the other kids but it's hard to gloss over the stratospheric levels of deceit this 'help' involves.)

I throw my fake designer 'Jenna' handbag on the hall console table, kick off my high heels and pull off the 'va va voom' bra that leaves livid red welts on my skin.

I can't afford to worry about the Hatfield Academy situation now. My agent has been sending me lots of, 'how are you getting on with the new book' messages. I have responded saying it's going well and haven't mentioned that the word count is hovering around three thousand. Pretty pathetic when you consider I've been writing this book for over six months and I don't have the excuse of a full-time day job.

When I got my first book deal, although it was a chunky amount of money, it didn't occur to me to give up work. I liked being a creative director. I could do both. (Back then I could still do anything.)

I flip open my laptop and take a deep breath. It's pointless to get hung up on my lack of progress with the book so far. Today is a new day – and one that's unhindered by the demands of any freelance copywriting. I'll quickly check my emails first though. There might be work ones.

I have to get it right with this new book. When I finally sent my agent, Kate, my second book it was months past the deadline, but she didn't say a word because I'd just had the first miscarriage.

'She's going to hate it,' I wailed to Stephen.

'Don't be silly,' he said. 'She'll love it.'

Meg said the same, reminded me I'd said no one would like my debut.

Kate took two weeks to call me. 'It's a bit… bleak.'

'Dark?'

'Bleak.'

I pushed my thumbs into my temples, thought about the announcement about my debut in *The Bookseller* another lifetime ago. My editor was quoted as saying she couldn't wait to share this wonderful story with the world. Kate said I was a talent to watch. 'I'll do a new draft.'

Silence buzzed down the line. 'What about your other idea? The one Felicia liked.'

I knew what Kate was saying: Write the idea you know your editor likes. Make it easy on yourself. I didn't, of course, instead telling her firmly that story didn't work.

Six weeks later, I delivered a new draft. My editor turned it down so it was sent out to other publishers. Seven months after that, my agent told me it was time to put that book to one side. No one wanted it, in other words. In a different universe, this would have floored me but, by that time, my misery was fully directed elsewhere.

Now I glance at my computer screen and see I have somehow fallen down a rabbit hole of looking at swimming costumes. There was an email about a half-price sale whose subject line told me I couldn't afford to miss it.

A ripple of self-loathing engulfs me. It's nearly three o'clock and I have done nothing with my day apart from going to Hatfield Academy. I *have* to write.

My stomach growls and I realise I haven't had any lunch. I can't think when I'm hungry. I wander into the kitchen and open the fridge.

The fridge is filthy. I'll give it a quick wipe down.

Thirty minutes later, I am still washing the last salad drawer. If a job is worth doing though…

I make myself a cheese sandwich and open Facebook on my phone. A guy I haven't seen since uni is travelling in Vietnam. I scroll through all the pictures thinking how gorgeous it is before posting a message saying it looks amazing and then deleting the message because, on reflection, a heart reaction is quite enough for someone I haven't seen in twenty years and may conceivably never see again.

I shouldn't be wasting time on social media. But then it is my lunch break. I open Twitter. This proves to be a mistake as forty-five minutes later I am still on there and engaged in a spat with a woman I don't know about trans rights.

I put my plate by the sink. What the hell am I doing engaging in pointless rows with people on Twitter? What do I think this numbskull is going to say? Oh, thanks for explaining that to me. I see it differently now.

Guilt washes through me. All writers procrastinate though. I remember asking a friend of mine who is a journalist how she turned in a blistering two thousand word opinion piece each and every week and she laughed and said that was easy: she spent the first three days of the week ignoring the task entirely, the next three in existential panic and the remaining hours before she had to file the copy frantically writing. As Alain de Botton said, 'Work finally begins when the fear of doing nothing exceeds the fear of doing it badly.'

I've hit that point, I queasily realise. I go back to my desk. There's still a lot of day left and I can work late. It's not like there's anybody who is going to want to share dinner or chat or watch a box set. I open my manuscript and read back the last chapter I wrote.

There's a considerable amount of pressure on this book. Firstly, because the last one was so long ago and secondly because no one seems to believe in it quite like I do. When I pitched the idea to my agent all those months ago her response was less than fulsome. 'It's going to be an honest and wry account of a marriage in freefall,' I said. 'It will be deliciously acid and raw. Sort of like a *Heartburn* for our times. Not that I'm comparing myself to Nora Ephron, of course.' I laughed nervously.

Kate chewed the end of her biro. 'Hmm, sounds like misery lit.'

'No,' I said, much more emphatically than I felt. 'It'll be funny. As heart-warming as it is heart-breaking.'

'Well, you're the writer.' (Subtitle: On your head be it. And don't forget how long it is since you've had a book out. Or that your last manuscript was utterly bleak and we couldn't find a single publisher who would touch it.)

Kate isn't the only one who seemed less than enticed by my pitch either. When I mentioned it to my mother, she asked if it wasn't just going to be a thinly veiled autobiography.

'All writers and, for that matter artists, are inspired by real life,' I snapped. 'And, anyway, I find that kind of comment so sexist. No one ever has a go at male authors for using their real-life experiences in their writing.'

My brother was even more annoying than my mum (having heard the pitch from her). 'Won't it just be very boring?'

Even Meg, my endlessly loyal best friend who managed to tell me with a straight face I looked beautiful in my teenage Goth phase, struggled to muster enthusiasm. 'I'm sure if you're writing it, it will be wonderful.'

Those words come back to me now as the cursor blinks accusingly on the blank screen.

The screen is still blank and I decide there's been enough procrastination, enough excuses, enough burying my head in the sand.

It's time to get the toaster fixed.

An hour later, I am standing in a snaking, ill-tempered queue for returns and exchanges. If there was ever a time when I have yearned for my (admittedly faux) celebrity privilege, it's now. Because if I was Jenna and not plain old Clare, I'd have been ushered to the front. The last few months have proved to me beyond doubt that celebrities get special treatment in any number of situations. Everyone goes out of their way to please me when I'm Jenna. Just look at Sam the teacher with his constant ministrations: 'Can I get you anything?', 'Sorry these chairs are so uncomfortable', 'You must be tired'. (Come to think of it, Sam is not a good example as that is how he appears to be with everyone. He is solicitous and kind with the kids and, the other day, Sandra in the school office told me he'd spent his whole Sunday assembling her flat-pack furniture and wouldn't so much as hear of her buying him a bottle of wine for his troubles.)

The queue inches forward fractionally and the man behind me reacts like Usain Bolt on the starting blocks so that he crashes into me from behind. 'Sorry,' he mutters, breathing garlic over me and not sounding very sorry at all.

Yeah, he'd definitely be nicer if I was Jenna. Not that I'd even be queuing.

Despite the fact it's November, it's sweltering hot in here (seriously, the heating must be set for about twenty seven-degrees. Have they not heard about climate change?). I set my coat and bag down at my feet and peel off my thick jumper.

'Hot, isn't it?' says the woman in front.

'Unbearably.'

What was I thinking telling the kids at Hatfield Academy I'd be at every rehearsal for the talent show? Quite apart from all the obvious issues with that, me committing to being at five more rehearsals will have serious implications in terms of my time. The rehearsals themselves may only be an hour (however long they feel) but I have to get myself there and back and even getting myself done up as Jenna takes over an hour. Truly, I don't think the woman has a low maintenance bone in her (perfectly toned) body.

The queue moves forward and, once again, the man behind crashes into me. This time I don't even get the muttered 'sorry'. In fact, he glares at me as if I am at fault for being in his way.

I dig my nails into my sweaty palms and stare longingly at the escalators that will take me away from this place. If I was Jenna I'd be halfway home by now. Just like if I'd been her when I was in that fancy boutique the other day, the assistants would have fawned all over me instead of making me feel as if I had no right to set foot in there. Maybe I'll go back and put that to the test one day? We've all seen *Pretty Woman*, right?

I shake the thought from my brain. Of course, I won't go back to the store dressed as Jenna.

'Why are only three out of the six checkouts in action?' says the woman in front, dabbing her top lip with a tissue.

'Goodness knows.'

She shakes her head. 'If we have to wait much longer, I may have to strip down to my bra and pants.'

I may have to come back on a different day pretending to be a celebrity.

Something sharp and heavy crashes into the back of my thigh and I look around to see it's the bulging carrier bag of the man behind me. I grit my teeth and force myself not to react. I'm only two people from the front of the queue now. Everything comes to those (non celebrities) who wait.

The woman behind the counter is called Lisa and wears a big round badge that tells me she is 'happy to help'.

'Is there something wrong with the heating? It's sweltering in here.'

Lisa gives an uninterested shrug.

No small talk then. Fair enough. If I was trapped in here all day long, I'd probably baulk at whingeing from people who might escape before nightfall. I heave the toaster out of the carrier bag and explain to Lisa that it's only toasting the bread on one side. I haven't had it very long and it started to malfunction within the first months.

'Got the receipt?' Lisa says, boredom seeping through her pores.

I hand it over and Lisa inspects it. 'The product has a one year warranty.'

'Yes?'

'And that's run out.'

'What? When?'

Lisa taps a cerise-coloured talon on the receipt and I look down to see I bought the toaster on the 7 November 2022. One year and one day ago. 'Oh, look I didn't realise. But, we're talking about one day, right?'

Lisa shrugs.

I can feel Usain Bolt's eyes boring into me and I don't even need to look at him to know that he's smiling.

My mind skitters around. I simply cannot walk out of this Hades of a store without having got some kind of result. 'Surely if it's faulty?'

Lisa shakes her head.

'I can't even get a repair?'

'Well, if you pay for one. But you'd have to organise that directly with the manufacturer and I dare say it would cost you more than the price of a new toaster.'

'That's ridiculous. No wonder the planet is screwed.'

Lisa shrugs.

'Look, is there anything you can do to help me please? I had no idea the warranty was up and it is only by one day. I know I should have checked the date on the receipt before I came, but I promise you there's no way I'd have spent an hour sweltering in this queue if I'd realised…' I let the words dry on my parched lips. Lisa isn't going to help me. I bet it would be a different story if she thought I was Jenna.

Chapter Twenty

September 2016

When Stephen gets home from work I am standing at the kitchen sink staring out of the window. I am still in my pyjamas and haven't even brushed my teeth.

'Hi,' he says coming up behind me and putting his arms around my waist. It flits through my mind that I don't smell great. 'I tried to call you a few times.'

'I had my phone switched off.'

He looks as if he is about to say something but thinks better of it. Everyone is like this around me now. As if I am as fragile as a bone-china cup. The only person who doesn't tread on eggshells around me is my father. 'The baby can't have been right,' he said. 'It's for the best. You'll get pregnant again.' My mum was annoyed with him but honestly it didn't upset me any more than all the people trying so hard to say the right thing. I'm equally angry with everyone.

I pull away from Stephen. I don't want him to hug me.

The same thoughts keep boomeranging. What could I have done differently? How could I have stopped this? I had a glass of wine before I found out I was pregnant. There was that day I sprinted for the bus. The one when I got really stressed at work.

And then, of course, there's the fact it took me a year to get pregnant. Everyone says that's not long but it felt like ages to me. Maybe next time it will take two years? Or not happen at all?

Stephen starts collecting the dirty mugs and plates I've left littered about the place and stacks them in the dishwasher. 'How was your—' He lets the sentence die on his tongue. He knows better than to ask me how my day was. 'How are you feeling?'

I shrug in response. 'The bin needs emptying.'

Stephen nods and pulls the bulging black bag from the stainless-steel drum.

I stare at the framed black-and-white wedding photographs on the wall. One captures us coming out of the church and laughing together, our heads dipped against the confetti that swirls through the air. Another is of us at the reception. We are locked in conversation and our own little bubble of happiness. And then there's my favourite one of all – our sweaty, joyful last dance; the triumphant end to the triumphant day. I ache for the people in those photographs.

We were so excited the day we went for the scan. The appointment was at eleven o'clock but we'd both taken the whole day off work. We were going to go to lunch at our favourite café afterwards. I'd even stopped feeling sick in the last few days so could actually look forward to eating. I was going to have a full English and ask for extra crispy bacon. We would take our time, order a second cup of tea. Decaf for me, of course.

The sonographer warned me the gel might feel a little cold. I smiled and told her not to worry, squeezed Stephen's hand and wondered how many scan pictures we should get. One for each of us, one for both sets of parents and maybe a couple of spares. Minutes later, the sonographer went quiet.

'We'll try again,' Stephen says now, snapping a bin bag off the roll.

'OH WELL THAT'S OKAY THEN. THIS BABY DOESN'T MATTER AT ALL BECAUSE WE'LL JUST MAKE ANOTHER ONE.'

'Sorry, sorry,' Stephen says, raising his hands up in the air. 'Stupid thing to say.'

I look at him and shake my head. Maybe I'm not equally angry with everyone?

'I'm asleep,' I say as Meg pokes her head around the bedroom door.

'I brought cake.'

'Home-made?' She nods. 'What kind?'

'Lemon drizzle.'

'Okay, I'm awake. Cut me a slab as big as my head please.'

Meg sits on the edge of the bed and pulls me into a hug. 'Will do. But first we need to get you into the shower.'

'Meanie.'

By the time I've showered, Meg has changed the sheets, opened the window and put a vase of asters on the chest of drawers. 'Cake now?'

I nod. 'It's literally the only reason I showered.'

I prop myself up against the pillows. Meg comes back with a tray that bears two steaming mugs of tea and two plates of cake. 'Where's Stephen?'

'I suggested he pop out for a bit. Take a bit of time for himself.'

'I was horrible to him earlier. Did he say?'

She shakes her head. 'No, and I'm sure you weren't.'

'I was. This is the best cake ever, by the way. You should give up your job immediately and become a cake lady.'

She laughs. 'I don't think I'd make as much as I do in HR. Although I would be happy if I never had to sit in on another person being fired. As soon as people see me, they know something is up.'

'I don't know why I was horrible to him. It's my body that's failed, not his.'

Meg puts her cake down and squeezes my arm. 'Don't say that. This is no one's fault.'

Tears roll down my cheeks and Meg gently takes my plate away from me and pulls me into a hug.

'It took me a whole year to get pregnant in the first place. Long enough that I thought it was never going to happen. We were so excited. And then I go and have a miscarriage. It's not fair.'

Meg strokes my hair. 'No, it's not.'

That's all she says. Not 'you'll get pregnant again' or 'miscarriage is very common' or 'at least you were only twelve weeks'. She just strokes my hair and lets me cry. And, if I didn't already love her, I'd love her just for that.

Chapter Twenty-One

November 2023

Jenna has written a novel. Well, of course, she has. They're all at it now, celebrities. As if knocking out a book is no big deal.

Jenna has created a breathy overexcited Instagram reel to tell her followers all about this magnum opus. She is wearing a face-splitting grin and a multi-coloured jumper which makes her look as if a rainbow has vomited over her. '*Huge* news guys.'

Is it huge news, Jenna? What's happening in Ukraine or the Middle East is huge news. I bloody hate the faux mateyness of 'guys' too.

'I've written my first ever novel. It's called *Sunny Side Up.*' She holds up the book.

'Eek! It feels so special to hold it in my hands.'

Eek? What is she – six?

'And I cannot wait for you all to read it.'

I can wait.

'I poured my absolute heart and soul into this.'

Of course you did.

'And I have loved writing every single word.'

Pah! That alone tells you she's not a proper writer. No proper writer loves writing every single word. Quite a large part of the writing process is resisting the urge to hurl your laptop out of the window. Or beat your head repeatedly against a hard surface. I'm supposed to be writing my book now and yet somehow it's eleven o'clock and I've yet to get down a single word.

'*Sunny Side Up* is about a breakfast TV presenter called Sophie.'

A thinly veiled version of herself then.

'Sophie appears to have the perfect life. Love, fame, you name it, Sophie has it all. But then things start to unravel…'

Why am I still watching this? It's not as if I don't have enough real world problems to deal with right now.

'…Sophie gets into all kinds of scrapes and bother.'

I roll my eyes so hard it's a wonder they go back to normal. 'Scrapes and bother'? I bet the book is mediocre and derivative and yet, despite that, has been snapped up by agents and publishers, all falling over themselves to bring it to market. And, because they've invested so heavily in it, the book will now have everything behind it. The marketing and publicity spend will be huge and the book everywhere, from your local supermarket to the sort of bookshops that would normally turn up their noses at a book with a pink cover and swirly type. There will be Tube posters and podcasts and reviews in the national press. The book will sell shedloads and both Jenna and her publisher will attribute that to its brilliance rather than seeing it as something predetermined – something they essentially bought.

'…Anyway, I'm going to have a book tour and details of that will be announced shortly but I'll be travelling up and down the country and I would love to see as many of you as possible.'

I'm not saying all celebrity books are bad. I love Graham Norton's books for example, and Ruth Jones's. But it pisses me off that it seems so easy for pretty much any celebrity to get a book deal and then that their books get so much money and care lavished upon them. It's not even just 'proper' celebrities either – TikTok comedians, Instagram cool girls, productivity hackers and 'wellness' peddlers are getting six-figure book deals.

It's all kind of depressing for us normal authors. Although, maybe if I spent a little less time and energy being angry about this and a little more on my own book, it would be a good thing all round.

Chapter Twenty-Two

I'm back at Hatfield Academy and finding that it might be possible to think bad things about a child with cancer as Alex is no easier to warm to than the first time I met him. He's relatively okay with me, well, the Jenna version of me, but he's curt, bordering on rude to pretty much everyone else.

He hasn't had a nice word to say about any of the three performances we've seen so far and is glowering over his Spiderman comic with a face that could sour milk. If I'm honest, the performances – a rendition of 'Rainbow' from Daisy, the dance/gymnastics mash-up, and a kid called Dylan whose talent is 'farting' with different parts of his body – have been less than stellar, but Alex's snipes and snarls are unbecoming, especially considering his classmates are doing this to raise money for him.

For my part, I have made a conscious decision to be positive. The person I used to be. Well, not actually her because obviously I'm being Jenna, but Jenna with a touch of old Clare. Which is probably a better fit. Jenna is relentlessly positive.

I don't want to be like Sam, though. He's about as useful as a newspaper over your head in a thunderstorm. Everything is 'lovely' or 'marvellous' or 'awesome'. The man has a low bar for awe.

I told Daisy that today's performance was a hundred times better than her previous one and I could see that she has worked very hard. But I think she can get it better still. How many times has she watched a video of Rihanna performing 'Rainbow'? How often does she listen to it? Practice is everything. I've used it to turn myself into a whole new person. I don't say the last bit.

I told the dance/gymnastics trio that their routine started strong and had a good bit at the end but lost focus in the middle.

I had nothing for the body farter.

Sam announces there's going to be a small break before the next act because the performer has mislaid her flute.

'*Flute?*' Alex says, his voice dripping with disdain.

Sam nods and smiles. He is wearing a dark blue shirt that really suits him and I'm reminded he could objectively be described as hot if I didn't subjectively find his unbridled puppy dog levels of enthusiasm so grating.

'I see you're a Spidey fan,' Sam says.

'I'm not some *baby*,' Alex says. 'But I collect vintage editions of the comic.'

I never would have spoken to one of my teachers that way but Sam's reaction is mild and unflustered. 'People of all ages enjoy comics actually. And it's great to see you reading.' Alex makes a harrumphing noise. 'Can you get me some crisps?'

'Please,' I say before I can stop myself.

Both Alex and Sam's heads snap around to look at me.

'Please,' Alex says.

'Your mum did say she'd packed some chia overnight oats for you,' Sam says.

'I think things are bad enough for me without that, don't you?'

On this, I am with Alex. When I had my first miscarriage, people brought cake and chocolate and lasagnes. By miscarriage four, they came with all manner of weird foods that would fix me. If I could just avoid the nightshade foods or cut out wheat or eat industrial quantities of quinoa. Did I know it was the world's only complete grain?

Sam scuttles off to get a packet of cheese and onion.

'Disneyland then?' I say to Alex. 'Is it the big rollercoasters you like?'

He shakes his head. 'Nah. I've done enough puking for a lifetime.'

I'd have put money on the big rides being the thing that's making Alex so keen to go to Disneyland. Let's face it, he's not a kid you can imagine being caught up in the magic.

'Mr Jackson fancies you, by the way.'

'Don't be silly,' I say, blushing furiously and hating myself for it.

Alex shrugs. 'He so does. You should have heard the way he was talking about you after the last rehearsal. How he couldn't believe you'd promised to come to all the rehearsals. How normal you are and how you muck in and help. How he reckons that there are a lot of people who aren't as nice as they seem on the telly but, if anything, you're even nicer.'

A change of subject is needed and fast. 'You haven't thought of being in the talent show yourself then?'

'Haven't got any talents.'

'Oh, I'm sure that's not true.'

'I'm not well enough.'

'Not even for a short act?'

Alex's eyes widen. I don't think he's used to being challenged. 'Nope.'

Sam returns slightly breathless. He approaches getting Alex's snacks as if he's fetching him an epi pen or a defibrillator.

'Excuse me,' he says stepping past me. Does he fancy me, or rather the Jenna version of me? No, of course, he doesn't. Alex, like eleven-year-old boys everywhere, just has that kind of nonsense on the brain.

Alex starts eating his crisps and the flautist takes to the stage for her rendition of 'Amazing Grace'.

'Well, that was less than amazing,' Alex mutters as she leaves the stage.

I bite the inside of my cheek to stop myself laughing.

Next up on stage is Joe the comedian. He starts with his llama joke and I feel a small glow of pride as I know it's me who gave him confidence in that. It's not actually me, of course, but I don't dwell on that.

'That was good, Joe,' I say, as he comes off stage.

Sam nods. 'Awesome.'

'I like your new stuff about breakfast club,' I say. 'You still need to speak up a bit though.'

'Thanks,' Joe says looking at his trainers. 'And I will.'

A screech comes from the back of the hall. A group of kids have been messing about throughout the rehearsal and, save for the odd 'sshh' or finger to his pursed lips, Sam hasn't done much about it. 'Seven J,' he says now. 'Don't forget we have a visitor.'

Joe is still standing staring at the floor. He scratches his neck. 'How are you feeling, Alex?'

'Just peachy.'

Joe's cheeks redden.

'He's just trying to be nice,' I say to Alex when Joe walks away, his head hanging low. I'm being a hypocrite though. When people used to constantly ask me how I was feeling, I often had to fight the urge to scream, 'How do you fucking well think?' and stab them with a bread knife.

Sam is twisting a button on his shirt. I imagine he's uncomfortable with me admonishing Alex, however gently.

'I know,' Alex says. 'But sometimes I just get sick of people asking. You know?'

'I do know,' I say. I really do.

More acts come and go, each one of them further testing my resolve to be positive. 'I'm just nipping to the loo,' I say to Sam.

'Of course, the staff toilets are down the corridor and to your right.'

I make my way across the hall as one of the poets takes to the stage and make a mental note not to hurry back.

I've already decided I'll use the kids' toilets and not the staff ones because, while the latter are probably nicer, I'd rather be scrutinised by a child I happen to bump into than another adult. So far, it's been surprisingly easy to limit the amount of people I interact with when I come here. After I made my rash promise to attend all the rehearsals, I told Sam I wanted to keep everything on the down low. 'That's so impressive,' he said. 'I imagine a lot of celebrities would use it to generate publicity.'

I open the door to the girls' toilets and am hit by such a powerful and unpleasant stench of stale urine and cheap air freshener, I nearly change my mind about using the staff toilets. I won't be in here for long though.

I hover over the toilet. I remember reading somewhere that it's injurious to your pelvic floor muscles to do this but there's no way I'm sitting down on this seat and, anyway, no one's going to know if my pelvic floor is less than perky.

A sniffing sound comes from a couple of cubicles down. Is it someone crying?

I consider knocking on the door but I probably wouldn't be able to help. From memory, I think I spent most of the time between eleven and sixteen in tears about something or other and no adult ever seemed to make it better.

I wash my hands. It's weird catching sight of myself all Jenna-ed up. I look so much better than usual. Happier too, which is odd. As if I've temporarily convinced myself I'm her and not me.

The person in the last cubicle is definitely crying. I guess I should at least ask if they're okay.

I look at my watch. It's twenty to one. Not long until I can finally get out of here.

I head for the door, my Jenna heels click-clacking across the dirty grey tiles.

I glance back at the cubicle the crying is coming from. For goodness' sake, the last thing I need right now is more drama.

I knock on the cubicle door. 'Are you okay?'

A pause. 'Fine.'

I recognise the voice. My brain whirs. 'Daisy?'

The door is flung open and sure enough there is Daisy, pink-nosed and snotty. 'What are you doing in these toilets? Don't they have like a VIP toilet?'

'I don't think so—'

'Well, the teachers' toilets then?'

'These were nearer. Anyway, never mind that, what's the matter?'

This sets Daisy off on a fresh wave of crying. 'I've got no friends,' she says, when she can finally get the words out.

'I'm sure that's not true,' I say, simultaneously realising that I have never seen Daisy looking as if she's part of a group. In fact, I don't think I've seen any of the other girls talk to her except when they've had to.

'*It is true*!' she says, hiccuping. 'Olivia and Gemma and Sophie and I were all mates at primary school but now Philippa has joined and they all hate me.'

'Why do you think they hate you?'

'I don't *think* they hate me, I *know* they do. Last weekend, they all went to Lakeside shopping centre together and I wasn't asked. And they always stop talking when I come into a room and make all these "jokes" about my clothes and stuff. Earlier, Philippa was saying that she managed to get her ears pierced in Kitty's Accessories even though she wasn't with her mum.'

I can't immediately place Philippa and then realise she's the one with nice singing voice who stood out for looking older the first time I came here.

Daisy wipes her eyes with a wodge of loo roll. 'She said she reckoned the others could all get away with it too, and then she looked at me and started laughing and the others joined in. Even Gemma.'

A visceral memory of being Daisy's age floods my body. My Philippa was called Alison. 'Oh, Daisy,' I say, patting her on her shaking shoulder. I'm tempted to go back into the hall and give those little bitches a piece of my mind but I'm aware that would be an extremely bad plan and not just because it's very un-Jenna behaviour. 'Have you talked to Mr Jackson about this?'

Daisy shakes her head so hard it's a wonder it doesn't fly off. 'No way can I tell a teacher! Not even Mr Jackson. That would make them hate me even more.'

Unfortunately, that's probably true. 'What about your parents?'

Daisy shakes her head again. 'I tried to talk to my mum but she never listens and always acts like everything is no big deal. Anyway, she's part of the problem.'

I think of my own mum telling teenage David and me that a mother's place is always in the wrong. 'Because?'

'She won't let me wear make-up or buy me cool clothes. Even my school uniform looks babyish because she bought everything way too big so I could grow into it.'

It crosses my mind that Daisy does look different to a lot of the other girls, and some of that is down to her not having hit puberty yet but, now that she mentions it, quite a few of the others do seem to wear a bit of eye make-up (even though I imagine it's against the school rules) and manage to make their uniforms look less, well, uniform. 'You could roll your skirt up at the waistband.'

'Won't Mr Jackson tell me off? They're supposed to come to the knee.'

I shrug. 'The others seem to get away with it.'

Daisy smiles for the first time since we've been in here. She rolls up her skirt and examines herself in the mirror. 'A bit better thanks. Oh, I wish my mum was more like you.'

A bubble of warmth spreads in my chest and I picture myself buying Daisy some mascara and maybe some of that Sunday Riley tinted lip balm I've seen so many of the others with and then giving it to her at the next rehearsal.

Wait though, tempting as it is to be the nice guy, should I really be buying make-up for a kid whose mum doesn't allow it? Even more importantly still, what message am I giving out? 'You know what, Daisy? You should be yourself.'

Daisy's shoulders sag and her head drops. 'That's what my mum says.'

I nod. 'Well, she's right.'

'She's mean is what she is. She won't even buy me that fluffy tote bag that all the TikTokkers have got. Says she bought me a perfectly good new school bag at the start of term and I should just use that.'

God, it must be hard being a parent. It's easy to forget that when you're so laser-focused on how hard it is not being one. 'I'm sure your mum wants the best for you.'

Daisy makes an indecipherable noise.

'You're lovely and you shouldn't have to change for anyone. Just be yourself.' Pretty strange coming from me right now, but that doesn't mean it's not good advice.

Chapter Twenty-Three

I am so agitated by the events at Hatfield Academy, I totally forget I am supposed to have a Zoom call with my agent.

A message pings into my inbox: *On the call if you're still free to catch up?*

Shit. Shit, shit, shit.

'Sorry, sorry,' I say, joining the call. 'I was writing and completely lost track of the time.'

Kate smiles. 'Well, I guess I can't complain about that.' Her brow furrows. 'You look different. Have you changed your hair?'

Christ, I am still Jenna-ed up. In my hurry to get on the Zoom, I totally forgot that. 'Err, I had a meeting in town this morning.' I move my laptop into the shadows. 'With, er, some of the ad agency people I work with.'

Kate nods. 'Well, you look very nice.' Her brow furrows. 'You remind me of someone actually. I can't think who.'

'Really?' I squeak. 'I'm just going to switch off my camera. The internet is a bit dodgy today.'

'Oh, it seems okay?'

'No, very patchy. You keep freezing.'

'Okay, no worries. I don't need to see you, just hear you.' She smiles. 'So, how's the new book going?'

I pause. Although recent events might suggest otherwise, I'm not a very good liar and I am especially keen not to deceive Kate who has been almost ridiculously loyal to me. This is the woman who stuck by my side when I delivered her a second book months late that no one wanted to publish. The woman who told me she'd wait and to concentrate solely on getting better when I went mad. The woman who never mentions the fact it's years since I made her a penny. 'Yeah… good.'

'When do you think you'll have something for me to read?'

Nausea bubbles in my belly. 'By Christmas? It won't be finished by then, of course, but I reckon I'll have the first forty thousand words or so.' Why did I say that? My current word count is five thousand and forty-two. We've still got five and a half weeks until Christmas though, so I should be able to do it. Especially if I spend more time actually writing the bloody thing and less time fannying around pretending to be Jenna.

'Are you sure you wouldn't like me to read what you've done so far?'

'No. No, thank you.' There's no way I can be honest about my lack of progress, firstly because it's been so long and secondly because I know Kate doesn't wholeheartedly believe in the premise of the book. We're in 'on my head, be it' territory.

I clear my throat and try to sound confident and in control as I tell Kate I want to polish what I have before I send it to her and that there's no point wasting her time with chapters that I'll end up cutting.

'Okay, whatever you think is best. By the way, I bumped into Felicia the other day and she was asking after you. Said she'd be excited to read whatever you write next.'

Felicia the editor who bought my debut novel. One of the biggest disappointments of my life, and there's a lot of competition for that spot, was when she turned down my second book.

Kate is telling me more about Felicia and how her career has really rocketed since she moved to a new independent publishing house. I zone out thinking about the new book and where I am (or more accurately where I'm not) with it. I've hardly written anything for weeks but that's only because I've been distracted by all this Jenna business, right? And I shouldn't worry that when I have sat down to write, the words haven't exactly been flowing? It's always hard to get yourself into a story.

Now I tune back into the conversation as Kate tells me about a big-name author Felicia has recently poached from one of the big publishing houses.

'That's great news.' Do I mean that? One of the hardest things about adult life is the seeming requirement to be pleased for people who were once a huge part of your life but then unceremoniously dumped you. I'm supposed to be happy for Felicia even though she once told me she wanted to publish my books 'until the end of time'. I'm meant to be gracious and charming about not just my ex-husband but also the woman he left me for. I have to make damn sure I hit the 'like' button on a happy social media post from a friend who dropped me like a proverbial hot potato when I had one too many miscarriages for them to deal with. (One too many for *them*?)

Kate and I wrap up the call with her telling me that she's looking forward to reading the new book and it will be perfect because she can use that quiet time between Christmas and New Year.

I snap my laptop shut with my heart racing. I can write forty thousand words in five and a half weeks. And I can keep believing in this book even when others don't. Of course I can.

*

It's a Cinderella moment – my transformation from Jenna back to me. I hang up the silk dress and change into my ratty sweatpants.

I hated having to lie to Kate about how well the book is going and I was already drained by my excursion to Hatfield Academy. The rehearsals are plenty bad enough in themselves without adding in trying to play agony aunt to Daisy. Not to mention the fact it's exhausting having to be someone else. To remember to speak like them, talk like them and laugh like them. *The Jungle Book* pops into my head: *I wanna be like youuuuuuuu*.

I sit down at my computer, open my manuscript and read back on what I wrote yesterday. Immediately, I want to delete it but I force myself not to. Remember my creative writing tutor telling us all you can't edit a blank page and that all first drafts are shit. Trouble is, so are my third drafts. And fourth and fifth.

My first book did okay. Well, more than okay. Good reviews, five weeks in *The Sunday Times* Bestsellers List. Looking back, I wish I'd enjoyed it more, soaked it in. But by then, Stephen and I had been trying for a year and I'd started to worry I'd never get pregnant. (Wrong worry!)

I mustn't think about any of that. I need to focus on the next scene in this manuscript and how Poppy my protagonist will navigate it. I force my fingers to keep moving across the keyboard. I used to love writing. I wish I could find a way back to being that person.

Poppy, my main character, still thinks she has the perfect life. Given I know what's coming, it's almost painful to write but I make myself keep going.

The doorbell rings. Meg can't be here already. She's coming after work. I look at the time on my computer and see it is after work. I have written a grand total of two hundred and four words. Pathetic.

Identity Crisis

I shut my laptop and open the door.

'Hey,' Meg says. 'You look nice.'

I glance down at my sweatpants but then I remember I still have my Jenna blow-dry and the remnants of her make-up.

Meg hands me a bottle of Cabernet Sauvignon. 'Open that quickly, will you? I've had a pig of a day. I'd just got to work when Lola's nursery phoned to say she had a temperature. And Alfie's teething again so he screams his head off every time I put him down. Sorry, boring.'

'You're allowed to moan about your kids, you know.' I want this to be true but it isn't entirely. I love Meg and I want to love her kids but that doesn't change the fact that every time I'm near them, I feel this visceral pain in my stomach, an ache of loss and longing, a thump of: *Why not me?* 'I realise that I'm a bitter evil cow but I make an exception for you.'

She laughs and I pour us both large glasses of wine.

Meg asks me how my day was. 'Fine.' I don't say anything about the excursion to Hatfield Academy. I haven't even told her about the lookalike work yet so I can't just casually mention I've somehow found myself impersonating a national treasure. 'I'm finding this book hard going.'

Meg is too nice to remind me I find every book hard going.

'I think I was a one book wonder.'

'Stop saying that. Of course you're not.'

I knew Meg was pregnant before she had a chance to tell me. I'd become pretty attuned to the signs by then having been pregnant twice myself. I pretended to be delighted and she pretended not to know it wasn't quite that simple. By the time she had Lola, I'd slotted in a third miscarriage, Stephen and I were fighting nearly all the time, and no publisher wanted my second book. 'My book is dead,' I said to Stephen. 'Like our babies.' He looked at me as if I was a monster before forcing a small unconvincing laugh. But I went to the hospital with flowers and a little yellow dress, and when Meg told me the birth had been unimaginably awful, I managed to say, 'Poor you,' not, 'Nice fucking problem to have.'

I rifle around in the fridge and put out a makeshift meal of dips and bits. 'I'm sorry, Meggie. I should have made us dinner. It's not even as if I have a proper job. Honestly, I don't know why you put up with me.'

'When you've spent all day with a four year old and a one year old, you're just grateful for someone who doesn't want you to watch *Peppa Pig* or play peekaboo or wipe their bum.'

'The night is young.'

'True,' Meg says, taking a swig of her wine. 'And anyway you know that, even if you did make me watch *Peppa* or play peekaboo or wipe your bum, we're still stuck with each other. Because what are we?'

'Sisters.'

Meg chinks her glass against mine. 'Sisters.'

Chapter Twenty-Four

So it turns out Jackie doesn't have any other Jonny Turners. Apparently, she used to but now he's retired from the business and become a yoga teacher.

This means I'm stuck with the dreadful Malcolm. Well, unless I want to give up taking double-act bookings, which doesn't seem wise when you consider the progress or rather lack thereof with my new book and the fact the freelance copywriting work comes in dribs and drabs. Being Jenna is the only income stream I can rely on right now.

Malcolm's nose does a small but perceptible wrinkle when he sees me. I guess he doesn't think my high street evening dress is suitably Jenna but as my bank balance is considerably smaller than hers, I'm having to rethink my policy of buying the sort of labels she favours. Anyway, screw Malcolm, I like this dress.

To celebrate the finest in insurance, we're in a hotel in Watford which one might label as 'pleasant' if you were feeling generous. The banqueting hall is an inoffensive pale-yellow room full of round tables with a stage at one end. A couple of chandeliers are doing the heavy lifting when it comes to the 'opulence' promised by the hotel website and the 'banquet' has begun with cream of mushroom soup and a bread roll.

Malcolm and I are not partaking in said meal as we have been ushered backstage to be briefed on the schedule for the evening. This is being done by a small rotund man who has a habit of plucking at his beard. 'So as soon as the starters are cleared, we'll start the show.' Pluck, pluck. 'If you could do about ten minutes of warm-up to get everyone in the mood. Just a hello and a few jokes.' Pluck, pluck. 'During that time, the mains will be served. A fricassee of chicken in a cream sauce. Something else for the vegetarians.' Pluck, pluck. 'Don't let the meal being served put you off your stride though. We've got a lot to get through tonight so, as soon as you've done your warm-up, start the awards. First up is Best Newcomer.' Pluck, pluck.

Nerves flutter in my stomach. Malcolm wrote the warm-up and sent it to me via Jackie. I added a couple of suggestions but see looking down at the script now that every single one of them has been ignored. Doesn't he realise I'm a writer? I give myself a mental shake. He doesn't and wouldn't care if he did. He's no more interested in my editorial input than those idiots at VOdz were when I tried to rewrite that speech, and it's a sad indictment of my self-esteem that this stings.

'The pinnacle of the night is Broker of the Year.' Pluck, pluck.

Malcolm and I are taken to the wings. A red-faced man in a too-tight suit introduces us. 'And please join me in giving a warm welcome to the stage to Jenna Cox and Jonny Turner.' He does a stagey wink. 'I can't *ensure* they're the real deal but I can promise we're in for a great night!'

Showtime. I follow Malcolm on to the stage.

'Jenna and I are so happy to be with you tonight,' Malcolm starts. 'As John said in his introduction, we're going to make sure you all have a wonderful evening. You won't need your "disappointing night" cover.'

IDENTITY CRISIS

There's a weak flutter of laughter but most people are more interested in their main courses and more importantly the free Merlot.

Malcolm looks at me and I know it's my turn to speak but I've completely forgotten my line.

'Although you might need your "hangover" cover.'

It's not my scripted line and Malcolm glares at me. After that, we get back on track though. I remember what I'm actually supposed to say, the chemistry between 'Jenna' and 'Jonny' seems authentic and we even get some big laughs, although admittedly I think they have more to do with the aforementioned Merlot than us.

By the time we start presenting the awards, the mood in the room is really quite jolly and when I mess up one of the categories, Malcolm rescues me in a way that could almost be described as gracious.

Finally, we reach the Broker of the Year award and I read out the names of the nominees and try not to be put off by a middle-aged pair just in front of me who are snogging like a couple of teenagers.

'And the winner is…' Malcolm pauses for effect. 'Sunny Patel.'

Sunny makes his way to the stage to collect the ugly glass trophy, which he holds aloft to applause from all those who aren't too drunk or too busy snogging to be aware of what's going on.

'Excellent,' beard plucker says as Malcolm and I come off stage. 'Your cab will be here in about ten minutes. But first I expect you must both need a comfort break.'

A what? Oh, he means a pee.

'Just the one cab?' Malcolm says.

'Yes.' Pluck, pluck.

I wait for Malcolm to start fussing about how Clapham is not on the way to Herne Hill. But he says nothing.

*

Much as I didn't fancy wandering the streets of Watford, sharing a cab with Malcolm isn't much better.

I've made several attempts at small talk since we got in, all of which have been rebuffed. When I said I thought the evening had gone quite well, it was met with a noncommittal 'hmm', when I asked what Malcolm had been up to in the day, he gave me a look that made me shrivel inside and said, 'Preparing,' and when I asked if he'd ever been a lookalike for anyone else, he said, 'Yes, Joan Collins.'

So now we are sitting in silence save for the strains of Magic FM.

My mind drifts to the situation with Hatfield Academy. Whatever possessed me to say I'd go to all the rehearsals? For that matter, what made me even become a lookalike? I never would have thought of it if I hadn't stumbled on that programme. How weird to think the course of your life can be changed by something you watched on telly. Especially since it was something that was served up to me as 'guilt-free TV' that I might enjoy because I'd watched *Below Deck* and *Married at First Sight*. I mean, we're not talking *Panorama*.

'You're good at doing her laugh.' Malcolm's voice startles me. 'But you need to smile much more.'

My face aches from bloody smiling. It felt as if every single time I stopped smiling tonight, Malcolm tapped the side of his mouth.

'And work on your body language. Jenna never slouches. That came very easily to Kara, what with her training as a principal ballet dancer.'

'Right.'

'Also that dress isn't quite right.'

'Who bloody asked you?' The words are out of my mouth before I can stop them but to my amazement Malcom laughs.

'I'm sorry,' I say eventually.

'No worries.'

'So Jackie says your first job in show business was when you were four?'

'Hmm, if you can call a sausage commercial a job in show business.' Malcolm shudders. 'I've never been able to put a sausage in my mouth since…'

He looks at me with a glint in his eye and we both burst out laughing.

'I had to eat about fifty of the things. No one told me I could spit.'

Juvenile as it is, we catch each other's eye and start laughing again. Uncontrollably like the real Jenna and Jonny.

Eventually we recover ourselves. 'So what do you do for a living?' Malcolm asks. Apart from this.'

'I'm a freelance advertising copywriter and a novelist. Or rather I'm supposed to be a novelist. My first and only book came out seven years ago and I haven't had anything published since. I had a few… er, problems over the years and it didn't make it very easy to be creative. Nobody wanted to publish my second book because it was terrible and now I'm trying to write a new one and that's looking as if it's going to be even worse. I don't even know if I can still call myself a writer.' Hot, fat tears start rolling down my cheeks. Oh for God's sake, why am I crying in front of Malcolm?

He hands me a tissue. 'Of course you can still call yourself a writer. You wrote one book and you can write another. And if you've had "problems" to deal with, well then of course that's going to hamper your creativity.'

'It's not supposed to,' I say through snotty sobs. 'Suffering is meant to fuel creativity.'

'Hmm, I think it depends.' His fingers go to the side of his mouth.

'Don't tell me you want me to smile now for pity's sake!'

'No, I just had an itch.'

And then we're both laughing again. Me, alongside the tears.

Chapter Twenty-Five

There are so many things I should be doing but I am lying on my bed watching Jenna's latest Instagram reel (work research, no?).

Today, she is wearing a chunky red funnel neck jumper and immaculately cut jeans. Her hair is piled up into the sort of 'messy' bun that only a hairdresser can create. But Jenna's killer accessory is an impossibly cute and tiny red cockapoo puppy. 'This is Scooby,' she says, bending down next to him. She lifts one of his front paws and makes him wave to camera. 'Say hello to everyone Scooby.'

Eurgh, dogs shouldn't be made to wave.

'Scooby belongs to my gorgeous sister Zara and her gorgeous husband Ben.'

I wonder if there is anyone in Jenna's life she doesn't describe as gorgeous?

'Zara and Ben have gone away for the weekend, which means that Auntie Jenna is looking after Scooby.'

Auntie Jenna.

'Isn't that right, Scooby?'

The dog cocks his head to one side and Jenna puts her crossed hands over her heart.

'Can you stand the cuteness, guys?'

Scooby starts jumping up and Jenna throws her head back in delighted laughter. Which just goes to show she knows very little about puppy training. I recently wrote an article entitled 'Ten Top Tips to Stop Your Puppy Jumping Up' and know that while the leaping all over you might seem sweet when your dog is little, it should be actively discouraged as you're unlikely to be so keen when they're big enough to flatten you.

Scooby has now discovered his reflection in a full-length mirror and is going crazy.

'Who's dat, Scooby? Who's dat?'

Lose the baby voice, woman. You're in your forties.

Jenna scoops Scooby into her arms and starts smothering his small curly head with kisses. 'Can you tell I'm in love with this pooch, guys?' Scooby licks her face in response (a bit unhygienic if you ask me).

Jenna grins to camera. (Has she changed her shade of lipstick? I hope not when I've spent a small fortune stocking up on Charlotte Tilbury's Pillow Talk.) 'Yep. Utterly, completely head over heels in love. In fact, y'know what this is, guys? It's puppy love.' She giggles and looks meaningfully to camera.

Surely, she's not going to sing 'Puppy Love'? Not even Jenna can be that cheesy?

She can. She is.

'And they called it puppy love…'

I have to admit she has a surprisingly good singing voice. The whole thing is still cringeworthy though, especially since Jenna doesn't seem to know most of the words and just 'la la las' her way through. Poor Scooby looks most confused.

I scroll down to read some of the many comments.

OMG, the cutest! And I don't just mean the puppy. ♥♥♥
I didn't know you could sing!!! Girrrrrrrrl, you're amazing!!!
You've got the voice of an angel!

Okay, she can hold a note but not sure she's got the 'voice of an angel'.

A-DOR-ABLE, the pair of you.
Love this video so much ♥♥♥
This has made my day!!!

Jenna only posted the video this morning and it's already had nearly half a million likes.

Some people can just do no wrong.

*

Note to self: Never ever set out to write a Nora Ephron book for our time.

Nora Ephron was a genius.

You are... not.

Chapter Twenty-Six

Stephen wants to have lunch with me. Like lunch is a thing we do. I reread his text message, searching for clues, but there are none.

If I wasn't struggling so much with the scene I'm trying to write, I'd probably say no. But anything beats sitting in front of my computer right now – even breaking bread with the man who smashed my heart into a million tiny pieces. Well, what was left of my heart by that time.

Stephen and I arrange to meet at the new deli on the high street. I'm glad we're not meeting up anywhere we used to go. I think that would be too much to bear, although it's fair to say the goalposts on that one have moved a few times.

For the rest of the morning I'm skittish and queasy. I abandon any pretence of trying to write and instead check Jenna's Instagram to see that the video of her singing 'Puppy Love' now has five million likes. I chuck my phone down in disgust and go to my wardrobe where I pull out various different outfits. For all the women's magazine articles on what to wear for various different occasions, I've never seen one on what to wear to have lunch with the man you once thought was your happy ever after but is now shacked up with someone else.

Stephen is already sitting down by the time I arrive. He looks a little tired and I allow myself a brief fantasy about him being up all night arguing with Tamara. Trouble in paradise.

'How's the new book going?'

'Okay,' I lie.

'Good. And what else have you been up to?'

Oh, you know, nothing out of the ordinary, just accidentally stealing the identity of a TV star and national treasure and pretending to be her to a bunch of school kids. Did I mention one of them has cancer? 'Not much.'

Stephen smiles the lopsided smile I used to find so irresistible. 'I wanted to talk to you about something.'

I nod slowly, already knowing I'm not going to want to hear this.

The waiter appears and asks if we're ready to order.

I ask for a cup of tea and a halloumi wrap. Stephen says he'll have the same. (So compatible!)

The waiter disappears and I look at my ex-husband. He really does look quite pale and there are dark circles under his eyes.

'Tamara's pregnant.'

I feel as if all the air has been knocked from my lungs.

'Twenty-two weeks.'

Longer than I ever managed. She'll have had two scans by now. They'll know things are looking good.

The coffee machine hisses and spits. Stephen fiddles with a button on his shirt, twisting it back and forth. 'I wanted to tell you myself.'

A wave of fury washes through me. What does he want – a sodding medal?

'Here we go,' says the waiter, setting down two halloumi wraps and steaming mugs of tea. 'Enjoy!'

I wait until he's walked away and look at Stephen. 'If you'll forgive me, I think I've rather lost my appetite.'

All afternoon I lay curled up on my bed. Like the juicy little baby inside Tamara's womb.

I can't even cry.

I don't know why it's a shock. There was never any suggestion that the problem lay with Stephen. Clearly his sperm are both abundant and good swimmers. Go Stephen.

At six o'clock I drag myself out of the house. The bus keeps stopping and starting and I begin to feel nauseous. I wonder if Tamara has had morning sickness? A memory rises of Stephen fussing around me with plain crackers and ginger tea. He knows the drill.

A toddler in a buggy is desperately trying to get her mother's attention but the mother is lost in her phone. I feel a sharp stab of hatred. I try to squash it down. Remind myself this could be the woman's only free moment in the day. She might be the most attentive, devoted mum.

Meg takes one look at me and shouts up to Adam asking him to bath the kids. She is still in her work clothes, and the expression 'stocking feet' flashes through my mind. Do people say that anymore?

The tears that wouldn't fall earlier come as soon as I start to speak. It's hard to get the words out.

'Oh, Clare,' Meg says, squeezing my hand.

I swipe at my eyes with the heel of my other hand and look at Meg. And suddenly I am hit by a revelation that feels like a punch to the gut. 'You knew.'

'I—'

I wrench my hand free of hers, jump up. 'You fucking knew.'

'Yes.'

'Do you see him?'

'No. Yes. Stephen came back with Adam one night after they bumped into each other on the train. I said hello, chatted for a bit. My loyalty will always be to you, Clare, you know that—'

'Did you invite them round for dinner to celebrate the happy news? Champagne for three and Nosecco for your new friend Tamara?'

'*Clare.*'

I head to the door, pull on my boots. From upstairs, I can hear the sounds of Lola chattering and Alfie singing 'The Wheels on the Bus' while Adam says things like, 'Don't put that in your hair,' and 'We'll find Mr Hippo in a minute.'

'Clare.' Meg's voice is small and imploring.

I slam the door behind me.

Chapter Twenty-Seven

Every time I go to Hatfield Academy, I berate myself for getting into this utterly ludicrous situation. But today I'm in an even worse mood than normal. Stephen's happy news has knocked me sideways and Meg's betrayal has achieved the seemingly impossible by making it even worse. The lack of progress on my new book is woeful and, while I can't really blame this on Tamara's pregnancy, it sure as hell hasn't helped.

Sam, in sharp contrast to me, is wearing his trademark face-splitting smile and assaulting me with his usual stream of happy chit-chat. Joe has a new joke which he's so excited for me to hear, Daisy's rendition of 'Rainbow' is getting better and better by the day, and I should judge for myself but he reckons Alex has a lot more colour in his cheeks today. And he's put on a little weight.

I wonder if Sam is ever down or grumpy. I mean, he must be, but it's hard to imagine.

'Y'all right?' Alex says as I sit down next to him. 'Cute puppy.'

It takes my brain a second to catch up and then I realise Alex is talking about Scooby.

'Yeah, my brother's dog.'

Alex's brow furrows. 'Sister's.'

Of course, it's me who has a brother. 'Sister's. Slip of the tongue.'

Alex gives me a bit of a funny look but then returns his attention to his iPhone.

The rehearsal does not get off to a good start with a magic show that lacks any magic.

My mind drifts to my lunch with Stephen. What does he expect from me? That I'll send Tamara my leftover prenatal vitamins, buy the baby a teddy bear, offer tips on how to prevent stretch marks (never get to full-term). Also, that smug, 'I wanted you to hear it from me.' Well, bully for you, Stephen, aren't you so fucking considerate?

'Very nice Deepak,' Sam says as the magical maestro leaves the stage. 'I particularly liked the levitating card trick.'

I tell you who I would have liked to have heard it from: Meg. My so-called best friend. I can't believe she knew and didn't tell me. Or for that matter that she and Adam have been hanging out with Stephen.

I tune back into the rehearsal and see Daisy taking to the stage. Her head hangs low, her small shoulders are slumped and she looks every bit as miserable as I feel. My mind flashes back to her crying in the toilets. How she brightened when I showed her how to roll up her skirt at the waistband but was then visibly disappointed by me telling her to be herself.

She murders 'Rainbow', which is a pity because if anyone is in need of a bit of praise right now, it's Daisy. 'Er, getting better. Maybe hold that end note a little longer.' She gives me a small, sad smile and, if my heart wasn't already shattered by my ex-husband and ex-best friend, this would surely do it.

Daisy is followed by the dance troupe who constantly step on each other's feet and almost completely fail to stay in time. They seem even more awkward than usual too. I snap 'penguin arms' three times in as many minutes.

'Can we take a break for a warm-up activity?' I say to Sam.

'I guess.'

'Well, we need to do *something*.'

If Sam notices my vinegary tone, it doesn't cause his smile to drop. 'Seven J, we're going to do a warm-up activity now, please. Ms Cox will lead it.'

'Everybody get yourself into a circle, please. Actually make that two circles, there are quite a few of us.'

The kids start milling about but Alex stays in his seat.

'Everybody,' I say looking at him.

'But I'm not in the show.'

'Neither am I.'

Alex's eyes flash but he gets to his feet.

'Right, this is a fun activity to loosen everyone up a bit. It's called Zip, Zap, Boing.'

The kids are still trying to organise themselves into two circles and I can't help but notice when Philippa smiles un-sweetly at Daisy and tells her there's more room in the other circle. Daisy looks like a deflated balloon and, if it wasn't for the fact I'm busy pretending to be a whole different person and keeping my own tsunami of emotions squashed down, I'd tell Philippa that she can go in the other circle. I settle for giving Daisy a smile. 'Right, there are three moves. The first is Zip.' I clasp my hands together with my thumbs raised and my index fingers pointing towards the person next to me. 'ZIP! Zip passes play to the person next to you and they can be on your left or your right.'

Some of the kids are looking confused while others are clearly bored and I question the wisdom of doing this on a day when

I'd rather just lie in a dark room and cry. But I remember loving this game when we did it in youth theatre and it made a big difference in terms of loosening people up. 'For Zap, you clasp your hands together in the same way but point your arms forward to Zap anyone in the circle—'

'Like you're shooting them?' Bethany offers.

'Umm, I guess. Anyway, the last move is Boing. You do a star jump and shout "Boing". This passes the Zip or Zap the way it has just come.' I demonstrate. 'When someone makes a mistake or hesitates for too long, they're out. The winners are the two people left in the circle at the end.'

'Er, perhaps we could have a practice round?' Sam says.

'I was going to suggest that.' My voice is still Jenna's but the testy tone is definitely my own.

We do the practice round and, much to my relief, everyone starts to get the hang of the game. In fact, by the time we start playing properly, some of the kids look as if they might even be enjoying themselves. I notice Alex hesitates a couple of times but doesn't go out and no one says anything. Apart from that everyone sticks to the rules.

'That was fun,' Bethany says when we finish.

'Yeah,' Sam adds. 'It was awesome. Did you enjoy it, Alex?'

Alex shrugs. 'It was all right.'

The rehearsal resumes with the rappers.

'Lame,' Alex mutters under his breath.

Next up is a whey-faced girl who reads a poem from behind a curtain of dark hair.

'Even more lame,' Alex says.

I'm on the verge of telling Alex to remember that this is all to raise money for him and the trip to Disneyland that seems off-brand, when he instructs Sam he needs a KitKat. To be fair, he does say please this time, but I'm pretty sure that's because he can feel my eyes boring into him.

'Sure,' Sam says. 'The vending machine on this floor is out of order though so I'll have to go upstairs.'

Joe takes to the stage and I realise I'm holding my breath. There's just something very likeable about the kid. Plus, I think it's ridiculously brave of anyone to do stand-up.

My good vibes don't seem to work though. Joe's routine is considerably less funny than it was last time and the new joke that he was apparently so excited for me to hear lacks any kind of punchline.

'Rubbish,' Alex mutters, his eyes never leaving his iPhone.

'At least he's trying,' I snap, before I can stop myself. 'It's easy to sit here and criticise.'

'In case you didn't realise, I'm not well.' Alex's words may be sarcastic but his voice is small.

I should stop then, back down. 'I know and that sucks. But if you're well enough to come to the rehearsals and mainline KitKats, then I reckon you could get up on stage and do something. And, if you can't, well, then maybe you shouldn't be quite so hard on everyone else.'

Sam reappears at that moment, takes in Alex's gaping mouth and slightly glassy eyes.

'Everything okay?'

'Everything is fine,' I say.

To my huge relief, Alex seems to quickly recover his equilibrium, although he's noticeably slower to snipe about his classmates. I imagine it's causing him almost physical pain not to say something about Bethany, aka Lizzo, who is on stage now and managing to achieve the seemingly impossible by being even worse than last time.

'Dylan isn't feeling good,' Sam says.

Join the club, mate.

'I'm going to take him to the school nurse. Will you be okay for five minutes?'

I'm not sure I'll ever be okay again but this doesn't seem to be an appropriate or Jenna-like response so I manage a half-hearted nod.

Sam disappears and I go back to pretending to listen to Bethany whose hair tossing and nail checking are making me feel bad as hell.

'Erm… very energetic,' I say as she finally comes off stage.

Philippa with the lovely singing voice, but apparently unlovely personality, takes to the stage just as Sam comes back into the room with Dylan, who I can't help but observe looks perfectly hale and hearty.

'That's good,' Sam says, sitting back down next to me. 'I was worried we wouldn't be able to get hold of either of Dylan's parents. They're both doctors. His mum is in theatre but we managed to contact his dad.'

'Hmm, pretty sure he'll diagnose his kid as a time waster who has pulled him away from people who are actually sick.' Why did I say that? Jenna doesn't do cynical. It's no good remembering to do her voice if the words I use it for are all wrong. 'Er...' I scrabble around for something more positive, or at least neutral to say. 'Dylan didn't stay with the school nurse, then?'

Sam shakes his head. 'He said he'd prefer to wait with us. That the rehearsal is a good distraction.'

That's one way of describing it.

Sam gestures towards the stage. 'Olivia's good, isn't she?'

I nod. 'Although, to be fair, Bethany is the polar opposite of a tough act to follow.'

Sam laughs.

More acts come and go and still it's not one o'clock. How on earth did I get myself into this?

'Oh, great,' Sam says, standing up. 'Here's Dylan's dad.'

I look towards the door and my stomach plummets as if I'm on a rollercoaster because standing there is none other than Doctor Reeves. I've seen a lot of gynaecologists in my time but Doctor Reeves is one who stands out in my memory.

Panic floods my body. Will he recognise me and therefore know immediately I'm not the real Jenna? I shove my face into my handbag and pretend to be intent on searching for something right at the very bottom.

Doctor Reeves and Sam talk for what feels forever and I am forced to keep my head down.

Will he recognise me? He saw much more of my vagina than my face. Plus, I must be one of thousands of patients he's seen over the years and I'm dressed up as a completely different person.

His face, though, with the wide set green eyes, slightly wonky nose and olive skin, is etched on my mind until the end of time.

Chapter Twenty-Eight

January 2019

Stephen and I haven't even got our coats off when Doctor Reeves starts rattling off things I have tested negative for: antiphospholipid antibodies, lupus anticoagulant, Factor V Leiden, prothrombin gene mutation.

'That's good news, right?' Stephen says.

'Absolutely,' Doctor Reeves says.

My heart thuds in my chest. 'But you said before there are no uterine problems and no cervical weakness?'

'That's right.'

'So *why* have three babies died inside me?'

I don't even have to look at my husband to know he will be wincing. No need to be aggressive with this kind doctor who's trying to help us. The doctor is unfazed though. He nods, rubs his hands together as if washing them. 'The truth is we don't know.'

Why don't you know? How come we can send humans into space and we still know so little about why one in five pregnancies end in a miscarriage? Is it because miscarriage is a 'woman's thing'?

'But what we do know is the tests have found nothing.'

Nothing. My body fizzes with rage and it's all I can do not to vault over the faux oak desk and shake this man who is supposed to have the answers. I wanted to walk out of here today knowing the problem. I wanted to be told there was a cure – a magic wand. If I did have a blood-clotting disorder, it could be treated with aspirin and heparin, if my cervix was weak, doctors could put in a special stitch, and if my womb was an odd shape, I could have surgery. But you can't fix 'nothing'.

'What would your advice be going forwards?' Stephen says.

More fury washes through me. When did my husband become the sort of person who says 'going forwards'? Why isn't he more upset? More angry? Does he not get how devastating this is?

Doctor Reeves launches into a monologue of fluff and platitudes which I zone out of for his own safety. We have waited what seems like forever for this appointment. NHS guidelines mean no one will even investigate recurrent miscarriages until you've had three in a row and, even when we hit that un-lovely milestone, we still had to wait months.

'...fifty per cent of couples who have had three miscarriages go on to have a healthy baby—'

'So fifty per cent don't?' My voice is quiet but menacing.

Stephen stares at me, his crumpled brow telling me he doesn't know why I'm behaving like this. The doctor is just trying to help. He's not helping though, is he, Stephen?

I clear my throat, 'So all the tests show—'

This time, it's Doctor Reeves who interrupts me. 'Nothing.'

How can it be nothing when it's everything?

We leave the warm fug of the hospital and step out into the cold, bright sunshine.

'You know what's bullshit?' I say, glancing across at my husband, whose face suggests he's adopted a mental-brace position. 'You get all this advice when you're pregnant: don't drink alcohol or caffeine, don't eat soft cheeses or rare meat, don't empty a cat litter tray. But, when you have a miscarriage, no doctor ever asks you if you might have eaten a rare steak or slab of Brie. By then, the accepted wisdom is, this couldn't have been prevented, that this just happened—'

'Clare.' He means, don't do this.

We walk along the Fulham Road, its chi-chi antiques shops, bustling cafés and overpriced delis blurring through the tears. Stephen takes my hand. 'Don't cry.'

This makes me cry even harder.

We pass an impossibly chic woman dressed head to toe in white and she stares at me for a second before averting her gaze.

'Do you want to get a cab home?' Stephen says.

I shake my head. 'Let's walk.'

A woman with a pram is coming towards us and I sense Stephen tense. I want to tell him that it's fine, that I've already reached peak misery and what's one more woman whose body has no problem holding on to a baby? It's not as if I can open Instagram right now without seeing yet another friend or former colleague showing off a scan picture. Even my best friend gave birth a couple of months ago.

As if on cue, my phone rings and I see it's Meg. She'll be asking how the appointment went. She's good like that. She'd never forget to check in, however many times Lola has got her up the night before. I hit decline.

Stephen's hand stiffens in mine. He wants to tell me I should speak to Meg. These days, there are lots of things he wants to tell me but doesn't dare.

'There's this woman called Alison on this Facebook group I've joined and she swears that Chinese medicine changed everything for her. She just gave birth to a healthy baby after seven miscarriages.'

If Stephen finds this news exciting, he hides it well.

We turn right toward the river.

'We could go private. There are therapies available privately you can't get on the NHS. Lymphocyte immunisation therapy, for example. A woman is given a transfusion of white blood cells from their partner before she becomes pregnant.' I don't mention this has been banned in the US outside of a research setting. 'I've found this one consultant called Harry Jarvis who is something of a celebrity among the recurrent miscarriage crowd. He's often mentioned in news stories about miracle babies.'

'I don't want to go private.'

'Look, I know my book money has all but drained away now but I'm feeling good about this new story I'm working on. And I could even pick up some freelance advertising work—'

'It's not the money.'

'What?'

Stephen pulls his hand away from mine, rakes it through his hair and stops walking. 'I can't do this anymore, Clare.'

I feel as if he has slapped me. 'WHAT DO YOU MEAN YOU CAN'T DO THIS ANYMORE?'

Stephen stares at the pavement. 'For the last four years, we've either been trying to get pregnant, pregnant or miscarrying—'

'WE?' I scream so loudly a woman with two young kids steers them towards the other side of the street.

Stephen sighs. 'You know what I mean.'

And I do know what he means because, yes, it was me who was pregnant and me who miscarried, but it happened to both of us and I tell people that all the time. Right now, I can't even give Stephen that though.

The silence stretches between us.

Eventually Stephen speaks. 'I think we just need to hit pause.'

'Great idea! I mean, I'm thirty-six so everyone knows the smart thing to do is to kick this into the long grass.'

'It doesn't have to be for long. I just want some time to get back to being us.'

'Unbelievable,' I say, turning on my heel.

'Wait, where are you going?'

'Somewhere you aren't.'

'Let's talk about this,' Stephen says, putting his hand on my arm.

I shake him off and start walking as fast as I can in the other direction. Because I thought I felt alone when we left Doctor Reeves. As if we'd been cut adrift into a choppy sea of Mumsnet chatter, private clinics, herbalists, nutritionists, quacks. But at least then I thought it was still 'we'.

Chapter Twenty-Nine

November 2023

Now I don't hold much with the idea of writing as therapy, and think you should have therapy as therapy, but there's no denying that sometimes it can feel good to put your anger on the page.

Which is why, for the first time in ages, I'm excited to be at my keyboard. Poppy, my main character, has just discovered her husband is cheating (the cheating is just the beginning, Poppy, you wait until he knocks up the woman he replaced you with). She is looking to seek revenge; the perfect way to get back at Amos.

I can't have her cutting up his clothes because that's way too much of a cliché.

I lean back in my chair and stretch out my neck. I haven't even de Jenna-ised myself yet. Normally, I take off 'her' clothes as soon as I walk through the door, grateful to get back to elasticated waistbands and things I can spill tea on without having an aneurysm, but today I was at my laptop within minutes of getting back from Hatfield Academy. I wonder how much time Jenna spent at her laptop writing the dubiously titled *Sunny Side Up*?

I look back at the blinking cursor.

I can't have Poppy hurling Amos's precious iPhone onto the stone floor because there's a chance Stephen will read this and wonder if it really was an accident that ended the life of his iPhone 10.

I can't have Poppy killing Amos because the book isn't a thriller.

I still can't wrap my head around what Stephen was expecting from me in terms of a response to his 'happy news'? Did he think buying me a cup of tea and a halloumi wrap would soften the blow?

Meg's behaviour is even more baffling. Stephen, after all, has form when it comes to ruining my life.

Maybe Poppy could kill Amos or at least maim him? In a non-thriller type of way?

A sort of Marian Keyes type of murder or maiming?

My agent's voice rises unbidden into my consciousness: *Make sure Poppy is likeable.*

The reader needs to be on her side. She needs to behave with dignity.

I strike a line through 'Poppy to murder Amos' in my notepad.

I feel bad about upsetting Alex earlier. He's a bit of a brat but he's a brat with cancer.

A piece clunks into place in my brain: I will give Amos cancer. That's perfect because I get to make him suffer (the least he deserves for being such a shitbag) but Poppy is blameless. She can even take him soup and magazines in hospital and, if that doesn't make her likeable, I don't know what does.

I'm finally getting out of my Jenna clothes when Jackie at Fake Faces calls. 'Have you seen that video of Jenna singing "Puppy Love"?'

Six million likes and counting. 'Yep, I've seen it.'

'It's very popular.'

'Or you could say pup-ular.'

Jackie doesn't laugh. 'The wedding you and Malcolm are doing. The bride just phoned me. She wants you to sing "Puppy Love".'

She what? 'Umm, I'm afraid I can't—'

'Why not?'

'I can't sing—'

'Acch, that doesn't matter.'

'No, I mean I *really* can't sing. Like tone deaf can't sing. I once had to sing in a school show and my mum got the giggles because I was so bad. The whole thing has entered into family folklore.'

'The bride was very insistent.'

'I'm sorry, Jackie, but there's absolutely no way.' There's enough wrong with my life already without an extra serving of humiliation.

Chapter Thirty

Nothing bonds people quicker than shared pain and for Malcolm and me, that pain is the gig we've just done.

'The groom was trashed when he arrived, right?'

'Oh yeah,' Malcolm says, nodding. 'He staggered down that aisle and slurred his way through his vows. It's a wonder he managed to get through the reception without puking.'

'His poor bride.'

Malcolm nods. 'Except…'

We both start laughing.

'Okay,' I say, holding my hands up. 'She was awful. But no one deserves him.'

Malcolm raises his over-plucked eyebrows. 'Do you remember her walking down the aisle hissing at her father out of the corner of her mouth? And I think she complained about pretty much everything – the photographer, the cake, us not mingling with enough of the guests, you not singing "Puppy Love".'

'I was never booked to sing. Jenna isn't a singer.'

'True, although that Instagram post has gone nuts. Anyway, even if you had sung, that bride wouldn't have been happy. There was no pleasing the woman.'

'She was deadly.'

Malcolm nods. 'They deserve each other.'

The two of us are back in what Malcom describes as our 'civvies' (non Jenna and Jonny clothes) in a dimly lit basement bar in Soho. At nearly two o'clock in the morning, the place exudes faded glamour but I know if I saw it in the daylight, there's no way I'd be tucking into this pizza.

'You married?'

'No.' I scratch my neck. 'He traded me in for someone with a more dependable uterus. Sorry, TMI.'

'S'okay. My husband traded me in for a twenty-five-year-old Polish model. I don't think he has much in the way of a dependable uterus but I definitely know how you feel.' Malcolm takes a sip of his wine. 'How long since he left?'

'Three years. You?'

'One. It was hell at first but now I'm enjoying being young, free and single again. Well, two out of three. Dating has changed so much since I last did it.'

'You're dating again?'

'Well, of course. Aren't you?'

I puff out my cheeks. 'Absolutely not. I'm done with men.'

Malcolm laughs. 'I know what you mean but isn't that a little extreme? I've found they make very good pets.'

I smile. 'Maybe. But I'm not sure I can face all the fuss. And it is really lovely never having to sit on a pissy loo seat.'

Malcolm does a stagey shudder. 'All pets need to be trained, darling.' He holds up his empty wine glass. 'One more for the road?'

'Umm... oh, go on then.' I scratch at a patch of eczema on the inside of my elbow. 'I thought Stephen and I were forever. Ach, that's a stupid thing to say, everyone who gets married thinks it's forever, even that couple today I imagine.'

'That doesn't make it any less painful when you don't get your forever.'

'Stephen and I started trying for a baby. I expected it to just happen. Like everything in my life had up until then. But it didn't. It took us a whole year to get pregnant – that's not actually that long but it felt long to me – and then I miscarried.'

'I'm sorry.'

The waiter brings over our wine and I take a grateful glug. 'Everyone told me that next time it would be different but I miscarried again.' A fat tear rolls off the end of my nose. Why am I crying in front of Malcolm? It's not as if he's my best friend just because we've survived a drunken groom and his angry bridezilla. Meg pops into my mind. She's left me countless messages since I walked out on her the other day and yesterday, in a moment of weakness, I nearly called her back but then I reminded myself that she'd known about Stephen's baby but still let me be blindsided. I'm not even sure I believe that Adam just bumped into Stephen on the train. They've probably kept in touch this whole time.

'Did you know you have to have three miscarriages before the NHS will give you tests to find out what's wrong with you? *Third time lucky.*' I wince as I hear the bitterness in my tone. 'Anyway, we had all the tests and they didn't show anything wrong. How rubbish is that? At least if you know what's wrong you've got some chance of fixing it.'

'Did you stop trying after that?'

I shake my head. 'Nope, although Stephen would have liked to. I had two more miscarriages.' I swipe the tears that are falling with my sleeve. 'God loves a trier. Only evidently in my case he doesn't.'

Malcolm rummages in his pocket and passes me a tissue.

'After the first miscarriage, I remember saying that it had brought Stephen and me even closer. But by miscarriage three we were fighting constantly. Every time it happened, he was upset for a bit and then he'd move on. I remember hearing him laughing on the phone to a mate and wanting to kill him. I always felt he didn't want a baby as much as I did. Which is an irony because now – surprise! – he's having one with someone else.'

'Ouch.'

I nod. Every fibre of my being is telling me to shut up now. I barely know Malcolm. I thought I hated him. But it seems I'm unable to stop the words spewing out of my mouth.

'Everything Stephen said annoyed me. He'd ask me how my writing had gone that day and it was all I could do not to scream, "HOW DO YOU BLOODY WELL THINK ARSEHOLE? CAN YOU IMAGINE BEING CREATIVE WHEN THE GUTS OF YOUR WORLD HAVE BEEN RIPPED OUT?" Honestly, I think we reached a point when he couldn't even say it looked as if it might rain.'

'So you lost your babies and your marriage?'

'Yeah. But also I didn't know who I was anymore – I wasn't a mother, I wasn't a wife, I wasn't a writer, I wasn't a creative director.'

'You lost yourself.'

Chapter Thirty-One

If there's one thing I could do without today it's a meeting with Hattie and Rosamund. But apparently there is much to be discussed on Lumiere skincare, so here I am sitting in the reception of The Leap Agency staring at the living wall while I wait for Rosamund to collect me.

It's three days since I emotionally vomited all over Malcolm and I am no less sad. I can't stop thinking about Stephen becoming a father. Remembering how, after the third miscarriage, he told me he wanted to 'hit pause'. Later, he even started to outline the advantages of us not having a baby. We could travel the world, enjoy long lie-ins, focus on each other. I know it wasn't that he didn't want a child – he did after all knock me up a couple more times – but it wasn't everything to him like it was for me. How come he now gets *my* everything?

Meg's betrayal weighs heavily too. If there was one person in the world I thought I could count on, it was her. A memory rises of my birthday in 2020. Stephen had left me, the country was in lockdown and I'd recently had miscarriage number five. I woke up desolate and utterly alone, grief the guilt-seeking torpedo homing in on the dark corners of my mind. But then I drew back my living-room curtains and saw Meg had been round before

I woke up and plastered signs to the windows: *Happy Birthday! We love you!* It was everything but not all because when I opened my front door, there was a box containing wrapped presents, a home-made chocolate fudge cake, a bottle of rosé and a packet of loo rolls (the hot ticket item of the pandemic and one Meg knew I was on the brink of running out of).

Rosamund appears in reception. She's dressed in children's TV presenter brights, which seem incongruous given her permanently sulky demeanour. She throws the thinnest of smiles in my direction. 'We're in Rocket Room.'

Rocket Room? Give me strength.

'The Lumiere client wasn't happy with the first round of concepts,' Rosamund says as I follow her up the spiral staircase. 'The work didn't make enough of the serum being scientifically proven to reduce fine lines.'

'I thought we couldn't say that?'

Rosamund shoots me the kind of look you might give a particularly irksome child.

'We can't. But we can imply it.'

We pass a couple of very young blokes playing table football. A crowd shouts from the sidelines. 'C'mon, Jonesy!' 'Play out from the back.' 'Gooooooal!'

Rosamund greets a few people by name, her face lighting up with the kind of smile I didn't know she possessed. 'I just love the creatives,' she simpers as we walk away.

I'm tempted to tell her that I'm a creative but am well aware that isn't how Rosamund sees me.

Hattie is perched on one of the gym balls that serve as seats in Rocket Room. 'Hey!' she says, tilting her phone towards us so we can see the video she's watching of a panda balancing a cup on its head. 'Isn't this the cutest?'

'Absolutely,' Rosamund says, nodding and clamping her fists to her chest.

'Thanks so much for coming in,' Hattie says to me. 'How are you doing?'

I don't love Hattie's brand of faux friendly but I'll take it any day of the week over Rosamund's barely concealed hostility. Besides, Hattie doesn't know it yet, but she's going to help me out today. I've decided to get Daisy one of the faux fur tote bags that so many of the other girls at Hatfield Academy have. It won't magically solve all her problems, of course, but it will put a smile on her face. It might also make me feel a little less guilty about the fact that the last time I saw Alex, I almost reduced him to tears. Sort of like offsetting your carbon footprint in terms of karma.

Unfortunately, the bags are sold out everywhere online, which is why I'm going to ask Hattie if I can buy hers. I imagine she might not want any money given she doesn't even like the thing.

'Did Ros fill you in on the problem with the Lumiere work?' Hattie says.

'Umm, kind of.' I sit down on one of the gym balls, which wobbles so much I almost face plant onto the conference table. 'She said they want to make more of it being scientifically proven. But that we can't say "scientifically proven". Any idea as to how I might do that?'

Rosamund's mouth bunches. 'Well, we're not copywriters.'

'Umm. Look, I'm a great believer in the power of words.' Once again, I nearly roll off my gym ball. 'But I can't say something without saying it.'

Hattie laughs as if I'm trying to be funny. 'Let's take a look at the client's written feedback, shall we?' She opens up my copy doc, which is covered in track changes. 'So the first concept was "Let's get glowing", which the client feels is too generic.'

Fair.

'Also, they don't feel it focuses enough on the collagen renewal and cell regeneration.'

'But I can't talk about that, right?'

'No,' Hattie says. 'But we can, y'know, totally create that vibe.'

It's going to be a very long meeting. I gaze through the glass wall to where a large man with a goatee is climbing on to the rope swing.

'Yeah, vibes,' Rosamund says. 'It's all about creating the right vibes.'

'I do think we need a clear message,' I say.

Hattie laughs. 'Let's stay positive.'

If I walk away from today with the tote bag, it will be worth this agony. I picture giving it to Daisy and how happy she'll be.

Rosamund is droning on about the amazing clinical trials we can't mention and I find myself zoning out and watching the guy on the swing as he flies higher and higher into the air. The only way he could appear more childlike is if someone was pushing him. When my dad used to take me and David to the swings, he'd tell us not to kick the clouds and we'd laugh as if he'd said the funniest thing in the whole world. Years later, when I was pregnant the first time, I told Stephen I couldn't wait to put our child on the swings and tell them not to kick the clouds. He grinned and said maybe we'd wait until they could sit up.

'…visible brightening,' Hattie says.

'Yeah,' Rosamund adds. 'Visible brightening. Totally.'

'Can I say that?'

Hattie shakes her head. 'Well, not actually say it.'

There's another thirty-eight minutes of that sort of nonsense (and, yes, I am absolutely counting each and every minute) before the dynamic duo grind to a halt and Rosamund asks me if everything is clear.

'Umm,' I say, glancing down at my blank notebook. 'I think so.' I wonder if now I've got the impersonator work coming in, I could phase out my work with The Leap Agency?

'I'll show you out,' Rosamund says.

'Actually, there was something I wanted to ask Hattie.'

'Oh?' Hattie says.

'Do you remember that fluffy tote bag your mum sent you?'

Hattie laughs. 'How could I forget?'

'I don't suppose you still have it?'

'Yeah, it's in my locker.'

Brilliant, I was imagining she'd have taken it home and I was going to have to persuade her to post it to me. 'Great, my niece is desperate for one, you see.' (Obviously, Daisy isn't my niece but I can hardly say I want the bag for some random kid I've met while pretending to be a national treasure.) 'And they're all sold out online. So I was wondering whether I could have yours?'

'Well, I'm not sure. It was a gift from my mum, you see.'

A gift you described as 'unspeakably awful'.

'But I guess I might be able to sell it to you.'

'At the right price,' Rosamund cuts in helpfully.

I force a smile. 'Okay, well they're seventeen pounds online.'

Hattie makes the same face she makes when I tell her I can't write a fifteen hundred word article in an hour. 'I'd take twenty-five.'

'But you don't even like it?' The words are out of my mouth before I can stop them.

'Actually, it has grown on me.'

Rosamund nods in agreement. 'Totally. It's kind of fun.'

'I'll give you twenty quid.' And a slap.

Hattie makes her exaggerated sad face. 'I think I'm going to have to say no.'

For goodness' sake. You hate the bag.

'Yeah,' Rosamund adds. 'Totally.'

'The thing is, this girl – my niece – is having a bit of a tricky time at school at the moment. Feeling a bit left out. And so many of the other girls have that bag and, while I know it won't solve all my niece's problems, I think it would make her feel she fits in a little bit better.'

Hattie looks at me blankly. And then I hand over twenty-five pounds. Because you can't appeal to someone's better nature when they don't have a better nature.

I walk away from The Leap Agency bubbling with irritation. I may have got the tote bag but what I didn't get was any sense of direction in terms of how I'm going to produce Lumiere copy the client likes. Good account people, and they seem rarer by the day, will push back when a client gives them unclear or unreasonable feedback but Rosamund and Hattie don't even seem to realise that's even an option.

I look up to see a man sitting on the kerb surrounded by a small clump of people. Poor thing must have come off his bike.

But as I get closer, I realise there is no bike to be seen and what lies upside down in the gutter is a large red skateboard.

I push my way through the throng. 'Toby. What happened? Are you okay?'

'Came off my board.'

'Reckon he's taken a bit of a knock to the head,' the woman kneeling beside Toby says in a thick Australian accent. 'You two know each other?'

'Umm, kind of.'

'I'll leave him with you then. He says he's okay but you'll want to keep an eye on him.'

She stands up and is obviously about to go and it's all I can do not to fall at her feet and see please stay because she looks so capable and I don't really know Toby that well. I can't even manage to keep my life under any sort of control so I certainly shouldn't be responsible for someone else's.

I sit down on the kerb next to Toby, the cold seeping through my jeans. 'We should get you checked out in A&E. UCH is only five minutes from here.' Scene of miscarriage three.

Toby shakes his head. 'I'm fine really.'

'You can never be too careful with a head injury—'

'Honestly, the only thing that's hurt badly is my pride.' He laughs.

'What happened?'

He shrugs. 'Dunno really. One minute I was on the board, the next I was face down on the tarmac. I don't think I was concentrating. It's been a bit of a day if you know what I mean?'

'Oh, I do know.'

Toby laughs and rakes his hand through his floppy fringe.

'Why is it a bad day?'

'Oh y'know the usual. Clients being dicks, account people being dicks. And we've got this new brief for TASK Furniture, which is one of the first ones where I've been in charge of the creative, and the client hates all the work we've shown them so far.'

'That's not good.'

Toby shakes his head. 'Not good at all. I've had the whole creative department working on it and we've presented loads of good ideas but not a single one of them seems to have landed.'

'I've been there.'

For a second, Toby's face shows a flicker of confusion. He thinks of me as a jobbing copywriter not a creative director but his innate good manners means he recovers himself almost instantly. 'Any tips?'

'Just keep on keeping on, I guess. What was their brief?'

'Affordable furniture for everyone.'

'Hmm.'

'Anyway, I'm sure you've got better things to do than sit here in the street talking to me about my work woes.' Toby slowly stands up.

'Are you sure you're okay?' I say, rising to my feet. 'You don't want to get checked over?'

'I'll be fine.' He picks up the skateboard.

'You're not getting back on that now?'

Toby laughs. 'Nah. Reckon I'll walk. I'm only going to the club. Which way are you headed?'

'To Tottenham Court Road.'

'Great, we can walk together.'

We fall into step chit-chatting about how we can't believe it's nearly the end of November now and how mad it is that Toby has already been at The Leap Agency for nearly a month and whether small agencies or big ones are better for creatives. Remembering Toby's mention of account people being dicks, I try to draw out a snipe at Rosamund and Hattie but get nothing back other than a non-committal, 'They seem nice,' and 'I haven't worked with them much.'

Notwithstanding my failure to get Toby to slag off the gruesome twosome, he's good company and, before I know it, the two of us are standing outside Tottenham Court Road Tube station.

'Thanks for coming to my rescue.'

'You're welcome. Hope your day improves. And hope you manage to crack the brief for TASK.'

Toby makes a pained face. 'God, me too.'

I say goodbye and then turn back. 'Wait, you've done a creative route about making the furniture your own, right?'

Toby's brow furrows. 'What do you mean?'

'Well, the thing about TASK furniture is there are so many hacks online for people to customise it.'

'Right, but I'm not sure that's something they want to talk about.'

Doubt flickers in the back of my mind. It's a long time since I have done this day to day. 'But they should do because it's a genuine point of difference between them and their competitors.'

'I guess.'

'Maybe the campaign idea is all about expressing your individuality. The tagline could be: *Make it your own.*'

Toby looks at me for a second before his face breaks into a grin. 'That's actually rather brilliant.'

'Well, I'm not sure about that.' I can feel a blush rising up my chest. 'Anyway, I'd better get going.'

'Brilliant,' Toby says firmly. 'And now you've come to my rescue on two fronts.'

I descend the stairs to the station, a small smile spreading across my face. I imagine Toby presenting my idea to TASK Furniture and them telling him they love it. Toby will say thanks but he can't really take the credit, it was actually the brainwave of a rather brilliant creative called Clare Palmer.

I press my card against the reader. When Toby gets out of the meeting with the TASK client, he'll phone me to say thank you. What a loss I am to the advertising industry and would I like to take a full-time job at The Leap Agency?

A man with a halo of frizzy blond hair shoves past me on the escalator.

Would I like a job at The Leap Agency? Probably not. But I'd like to be asked. And I'd like to see Rosamund and Hattie's faces when they hear about it.

Chapter Thirty-Two

Today finds me in a bitterly cold studio off the A40 on a filmset. Malcolm and I are taking part in a shoot for a TV ad for a new range of cat treats. I was more than a little apprehensive about seeing Malcolm after my emotional meltdown the other night but mercifully he's made no mention of it and is acting normal. (I say 'normal'. As normal as you can be when you're a. Malcolm and b. all dressed up as someone else.)

When I properly worked in advertising instead of hanging around on the edges of that world as a freelancer, I did lots of shoots and the one thing that united every single one of them is that there was always lots of hanging around. Today's shoot is no exception and Malcolm and I are currently sitting at the edge of the set on our fourth coffee in the space of an hour while waiting for Luna, one of the star cats, to perform the leap that her handler is adamant she will be happy to do.

Malcolm takes a sip of his coffee and winces. 'This stuff really is vile.'

'It's awful but at least it's warm. I think I've lost the circulation in my feet.'

'It's freezing. You'd think they'd make some attempt to keep the talent warm.' He rubs his gloved palms together. 'I still don't fully understand what our role is in this commercial, except that they're insistent we're playing impersonators not the actual Jonny and Jenna.'

'Hmm, I think it's about cats not accepting pale imitations or second best.' I stamp my feet up and down. 'That's why they reject the competitor cat treats and why, at the end of the commercial, they won't let us stroke them. Because we're impersonators not the real thing, you see.'

Malcolm sniffs. 'Sounds like bollocks to me.'

'Yeah, not a script I'd have approved if I was the creative director.'

The cat handler bends down to Luna's level and offers her yet another cat treat. Luna glances at it disdainfully and stalks away with her tail in the air.

'Do you ever wonder what real celebrities think of lookalikes and impersonators?' I say.

Malcolm scrapes his hand through his hair. He's clearly been at the dye again as it's now an almost bluish black. 'I think it's a mixed bag. Keith has met Elton several times and even had lunch with him and David in the south of France. ABBA gave FABBA free tickets to *ABBA Voyage* and they got the full VIP treatment when they got there. But Sarah Anne has been on a chat show with Naomi and apparently she was positively glacial in the green room.'

Suzanne, the heavily pregnant make-up artist, asks if she can check our make-up.

'Sure,' we chorus.

I try not to focus on Suzanne's enormous bump as she pulls a big powder brush from her kit and starts dusting it across my nose.

'You know I've met Jonny,' Malcolm says to me as Suzanne waddles away.

'I did not know.'

The agency creative team, neither of whom look much older than the kids I'll be seeing at Hatfield Academy tomorrow, are approaching the director with a murderous look in their eyes. Earlier we heard them berating him for Luna's lack of athleticism.

'My God, advertising people are such dicks,' Malcolm says. 'No offence, darling.'

I roll my eyes. I was worried about taking this job when Jackie first mentioned it – it seemed as if my real life and my Jenna life were getting uncomfortably close and that, as advertising is something of a small world, I might bump into someone I know. It's not a production company or an advertising agency I've ever come across before though. 'So what was Jonny like?'

Malcolm leans forward, a glint in his eye that tells me he adores this kind of chat and is pulling up his metaphorical picket fence over which to spill the gossip. 'Well, physically gorgeous.'

'Obviously.'

'He was also very warm and charming. Told me he was flattered by the comparison and, frankly he'd kill for my bone structure.'

'Well, who wouldn't?'

A harassed looking runner in jeans that stop three inches above his ankles asks us if we'd like another coffee.

'I think I'm fine.' I glance across the set and see that Luna is now back in her cat carrier and there is a tense huddle going on between clumps of people from the production company and the advertising agency. We could be some time. 'Oh, you know what? I will have one more coffee thank you.'

'Me too, thanks,' Malcolm says. He turns back to me. 'So, as I was saying, Jonny was charm and schmooze itself. But…' He pauses for dramatic effect. 'Then I overheard him talking to his publicist when he thought I was out of earshot and he wasn't very charming at all.'

'What did he say?'

'I'd rather not repeat it.'

'MALCOLM! You have to tell me.'

Malcolm does a stagey 'let me think about that' face. 'He described me as a "tragic little parasite".'

I clamp my hand to my mouth. 'Nooo! That's horrible.'

Malcolm nods. 'I know. Especially when you think of the love and care I've poured into all this. How careful I am to only behave in a way that reflects well on him and his image. And it's not as if I'm a nobody. I've—'

'Been in the business since you were four years old. Appeared in Hollywood movies and in the West End. Rubbed shoulders with the A-list.'

The corners of Malcolm's lips twitch. 'Are you mocking me, darling?'

'Only slightly.'

One of the agency creatives is shouting now. If the cat doesn't leap, there is no commercial. It's central to the idea. The cameraman and the first assistant director, both of whom look old enough to have fathered the shouter, look on in disgust. Meanwhile, a couple of the sparkies have got the giggles.

I take a sip of the coffee. 'This is going to be a looooooooong day. And going back to Jonny, I find that so disappointing when his public persona is all about being "Mr Nice Guy".'

Malcolm nods. 'I know. Jenna is probably the same. In fact, I'd wager a lot of celebrities are big old fakes.'

'Probably,' I say, laughing. 'But I guess you and I aren't in the best position to talk about people being fake.'

Chapter Thirty-Three

I put my key in the door to my flat suppressing a sigh of relief. It seems a very long time since I left here at five o'clock this morning and I am tired, cold and sick of having to keep up my 'Jenna' smile.

I throw my keys on the side and collapse on the sofa before gratefully pulling off my high-heeled boots (damn Jenna for her fondness for impractical footwear). The shoot finished, or wrapped to use the correct parlance, relatively early at seven o'clock so the evening lies ahead of me. There are many things I could and probably should do: spend a few hours working on my book, call my parents, clean the bathroom.

I fish my phone out of my fake designer 'Jenna' bag and open Instagram. Jenna is at a film premiere this evening. She has posted a picture of her on the red carpet looking impossibly glamorous with softly curled hair, a huge radiant smile and a full-length dark green lacy dress. I glance down at the cream trousers I managed to splatter with ketchup at lunch.

Eek, so excited to be out out!!!
Dress by @victoriabeckham
Styled by @georgieglennstylist
Glam by @thesquadlondon

She'll be inside by now quaffing champagne and rubbing shoulders with the great and the good. And, it's not that I'd like to swap places, not really, but the silence is bouncing off these walls in a way that's almost deafening.

I scroll to another post.

Only 12 more sleeps until Sunny Side Up *hits the shelves!!!*

What adult talks about the number of sleeps? Maybe I'm just jealous though? I can't think of anything that's coming up in my life I'd want to count the number of sleeps to.

Twenty-two more sleeps until I fail to deliver my agent the forty thousand words I've promised her!

A hundred and nineteen more sleeps until the man I thought was the love of my life has a baby with someone else!

One more sleep until I have to go back to Hatfield Academy and deceive an innocent bunch of schoolchildren and their teacher!

This is ridiculous. I should get off this sofa and do something. Instead, I scroll to one of Jenna's reels. It's from a couple of months ago, before I met Sam and got sucked into this whole Hatfield Academy thing. Jenna is on holiday in Mauritius. There's footage of her on the icing sugar sands looking toned and lithe in a teeny-tiny bikini (mental note: never accept an impersonator job that involves swimwear), her lying in the hammock by the turquoise pool of her massive over-water villa and her scuba diving amongst brightly coloured tropical fish. There are also lots of photographs of her and her 'bestie', faces pressed together as they grin at the camera. Meg flits into my mind and I swallow hard.

Think we've found paradise!!! Having the most incredible time at the Azure Beach Resort. One of the most beautiful places I've on Instagram. Everyone knows that what you see on social media isn't reality. Jenna doesn't post photos of herself with a head cold or a hangover. There are no reels of her wandering around Tesco desperately searching the aisles for something to make for dinner. No record of the days when she feels utterly and completely alone in the worst kind of way. It's stupid to compare my life to hers.

Chapter Thirty-Four

I am transforming myself into Jenna for another visit to Hatfield Academy and, while this is always a surreal experience, today there is an extra layer because I am utterly and completely furious with Jenna.

Yesterday, at the hairdresser, I bumped into a writer friend of mine I haven't seen or spoken to for ages. (Many friends fell by the wayside during the miscarriage and mental years.)

She told me that her last book hadn't sold well and her publisher hadn't renewed her contract, which meant she'd had to take a ghostwriting job to pay the bills. I immediately assumed this was an autobiography but Nelly shook her head. 'A novel. It's for a celebrity. The publisher are counting on it selling shedloads because of the reach of her brand.'

'Right. And you're getting your name on the cover? Along with the celebrity?'

Nelly laughed bitterly. 'Er, no. Not so much as a mention in the acknowledgements.'

'That's terrible. Who's the celeb?'

Nelly looked at the ground. 'I really shouldn't tell you. I've signed a non-disclosure agreement.' And then she said the name I was already somehow expecting to hear.

I look in the mirror, my hand trembling unhelpfully as I start doing my winged eyeliner. Remember Jenna's stupid '12 more sleeps' post about *Sunny Side Up*. That's nothing compared to her video about the book though – banging on about how it was so special to hold it in her hands and how she'd poured her heart and soul into it. And the utter gall of saying she'd 'loved writing every single word'. You didn't write a single word!

I reach for a cotton bud and some eye make-up remover to remove my shaky left wing.

'Lying cow,' I say to the Jenna in the mirror. And, yes, I see the irony.

I am still fizzing with irritation as I follow Sam down the school corridor but know I must force *Sunny Side Up* from my mind.

'Your fifth visit to Hatfield Academy,' Sam says. 'How did that happen?'

Good question.

Sam opens the door to the hall, which is buzzing with noise and activity.

'Hi,' Alex says as I place my bag and coat down on the chair next to him. My stomach knots remembering how sharp I was with him last time I was here. Not exactly my finest hour. He doesn't seem to be harbouring a grudge, thank goodness.

I scan the room and see Daisy sitting alone at the back. 'I'm just going to give Daisy a few notes on "Rainbow".'

'Great,' Sam says, giving me a face-splitting smile.

Alex grunts in the affirmative.

As I draw closer to Daisy, I see that her eyes are red and puffy.

'Are you going to tell me I shouldn't perform?' she says.

'What? No. Why, would I do that?'

'Philippa says I'm rubbish and she can tell you think so too just by the look on your face whenever I perform.'

Little cow. 'You're not rubbish. Actually, I've got you a little present.'

'Me?'

'Yes, you.' I reach into my bag, pull out the tote bag and hand it over.

Daisy's whole face lights up and suddenly it doesn't matter that I was fleeced by horrible Hattie because I'd have paid three times what I did to have this moment.

'OMG, I can't believe it! It's like the nicest thing I've *ever* had. Thank you so much.'

'Your mum won't mind, right?' Too late to worry about that now, Clare.

Daisy shakes her head. 'Not as long as she didn't have to pay for it.'

'Great. Reckon it will help you be Rihanna?'

Daisy laughs. 'I thought you said I should just be myself?'

'Have aliens kidnapped Alex and inhabited his body?' I whisper to Sam.

Sam laughs and it makes his eyes crinkle rather attractively. Not that I notice such things, of course, but, if I did… 'He does seem to be in a good mood today. I thought it might be something you'd said to him.'

Sam has clearly forgotten the last time I saw Alex he was virtually in tears. 'I can't believe he's agreed to be part of the show. Oh, he's coming back from the loo.'

Alex sits down next to us, grunts in my direction and reaches into his rucksack for a Spiderman comic. As he does so, out falls a small Calpol pink pot with a cartoon princess on it. Alex turns as pink as the pot and rolls his eyes. 'My little sister's lip balm. I was moaning about having chapped lips this morning and she insisted I take it. I did try to tell her it isn't great for my image.'

I laugh. 'I didn't know you have a sister.'

'Yeah. Amy.' A smile spreads across his face. 'She's six and a right pain in the bum.'

'It's great you've decided to MC the show.'

Alex shrugs but there's a hint of a smile there too. 'Might as well. If I've got to watch it anyway.'

Daisy finishes 'Rainbow', leaves the stage and immediately picks up the fluffy tote bag which she left at the side and has already stuffed with her possessions.

'That performance was so much better,' I say to her.

'Yeah,' Alex adds. 'It was all right.'

Daisy, Sam and I all stare at him. Where are the snipes and the scowls? 'I still can't get the chorus right. Can you show me how it should be?'

'Oh, I can't sing.' The words are out of my mouth before I realise what I've said. People are still talking about Jenna having 'the voice of an angel' and still sharing that wretched video of her singing 'Puppy Love' to poor Scooby. 'Er, I can't sing today because I have a bit of a sore throat.' I cough theatrically. 'Just study the Rihanna video again and again and you'll get it.'

Daisy and Alex both give me a bit of a funny look but then Daisy says okay and shuffles off.

'I'm just going to grab a KitKat from the vending machine,' Alex says.

'Do you want me to get it for you?' Sam says.

Alex shakes his head. 'Nah, y'all right.'

on Instagram. Everyone knows that what you see on social media isn't reality. Jenna doesn't post photos of herself with a head cold or a hangover. There are no reels of her wandering around Tesco desperately searching the aisles for something to make for dinner. No record of the days when she feels utterly and completely alone in the worst kind of way. It's stupid to compare my life to hers.

ever visited but the best thing is being able to share it with my gorgeous bestie @sarahhyam

The last holiday I went on was with Stephen over three years ago. Our marriage was over by that stage but we thought we could save it with a 'blow the budget' trip to the west coast of America. Instead, we argued our way along the Pacific Coast Highway, barely registering the sweeping views of the ocean. Stephen left a wine tasting in Napa early because I was being 'insufferable' (I was) and all I remember of the breathtaking (in all senses) hikes in Yosemite was how much I cried.

Since then, I haven't had either the budget or the heart to go on holiday. It's difficult to find someone to go with too. Meg has offered but I felt bad taking up her precious annual leave when she could be with her husband and kids. Not an issue now, anyway. Meg can go on holiday with Stephen and Tamara.

Another reel. Jenna at a glamorous party, a champagne coupe in her perfectly manicured hand, her head thrown back in laughter. To be fair, I've been to a few luxe parties myself recently, as the Leapsters discovered when I said I'd been to both The Yard and Annabel's. Not quite the same when you take into account me having attended those parties impersonating Jenna though, is it?

Another reel. Jenna hanging upside down in a huge light-drenched white aerial yoga studio (mental note: never accept an impersonator gig that involves yoga).

Another reel. Jenna at a big family lunch. Twelve or so people of different generations crowded around a table that's crammed with huge steaming plates of grilled shellfish and exotic salads. Happy, smiling faces all around.

I close the app and throw my phone on the coffee table. It's ridiculous to compare my life to the snapshot I see of Jenna's

Chapter Thirty-Four

I am transforming myself into Jenna for another visit to Hatfield Academy and, while this is always a surreal experience, today there is an extra layer because I am utterly and completely furious with Jenna.

Yesterday, at the hairdresser, I bumped into a writer friend of mine I haven't seen or spoken to for ages. (Many friends fell by the wayside during the miscarriage and mental years.)

She told me that her last book hadn't sold well and her publisher hadn't renewed her contract, which meant she'd had to take a ghostwriting job to pay the bills. I immediately assumed this was an autobiography but Nelly shook her head. 'A novel. It's for a celebrity. The publisher are counting on it selling shedloads because of the reach of her brand.'

'Right. And you're getting your name on the cover? Along with the celebrity?'

Nelly laughed bitterly. 'Er, no. Not so much as a mention in the acknowledgements.'

'That's terrible. Who's the celeb?'

Nelly looked at the ground. 'I really shouldn't tell you. I've signed a non-disclosure agreement.' And then she said the name I was already somehow expecting to hear.

I look in the mirror, my hand trembling unhelpfully as I start doing my winged eyeliner. Remember Jenna's stupid '12 more sleeps' post about *Sunny Side Up*. That's nothing compared to her video about the book though – banging on about how it was so special to hold it in her hands and how she'd poured her heart and soul into it. And the utter gall of saying she'd 'loved writing every single word'. You didn't write a single word!

I reach for a cotton bud and some eye make-up remover to remove my shaky left wing.

'Lying cow,' I say to the Jenna in the mirror. And, yes, I see the irony.

I am still fizzing with irritation as I follow Sam down the school corridor but know I must force *Sunny Side Up* from my mind.

'Your fifth visit to Hatfield Academy,' Sam says. 'How did that happen?'

Good question.

Sam opens the door to the hall, which is buzzing with noise and activity.

'Hi,' Alex says as I place my bag and coat down on the chair next to him. My stomach knots remembering how sharp I was with him last time I was here. Not exactly my finest hour. He doesn't seem to be harbouring a grudge, thank goodness.

I scan the room and see Daisy sitting alone at the back. 'I'm just going to give Daisy a few notes on "Rainbow".'

'Great,' Sam says, giving me a face-splitting smile.

Alex grunts in the affirmative.

As I draw closer to Daisy, I see that her eyes are red and puffy.

'Are you going to tell me I shouldn't perform?' she says.

'What? No. Why, would I do that?'

'Philippa says I'm rubbish and she can tell you think so too just by the look on your face whenever I perform.'

Little cow. 'You're not rubbish. Actually, I've got you a little present.'

'Me?'

'Yes, you.' I reach into my bag, pull out the tote bag and hand it over.

Daisy's whole face lights up and suddenly it doesn't matter that I was fleeced by horrible Hattie because I'd have paid three times what I did to have this moment.

'OMG, I can't believe it! It's like the nicest thing I've *ever* had. Thank you so much.'

'Your mum won't mind, right?' Too late to worry about that now, Clare.

Daisy shakes her head. 'Not as long as she didn't have to pay for it.'

'Great. Reckon it will help you be Rihanna?'

Daisy laughs. 'I thought you said I should just be myself?'

'Have aliens kidnapped Alex and inhabited his body?' I whisper to Sam.

Sam laughs and it makes his eyes crinkle rather attractively. Not that I notice such things, of course, but, if I did... 'He does seem to be in a good mood today. I thought it might be something you'd said to him.'

Sam has clearly forgotten the last time I saw Alex he was virtually in tears. 'I can't believe he's agreed to be part of the show. Oh, he's coming back from the loo.'

Alex sits down next to us, grunts in my direction and reaches into his rucksack for a Spiderman comic. As he does so, out falls a small Calpol pink pot with a cartoon princess on it. Alex turns as pink as the pot and rolls his eyes. 'My little sister's lip balm. I was moaning about having chapped lips this morning and she insisted I take it. I did try to tell her it isn't great for my image.'

I laugh. 'I didn't know you have a sister.'

'Yeah. Amy.' A smile spreads across his face. 'She's six and a right pain in the bum.'

'It's great you've decided to MC the show.'

Alex shrugs but there's a hint of a smile there too. 'Might as well. If I've got to watch it anyway.'

Daisy finishes 'Rainbow', leaves the stage and immediately picks up the fluffy tote bag which she left at the side and has already stuffed with her possessions.

'That performance was so much better,' I say to her.

'Yeah,' Alex adds. 'It was all right.'

Daisy, Sam and I all stare at him. Where are the snipes and the scowls? 'I still can't get the chorus right. Can you show me how it should be?'

'Oh, I can't sing.' The words are out of my mouth before I realise what I've said. People are still talking about Jenna having 'the voice of an angel' and still sharing that wretched video of her singing 'Puppy Love' to poor Scooby. 'Er, I can't sing today because I have a bit of a sore throat.' I cough theatrically. 'Just study the Rihanna video again and again and you'll get it.'

Daisy and Alex both give me a bit of a funny look but then Daisy says okay and shuffles off.

'I'm just going to grab a KitKat from the vending machine,' Alex says.

'Do you want me to get it for you?' Sam says.

Alex shakes his head. 'Nah, y'all right.'

Aliens, I mouth to Sam as Alex disappears and the rappers take to the stage.

'Oh, by the way,' Sam says. 'I have great news. Dylan's dad has offered to come and help out with our last two rehearsals. Apparently, he's on a sabbatical at the moment and he was quite the performer at med school.'

My stomach lurches. 'Dylan's dad?' What if he has a really good memory and not just for vaginas? I can't keep my head buried in my handbag throughout two whole rehearsals. 'Err, I'm not sure that's a good idea.'

'Really? I thought you'd say we need all the help we can get.'

'Umm—'

'I mean it can't do any harm, can it?'

Sweat prickles my armpits. 'Well, actually I think it could. Things have got so much better recently.' I pause half expecting Sam to laugh in my face but of course he's way too nice for that. 'So, even though it's kind of Dylan's dad, I'm not sure it's a good idea to bring in amateurs.' Coming from the amateur of all amateurs.

Sam looks at me quizzically for a second before saying, fine, whatever I think is best.

My mind churns as I watch the rappers. Bloody celebrities always seem to get their own way and even though real me is pleased on this occasion, I feel guilty, not least of all because Dylan's dad could well be way more useful than I am.

'Who's up next?' Sam says as Alex returns with his KitKat and the rappers come off stage.

'Me,' the flautist says appearing out of nowhere.

'Brilliant,' Alex mutters.

Sam and I exchange small smiles. The real Alex is still in there.

A woman in a Christmas jumper so unpleasant it's virtually a contraceptive appears at the door and beckons Sam towards her.

'Y'know I said before that Mr Jackson fancies you?' Alex says as soon as Sam is out of earshot.

'I'm not even going to dignify that with an answer.'

'Yeah, well, I reckon you like him too. Even though you're a celeb, so technically out of his league.'

'Don't be ridiculous,' I say, blushing furiously and keeping my eyes fixed on the stage.

Alex, meanwhile, sits there with a big infuriating grin which doesn't slip even when 'Amazing Grace' becomes particularly discordant.

'Very, err… err… spirited,' I say as the flautist leaves the stage and Sam returns to his seat. Why am I getting so flustered? Pathetic with a capital 'P'.

Joe takes to the stage, all pimples and shuffling feet.

'Penguin arms,' I shout.

Joe straightens up and launches into his routine. He's got a new joke about The Simpsons which Alex actually laughs at. Sam and I exchange glances and I mouth *aliens* again. To be fair though, Joe's routine is better. Come to think of it, every act I've seen so far has been much improved. Which I suppose is lucky given the show is in a couple of weeks. It hits me suddenly that the dress rehearsal is the last time I'll ever see these kids and, even though I'm desperate to stop having to pretend to be Jenna (except for impersonator gigs which are different), I'm also a bit sad about that. 'I can't believe the show is the week after next.'

'I can't believe you can't come,' Alex says.

I scratch my neck. 'It's a shame. But I'll be here next week. And at the dress rehearsal.'

Alex nods. 'Definitely? You know the date – the thirteenth of December?'

'I know the date and I'll definitely be here.' My stomach knots. On days like today, when things are going well, I get flashes of thinking I've helped Alex and the other kids a bit. But then I remind myself that I haven't done anything but lie and deceive and, if there's been any good done at all, it's by fake Jenna.

'Why can't you come on the fourteenth?' Alex says.

'*Alex*,' Sam says. 'Ms Cox is filming on the fourteenth. She told us that already. And we're very lucky she's spent as much time with us as she has.'

A few more acts come and go and I offer up some notes while Sam tells them they're 'awesome' or 'great' or 'brilliant' and alien Alex manages 'all right'.

The last on the bill are the dance troupe. Unlike their classmates, they have not improved. If anything, they've gone backwards and even Sam's smile seems to have dropped.

'Okay,' I say getting up from my seat. Let's have a look at that cha-cha, shall we?' I go up to the stage. 'Side, rock, step.' I demonstrate, wishing I was wearing my usual trainers instead of the teetering high heels favoured by Jenna. 'Side, rock, step together. Now forward and backward with the—' Suddenly my ankle rolls beneath me. 'Ouch.'

'Are you okay?' Lucy says.

'Fine,' I say, clutching my ankle and trying to ignore the searing pain shooting up my leg.

Sam appears beside me on stage.

'I'm fine,' I say, wincing. 'Absolutely fine.'

Chapter Thirty-Five

'You've got a car coming to pick you up, right?'

I nearly laugh in Sam's face until I remember he thinks I'm a big celebrity and also that I'm in too much pain to laugh anyway. My ankle is throbbing like hell and has swelled up and turned lividly purple. 'I haven't but I'll order a cab.'

'I'll drive you. My car is a bit shabby but as long as you don't mind slumming it?'

Now what am I supposed to say? Because obviously I don't want Sam anywhere near my house but now it's deeply ungracious to insist on a cab. 'I don't want to put you to any trouble.'

'It's no trouble.'

I force a smile and attempt to get up from my seat but, as soon as I try to put weight on my left leg it's apparent that isn't going to happen. 'Fuck,' I say in a very un-Jenna way.

'Here,' Sam says, offering me his arm. 'Lean on me.'

I have little choice but to cooperate and the two of us limp slowly out of the hall and down the school corridors. Up close, he smells good – not of some fancy aftershave but of clean skin and washing that's just been taken off the line. Stop it, I tell myself, the pain is making you delirious. 'Sorry, this is taking forever.'

'Don't be silly. There's no rush.'

Eventually we come to a beaten-up red Ford Fiesta. 'This is me,' Sam says, opening the passenger door for me. I wince as I manoeuvre myself into the seat. 'I really think I should take you to hospital and get that looked at.'

'I'll be fine.' There's no way I can go to hospital. What name would I give? I'm also desperate to be back in my own home and out of these ridiculous Jenna clothes now. My ratty sweatpants won't fix my ankle but these horrendously tight jeans cutting into my belly are finishing me off. Even my Jenna false eyelashes feel too heavy suddenly. And let's not forget it was 'Jenna' heels that got me into this mess.

Sam clicks his seat belt into the holder. 'Sorry again about my car. Not exactly a limo. But y'know, teacher's salary and all that.'

I'm just about to tell Sam he could supplement his income by being a Ryan Reynolds lookalike when I realise that the very last subject on earth I should bring up is lookalikes. Because, somehow, and this will never not amaze me, Sam believes I'm the real Jenna Cox. Christ on a bike.

Sam pulls out of the parking space. 'All the kids were so much better today, weren't they?'

'They really were.'

'That's down to you and all the great advice you've given them.'

A heat rises through my chest. I don't deserve any praise. I'm nothing but a liar and a fraud.

'How lucky was it that I saw you in the street that night?'

I force a smile.

'I actually had some great news from the Headteacher today. She's managed to secure budget to hire a part-time drama teacher next term. I think me banging on about how the kids have blossomed under you really helped. Not that an ordinary drama teacher will be as good as you, of course. Maybe I could tempt you to apply?' He laughs. 'The head did say she'd consider someone without a traditional teaching background.'

'Yeah, I don't think I've got the patience.' I wince as we go over a speed bump.

'You're in a lot of pain, aren't you?'

'I'm okay. I'm pleased for you about the drama teacher. And I'm pleased Alex has decided to be part of the show. I think he'll be a good MC.'

'Me too. And again, I've got you to thank for that. I have no idea what you said to him at the last rehearsal but he was a different kid today. Volunteering to be the MC but also just so much less...'

'Snipey?'

Sam laughs. 'Yeah. He's an incredible kid though. I'm in awe of the way he handles his illness. I've rarely heard him moan about how he's feeling.'

'That is amazing.' I've never consciously registered this but, now Sam says it, I realise how true it is. 'Oh, look at this big traffic jam. I feel awful taking up so much of your free time.'

'It's fine. I'm not doing anything this evening anyway.'

I wonder if Sam's not doing anything is with a partner. Not that it matters to me obviously.

'Are you hot?'

'I'd like to think so.' I say, laughing.

Sam laughs too. 'I mean this as a compliment when I say you're not like I imagined you'd be. You're not very celeb-y.'

That's because I'm not a celeb. 'Er, thanks.'

'Like I said, it's a compliment.'

'It's the next turning on the right, by the way.'

Sam flicks on the indicator and turns into my road.

'It's just a bit further down on the left. The one with the red door.'

Sam pulls into a parking space. 'Stay there and I'll come and help you out.'

I'm about to tell him I'm fine when I realise I'm really not. 'Thanks.'

Sam comes to the passenger side and opens the door. 'Okay, put your hands on my shoulders and let me do the work.'

I do as instructed trying not to be distracted by the clean washing smell. Slowly and carefully, we make it to the front door.

'Tell me you live on the ground floor?'

I should lie, of course, but my brain doesn't work quickly enough. 'Third.'

'Okay, let me help you up the stairs.'

'There's no need. I can manage.' How can you manage, Clare? *How?*

'Don't be silly.'

I mumble an embarrassed thanks and open the front door.

'Right,' Sam says as we reach the bottom of the stairs. 'Ready.'

We start to very slowly climb the steps, me leaning heavily on Sam. 'Ouch,' I say before I can stop myself.

'It would be easier if I carried you.'

'What? No, I can't let you do that.'

'Sure? It would be a lot quicker.'

'Let's keep going like this.'

We inch our way up another two steps, me trying hard not to cry with how much it hurts.

'Let me carry you.'

'No. You'll hurt your back.'

Sam laughs. 'Do I look like that much of a weakling?'

Before I can answer, he scoops me up into his arms. I can feel the heat of his body through his shirt. 'Don't drop me.' Christ, what a stupid thing to say!

He grins. 'I'll try not to.'

We make it up the stairs. 'This is me on the right.'

Sam gently and carefully puts me down. 'Are you going to be okay?'

'Yes. Thank you.'

'Okay, well, see you at the next rehearsal.'

'Yeah, and thanks again for looking after me.'

'You're welcome.' He turns to head down the stairs.

'I feel as if I should at least offer you a cup of tea.'

Sam smiles. 'A cup of tea would be lovely. But I'll make it for you. We need to get that leg elevated.'

Chapter Thirty-Six

I am on the sofa with my leg propped up on a stack of cushions and a bag of frozen peas on my ankle. As soon as I invited Sam in for a cup of tea, I wanted to suck the words back into my mouth. How on earth was I going to get away with living somewhere so un-celeb-y? It was such a stupid and avoidable mistake and one I'm sure I wouldn't have made if I wasn't distracted by being in pain. I am in luck though as Sam merely commented that he might have known my home would be 'lovely but normal' and this was further proof of me being 'incredibly down to earth'.

He is now bustling around my kitchen and I'm running a quick mental check to see if there's anything in the flat that gives away my true identity. But I'm not the type to leave mail lying around and I haven't had any photographs on display since Stephen left me. No one wants constant reminders of happy days when those days feel like another lifetime ago.

'Here we go,' Sam says, placing a steaming mug of tea into my hands. 'Are the painkillers kicking in yet?'

'Starting to.'

'Good.' He raises his mug. 'Cheers. Here's to you making a speedy recovery and to the show going well.'

'Cheers.' I take a sip of my drink. 'You make a half decent cuppa.'

'Ha, not even a pretty face.'

'I wouldn't say that.' What the hell is wrong with me? 'Have you always been a teacher?'

Sam shakes his head. 'Nope. I used to be in advertising—'

'No way. So did…' No, you didn't because you're Jenna, idiot! 'So did lots of people I know.'

It's a strange thing to say and Sam's face crumples for a second but then he carries on. 'I had a midlife crisis and decided I wanted to do something more worthwhile.' He grins and rolls his eyes. 'Jeez, I sound corny. I've been a teacher for nearly five years now.'

'Well, you're obviously a good one. All the kids love you.'

'Yeah, but not when I'm making them read Chaucer.'

'Well, love is rarely unconditional.'

Sam smiles. 'I'm very lucky to be doing something I enjoy as much as I do. Don't get me wrong, teaching definitely has its downsides but, on a good day, there's nothing better. Did you always know you wanted to go into show business?'

'Err… I guess.'

'Sorry, you must get sick of being asked about your work.' He gets up and moves towards the bookshelves. 'I see you're a fellow bookworm. What are you into?'

'A mixture of stuff. I don't really understand people who stick rigidly to one genre. I mean, I like roast potatoes but I wouldn't like to eat nothing else for the rest of my life.'

Sam laughs. 'I can think of worse things. My ex-wife used to tease me I ought to start a potato appreciation society.'

'Ex-wife?' Why, Clare, why?

Sam's face clouds. 'Yeah. I wouldn't wish a divorce on my worst enemy but I'm over it now. We've stayed on good terms too.' He turns back towards the bookshelves. 'Oh, you've got the Jackson Brodie series.'

Him being divorced makes no difference to me, although I wish my brain would send an appropriate message to my sweaty palms and racing heart.

'I'm a big Kate Atkinson fan,' Sam says.

'Me too.'

'Oh, but you like this author even more.'

I freeze because in Sam's hand is a copy of my book.

'Clare Palmer. She must be good because you've got six copies of the same book.'

My author copies. 'Umm, I think I was a bit stuck for inspiration when it came to Christmas presents one year but then I forgot I'd bought them and got people other things. You know how it is.'

'Hmm.' Sam is reading the blurb on the back of the cover. 'It sounds good. I might get myself a copy.'

'Take one of those.'

'Oh, no, I wasn't hinting.'

'I know but I don't need six copies and anyway it's the least I can do after you've driven me home, carried me up the stairs and played nurse.'

He smiles. 'Thanks. I love discovering a new author.'

If only you knew.

I have no idea how we got here. One minute Sam and I were having a cup of tea and now it's eleven o'clock at night and all I want is to lean across the sofa and kiss him.

Which is insane. And CANNOT happen.

The tea morphed into a glass of wine, the wine into dinner, which Sam insisted on cooking because I was to stay put and keep that leg elevated. He scrabbled around in the virtually empty fridge and produced a delicious bowl of lemony orecchiette with peas and pancetta. And all the time we talked and talked and it was the weirdest thing because, even though I am quite literally pretending to be someone else, I am so comfortable with Sam – as if I am properly myself. Yes, my hair and make-up and clothes are my Jenna ones, but that's where the pretending stops. (This is only possible because the real Jenna affords me a clean slate in terms of the person inside. Her public persona is a study in everywoman blandness and, although she shares frequently on social media, her candour and 'realness' are a sham and her 'opinions' innocuous and universal: Be the best you can be, life is for living, my friends and family mean the world.)

It's been the real me who has spent this evening getting to know Sam better then. And what a revelation that has been because, while I suppose I knew he was funny and smart and an all-round good guy, now it's as if those things are flashing in neon in front of my eyes.

'I think you're ready for a new ice pack.' Sam removes the half-melted bag of peas from my ankle and, as his fingers graze my bare skin, heat ripples through my body. Jesus, Clare, get a grip of yourself. You're done with men, remember. Also – small detail – Sam thinks you're someone else.

'Is Alex going to be okay?'

'I'm not sure,' Sam says, his back to me as he rummages around in my freezer. 'I hope so but apparently his prognosis is uncertain.'

'Life is so shit, isn't it?' See, definitely the real me.

Sam places a fresh bag of frozen peas gently on my ankle. 'I know what you mean. It's awful to see a kid have to deal with something like that. But, and I don't want to sound all Californian on you, life is beautiful too.'

'Hmm. I think a lot of the people who say that haven't had many tough breaks.'

'I've had tough breaks.'

'Yeah, I know you've been through a divorce but *tough* tough breaks.' Like five babies dying inside you. Like losing everything including yourself.

'My whole family died in separate incidents over a period of six months. My mum, my brother, my dad.'

'I'm sorry.' A pointless little phrase if ever there was one but what else can I say?

Sam's face has clouded. He's somewhere else. 'My mum had a heart attack. She was fifty-five and apparently in perfect health. Not overweight, hardly drank, a non-smoker. Two months later, my brother was in a freak accident on a construction site and then three months after that, my dad took his own life.'

'My God.'

Sam looks up, his bright blue eyes full of pain. 'Yeah, it was pretty full-on and, for a while I sank into a deep depression. I did everything in my power to push my wife away and eventually I managed that. I sat around feeling sorry for myself and hating the world. One day I was in the corner shop and I saw a guy about the same age as me and he had a baby in a pushchair and a woman with him, who was obviously his mum, and they were fussing around the baby and I hated them, but specifically him, so so much. Resented the hell out of him because he had everything. But then I remembered that saying about how resentment is like drinking poison and waiting for the other person to die and from that moment on, I realised I had to try to let go of the anger and the bitterness. That it was time to start living again, not just for me but for my mum and my brother and my dad as well.' He gives a sad little laugh. 'I even decided to take up showering again.' He shakes his head. 'I'm sorry, I didn't mean to hit you with all this heavy stuff. I was having such a nice evening too.'

Without thinking, I reach across and put my hand on his arm. 'I'm sorry you lost your family.'

'Thank you,' he says, holding my gaze. 'Well, I make a terrible nurse, don't I? It's all me me me.'

I smile.

'How is the ankle?'

'A little better thank you. Would you like another glass of wine?'

'I'd better not as I'm driving.'

Stay. 'I've had a nice evening too.'

Sam smiles.

And then I do something unbelievably stupid. I lean forward and put my lips on Sam's. For a second, he hesitates but then he is kissing me back and damn him if he isn't the most amazing kisser because a voice in my head is screaming at me to STOP but somehow I can't.

Chapter Thirty-Seven

FUUUUUUUUUCK!
I am pacing around the bathroom sweating and crying. What the hell was I thinking?

(You weren't thinking.)

It's nearly six o'clock, which means any minute now Sam is going to wake up. In my bed. And I don't know whether he thought last night was a one-off thing (or, to be more accurate, a four-off thing) or whether he thinks it's the start of something, but one thing is for certain and that's that he thinks I'm Jenna.

I sink down to my haunches with my back against the heated towel rail. Perhaps I can tell him the truth?

No, of course, I can't. I mean, how would that go: So, Sam, a funny thing...

Maybe I'll just hide in here until he leaves? That seems like a good plan. As if on cue, there's a knock at the door though. 'Jenna? You okay?'

'Fine.' A series of images from last night flash through my mind. Unhelpful to say the least.

'I'll put the kettle on.'

I stare at myself in the bathroom mirror. Part Jenna, part me and a lot monster. That poor bloke.

'Tea or coffee?' Sam says when I finally give in to the fact it's not an option to hide in the bathroom indefinitely.

I can't look at him. 'Tea please.'

'How's the ankle this morning?'

Painful but not nearly as painful as my heart. 'Not too bad, thanks.'

Sam puts a cup of tea down on the side table next to me. He has remembered just how I like it – I'm talking the exact Pantone shade – and for some reason this makes a lump rise in my throat. Like that's the thing to get upset about.

Sam reaches out and runs his finger along my cheekbone and a jolt of electricity shoots through me. He's looking particularly Ryan Reynolds-y this morning.

'About last night,' I blurt, wincing at the cliché. 'It was lovely.'

'I thought so too.'

Stop making this harder. 'But it can't happen again.'

Sam stops stroking my face and his eyes cloud. 'Right. Of course. Because people like you don't date people like me.'

'No, it's not that.'

Sam looks at me: what the hell is it then? And, of course, I have no answer. Or no answer I can give Sam.

Chapter Thirty-Eight

I haven't moved from the sofa since Sam left. Or stopped crying. Big, snotty, hiccupy sobs that make me feel as if I can't breathe.

I hate what I did to him. It will take me a long time to forget the pain in his eyes and the quiet dignity he behaved with. He even reminded me to keep icing my ankle.

But it's not just about the shame of behaving so badly to someone who deserves so much better, there's also the simple fact that I like Sam in a way I'd forgotten I could. I wasn't lying when I told Malcolm I'd given up men. I haven't been on a single date since Stephen left. Not just that, but I haven't even felt a flicker of interest. Until last night.

Sam will be at school now. I wonder if he's managing to be his usual, upbeat self? He seemed so flat and sad but maybe I'm flattering myself (Jenna?) and he has one-night stands all the time. He looked crushed though.

I can't write now, I'm in no fit state. I pick up my phone and scroll through Twitter.

Jonny Turner is trending for some reason.

Turner's TV career over...
Affair with a younger male colleague...
Accusations of grooming...

My heart pounds. If Jonny Turner's career is over, then so is Malcolm's. He's always going on about being a proper performer but I'm pretty sure the majority of his livelihood comes from his Jonny lookalike work.

I try his number but it goes straight to voicemail.

I type out a message, *Are you okay?* I delete it immediately and call a cab.

I hammer on Malcolm's door. I know he's in there. I saw the living-room curtains twitch a minute ago.

'Malcolm,' I call through the letterbox. 'Hello.'

The door swings open and I narrowly avoid falling flat on my face on the doormat.

'What are you doing here?' Malcolm says.

'I came to see if you were all right.'

'Never better. Who needs a career, right?'

'May I come in?'

'I'd rather you didn't,' Malcolm says, stepping aside to let me past. 'What have you done to your ankle?'

'Sprained it. I was trying to show someone a dance move.'

'I see.' Malcolm shows me into the living room. It's very much a more-is-more aesthetic – I'm talking colour, pattern, texture and lots of furniture which would be described as a piece. Today it feels grey and flat though. The swagged curtains remain shut and there's an ashtray that's full of spent cigarettes and half-drunk cups of coffee littered about the place.

I sit down on the leopard print sofa. 'Have you spoken to Jackie?'

Malcolm shrugs. 'Yeah, but there's nothing she can do, is there? Jonny Turner is about as employable as a convicted serial killer, which means exactly the same is true for me.'

'But you've got other work, right?'

Malcolm gives me a look which, even in this dim light, I can see is not what one would describe as friendly. 'Oh yeah, there's that movie with Scorsese and the Lloyd Webber musical. Oh, and don't forget I'm headlining at Glasto this year.'

We sit in silence, my ankle throbbing. Why did I come here? As if things aren't bad enough today. 'It'll be okay,' I say eventually.

'How?' Malcolm's voice cracks. 'How will it be okay?'

Chapter Thirty-Nine

August 2019

I am pregnant. Hurrah.

Except when you've had three previous miscarriages there's no whooping and cheering. No one's buying Babygros or thinking what colour to paint the nursery.

Instead, we are living at the fork of two alternative lives. Trying to think as little as possible about what's going on inside my body while thinking about it almost constantly.

Baby or miscarriage?

There's an extra dimension too. Stephen and I have failed to resolve things since the row that revealed that, while I wanted to go private or turn to traditional Chinese medicine or do whatever the hell else it took to stay pregnant, he wanted to 'hit pause' and not do 'this' anymore. In the seven months since, we've often revisited the conversation and it has usually turned into a row.

One particularly bitter recent exchange saw me trying to discuss adoption or surrogacy and Stephen responding by once again extolling the virtues of a child-free life – more freedom! More spontaneity! More money! I shook my head in disbelief, told him his hard sell reminded me of my advertising days and slammed the front door behind me before spending three nights on Meg and Adam's sofa. (Ironically, seven-month-old Lola was teething at the time and screamed so constantly, one might have thought Stephen had employed her to make his case.)

Now when I rush to the loo praying I won't find blood in my knickers, there's a little part of my brain questioning whether, if I do lose this baby, Stephen might be relieved.

To be fair to him, he's done a good job of acting – and I hope it's not just acting – as if this wouldn't be the case. He brings me ginger tea and dry crackers, rubs my shoulders and assiduously notes the Early Pregnancy Unit appointments in his calendar. He reminds me of the plethora of stories of miracle babies born to people in our position.

Neither of us can say if we will join their ranks. The future's not ours to know as the song intones. And yet I do know. Somewhere deep inside me. I know I will lose this baby and I know I will lose my husband.

Chapter Forty

December 2023

It's a week since I slept with Sam and then told him nothing could happen between us ever again. I'm transforming myself into Jenna in preparation for the penultimate talent show rehearsal at Hatfield Academy. But no amount of Charlotte Tilbury make-up, expensive clothes or faux diamonds can ready me for what's ahead.

I am dreading seeing Sam. Either he'll be offish, which will be awkward, or he'll be nice which will be even more unbearable.

And that's not even to start on how I feel about seeing the kids. Alex who, underneath his brittle exterior (hi, kettle!), has a soft underbelly. An eleven year old who's having to cope with things that no eleven year old should. Joe whose smile when one of his jokes lands could melt the hardest of hearts. Daisy who listens to my notes about her singing as if I am Rihanna, and the talentless dance troupe who never stop trying.

My ankle is still sore so Jenna will have to wear trainers today. I lace them wondering as I do if I should pull a sickie. What difference will it really make if I don't go to these last two rehearsals? It's something of a miracle no one has uncovered me as a fraud so perhaps it's best to quit while I'm ahead?

My laptop glares at me from the corner of the room. Yes, it says, if you don't go to the rehearsal, you can actually get some writing done.

I want to say goodbye to the kids though. And Sam, for that matter. I owe them all that much at least. Before I can think too much more about it, I grab the knock-off designer handbag I use for Jenna and slam my front door behind me.

I limp slowly down the stairs trying not to think about Sam carrying me up them. The feeling of his body next to mine, the fresh clean washing smell, the laughter lines around his eyes.

Once I'm in the back of a cab (no walk to the bus stop with my ankle like this), I call Malcolm. I'm expecting it to go to voicemail but he picks up. 'Hi, I've been trying to call you for days.'

'I know.'

'How are you doing?'

'Oh, marvellous. Who needs a livelihood or indeed a reason to get up in the mornings? Sorry, darling, I shouldn't be a bitch to you. I know you're trying to be kind.'

'S'okay.'

'Are you still getting lookalike bookings yourself? Or do people not want Jenna without Jonny?'

'I haven't had any since it happened.' I'm conflicted about this. On the one hand, my sorry looking bank balance needs all the help it can get, on the other, all this business with Hatfield Academy has left me feeling a bit queasy about passing myself off as Jenna, even when I'm doing it in a professional context.

'At least you've got the writing to fall back on.'

'Hmm. Listen, I was thinking of popping over to see you later.'

'I wouldn't, darling. I'm not much company.'

'Don't be silly. I'll come over about six if that's okay? Bring you some dinner. Anything you particularly fancy?'

'A litre bottle of vodka and something to live for?'

'I'll see what I can do.'

I end the call to Malcolm and, almost immediately, Meg's name flashes up on my phone. I hit decline. She tries to call me most days, leaves me long voice notes which I don't listen to and messages I delete without reading. I don't want to hear that she's sorry. Sorry is just a word. She and Adam can be friends with Stephen and Tamara. Maybe Lola and Alfie have some toys and clothes they've outgrown which can be passed on to the baby?

'Excuse me,' the cab driver says.

I know what's coming. He did a noticeable double take when I got into the car and has glanced at me repeatedly in the rear-view mirror. 'It's you, isn't it?'

People always say this. It's such a nonsense. Everyone is 'you'.

'I've been a fan since you were first on the telly.'

I force a big wide Jenna smile. 'Thanks.'

'And me and the wife and kids love *You've Got It*. We never miss an episode. Who is your favourite contestant? We liked Josh.'

'Er, yeah. He was a sweetie.'

The driver shakes his head. 'I can't believe you're in the back of my cab. My wife is going to your book signing next week. The one in Waterstone's Piccadilly.'

'Ahh, well, tell her to say hello.' God knows why I come out with this. It's just what pops into my head – the sort of thing I imagine Jenna would say. And surely if some random woman at her book signing tells Jenna she's the wife of the cab driver who drove her the other day, Jenna is unlikely to drill into that too deeply and will instead just nod and smile?

The driver smiles, his already puffy red face seeming to get a little puffier and a little redder. 'I will. Her name is Janice. Janice Gregory.'

'I look forward to meeting her,' I say, squashing down a wave of queasiness. One more lie to add to the ever-growing list.

Chapter Forty-One

Sam is nice which makes me think three things:

1. Well, of course he is.
2. Is there anything hotter than an emotionally intelligent man?
3. Today would be a hell of a lot easier for me if he was being an arsehole. (Also fat and bald, please, and thank you.)

'How's the ankle?' he says as we make our way slowly down the school corridor. (He did offer me his arm but was visibly relieved when I said I was okay on my own.)

'A lot better than it was but still quite swollen. I won't be running any marathons anytime soon.'

Sam smiles but his eyes don't crinkle. 'Well, I'm glad it's getting better at least.'

'Yeah. Thanks for looking after me when it happened, by the way.' That's right, Clare, remind him of the other night. Elegant.

'I'm sorry to hear about Jonny Turner. You must be upset about it.'

'Yeah.' I think about Malcolm asking me for vodka and something to live for. Jackie told me that when his husband left him he sunk into this black hole she was worried he might never pull himself out of. That he has only been himself again in the last few months.

'I can't help feeling sorry for him,' Sam says. 'I know what he did was wrong but it's scary to lose everything overnight like that. And some of the stuff in the newspapers is unnecessarily vitriolic, if you ask me. What happened to "let he who is without sin cast the first stone"?'

'I agree.'

'And there's a nasty homophobic undertone.'

'Yeah.' In another life where he didn't think I was a completely different person, I could have something with this man. A real connection. I shake the thought from my brain.

Sam opens the door to the hallway and I am hit by the smell of nerves and Lynx Africa. 'No Alex today?' I say, fear dragging at my stomach. Please, please don't let something have happened to Alex.

'No, he's here,' Sam says. 'He needed to talk to the Headteacher for some reason.'

The rehearsal gets under way and, although the first act on stage are the woeful rappers, it's great to have something to distract me from real life. Well, my real fake life.

'Awesome,' Sam says as the boys leave the stage.

'Yeah great,' I say vaguely because with the show so close it's a bit late to hope they're going to morph into Jay-Z.

'Who's next on stage?' Sam asks.

'Joe,' Daisy says. 'But he's gone to the toilet.'

'Ah, okay,' Sam says. 'Well let's give him a couple of minutes.'

Daisy nods and then looks at me through her eyelashes. 'So you and Vince Matty?'

My stomach drops as if I'm on a rollercoaster. 'Er—'

Daisy, who has the fluffy tote bag welded to her side (*et tu* Brutus), shows me her phone. 'I saw it on Instagram.' I look at the screen and see a selfie of Jenna with Vince Matty. They're in front of a huge glittering Christmas tree in what looks like an idyllic country cottage, their cheeks pressed together and huge smiles plastered across their faces. They are together and this is their announcement to the world – their hard launch. Nausea swirls in my belly and I can hardly bear to look at Sam's stricken face.

'Daisy,' he says eventually. 'Ms Cox's personal life is none of your business. Plus, you know that Instagram is for people over at the age of thirteen. And you know the rules about phones in school time.'

'But Alex is on his phone all the time.'

Sam gives her a look I wouldn't have thought he was capable of. 'Put it away now.'

Chapter Forty-Two

Sam and I sit in stony silence watching Joe's act. I desperately want to say something to him, but what? I'm not with Vince Matty. I've never even met the guy and actually he may have been voted as one of last year's hottest stars but I think he has a preternaturally big head.

'That was great, Joe,' I say as he leaves the stage. 'But don't forget to lose the penguin arms.'

I look across to Sam waiting for the requisite 'awesome' or 'fabulous' but he stays silent, his eyes fixed on the middle distance.

'That llama joke is really a banger.' The very least I can do today is lavish the kids with praise. With the show next week, and Sam out of cheerleading commission, it's up to me to build their confidence.

Joe shuffles off and I glance at Sam. He looks so sad and it's all I can do not to reach across and stroke his cheek. Tell him that everything is not as it seems and I'd take him over Vince Matty any day.

The hall doors open and in bursts Alex. For a kid who habitually plays sulky preteen to perfection, he's wearing an enormous grin and bouncing with restless energy. 'I've got the *best* news!'

'You're better?' I say.

'Yeah, they found a cure for cancer overnight.' Alex rolls his eyes. 'Nah, not that. But I talked to Mrs Gray about moving the date of the show to the thirteenth instead of the fourteenth so you can come. She took a bit of persuading but in the end she saw that we'd raise way more money with you here and that, if we're ready for a dress rehearsal on the thirteenth, well, then we're ready for the actual show.'

My stomach lurches. '*What?*'

'Mrs Gray said that?' Sam says, snapped suddenly from his catatonic state.

'Yeah,' Alex says. 'She says she wouldn't normally agree to it but these aren't normal circumstances.'

On that much at least the Headteacher and I are aligned.

Sam blinks like a man trying to shake off a terrible nightmare. 'But, but—'

'Mrs Gray says as long as you're fine with it, then so is she.'

'And what about me?' I say.

Alex looks at me. 'What about you? You've said a million times how much you wish you could be at the show. And I know you're free on the thirteenth because you were coming to the dress rehearsal.'

'Everyone is expecting the show to be on the Thursday,' Sam says. 'People have booked tickets.'

'Yeah,' Alex says. 'But those people are our parents. It's not like they won't come if we change the day.'

'What about if they've made arrangements to take time off work?' Sam says. 'On Thursday?'

Alex shrugs. 'Mrs Gray thought of that too. But she thinks people will "forgive the inconvenience".'

'Well, I'm still not sure,' Sam says. 'What about the other performers?'

Alex laughs. 'They'll be cool with it. We can do the show on the fourteenth and sell no tickets to anyone apart from our parents or we can do it on the thirteenth and sell a gazillion tickets.'

A wave of nausea washes through me. How did I get here and how the hell am I going to get out of it?

'OMG,' Daisy says, appearing out of nowhere. 'You could even sing "Puppy Love" at the end.'

'Yeah,' Alex says. 'That would be great.'

'I can't sing,' I say.

'What?' Daisy and Alex say in unison.

'Er, I can't sing at your show because it's about *your* talent.'

Alex shrugs. 'Whatever. The important thing is you're here. Mrs Gray reckons if you are, the newspapers might even turn up. She said it's definitely a story.'

'There can't be any newspapers,' I say, my voice going up an octave. 'If I'm going to do this, it has to be on the down low.'

'Why?' Alex says.

'Umm… well, I didn't do this for the publicity. My team don't even know I come here.' That's for bloody sure.

Alex gives me a look that belies his age. 'You'll come to the show though? If it's on the thirteenth?'

Sam clears his throat. 'I'm not going to agree to this date change unless I'm one hundred per cent sure that everyone involved in the show is okay with it.'

Alex nods. 'Right, well, why don't we put it to a vote?'

Chapter Forty-Three

Rain lashes against the windows. Biblical, apocalyptic rain, the sort you feel will never stop. I limp around my flat feeling sick with panic.

I have managed to pretend to be Jenna to Sam and the kids of 7J. I have even fooled the odd parent or member of staff who's poked their head around the door or seen me in passing, but there's no way I can get a whole audience of adults to buy it, especially as one member of that audience has previously met the real me. (What are the odds on Dylan's dad being one of my former gynaecologists? Granted, I saw a fair few but it does feel a bit unlucky.) And then, of course, there's the risk that someone leaks this to the press. I may have asked to keep it quiet but it just needs one loose-lipped parent to pick up the phone and I'm busted.

I could skip the country? Grab my passport and a bag of possessions and never be seen in London again. Not many people would even notice I'm gone. My parents, my long-suffering agent (although I could continue to *not* write my book from anywhere).

The only viable option is to wait until the day of the show and then say I'm unwell. Some terrible stomach bug that makes leaving the bathroom floor an impossibility. I don't feel good about letting down Sam, Alex and the other kids but what are my choices?

My ankle throbs and I wash down a couple of max-strength painkillers, the thought flashing through my mind that being in pain is the very least I deserve given everything I have done.

I reach for my lip balm, a memory flitting into my consciousness of the pink pot with the cartoon princess on it that rolled out of Alex's pocket. How he described his little sister as 'a right pain' but his whole face lit up at the mention of her. And that's when I realise that the princess on the pot wasn't any old princess, she was a Disney princess, and I finally understand exactly why Alex is so keen to go to Disneyland. I blink back tears.

I go to Jenna's grid on Instagram. Look at the photo of her and Vince again. They really are the epitome of smug togetherness. Like they're the first people in the whole world to be in love. Well, just you wait until it all goes wrong. Stephen and I looked like that once and now he's having a baby with someone else.

Jenna has posted something new too. A reminder she'll be at Waterstones Piccadilly next Tuesday evening. She 'can't wait to chat about all things *Sunny Side Up*'.

All things? Like the fact you didn't write it?

I wander over to the bookshelf and absent-mindedly pull one of my books off the shelf. Think about Sam doing the same. I wonder if he'll still read the copy I gave him. I'd like him to read it as it would give him a little glimpse of the person I am. Or the person I was. Not that Sam knows it's me, of course, or would even think about reading it if he knew it was.

Tears roll down my cheeks and I stand in the chill grey light listening to the ceaseless rain. I had such a bright future ahead of me once.

I sit down at my desk and open my computer. Although Jackie assures me there will be solo gigs as Jenna on offer again in the future, after everything that's happened at Hatfield Academy, I'm not sure I have the stomach for it. Which means I have no other source of income other than this book and my less than reliable freelance copywriting work.

I have to put all this mess out of my head. I can't think about how awful it will be to tell Hatfield Academy I won't be at the talent show. Can't dwell on how that will land with Alex and the other kids or, for that matter, Sam.

Equally, I can't afford to think about Stephen and his baby or the row with Meg or how worried I am about Malcolm.

All I can focus on now is my fictional world.

Chapter Forty-Four

Since hope, joy and career opportunities are not to be found on the shelves of Tesco Express, it's very difficult to know what to get to take to Malcolm's. I pick up a packet of sausages, remember the conversation about how Malcolm hasn't been able to stomach them since making that TV commercial for sausages at the age of four and put them back on the shelf.

I reach for a packet of sea bass fillets. Everyone likes sea bass. (Although Malcolm doesn't much like anything right now.)

I chuck a few more items in my basket and then queue up to pay. As there is only one assistant manning the tills, I have no choice but to go for self-checkout, although it's hard to put my hatred for it into words. The sheer nerve of these big companies pretending all this is being done for our convenience rather than their profits. Yeah, because it would be so inconvenient for us to have competent humans checking out the shopping we're paying a small fortune for.

I attempt to scan the sea bass fillets but the machine stubbornly refuses to acknowledge the barcode. A bored looking assistant appears, looks at me contemptuously and wordlessly attempts to scan it. To my huge relief, the machine does not bleep for him either.

'Not sure what's wrong with it?' I say trying and failing to get the rather pathetic note of triumph out of my voice.

The assistant doesn't dignify this with an answer, instead keying in numbers before putting the sea bass in the bagging area. (The bagging area where there will surely and mystifyingly be unexpected items any minute now.)

My phone rings as I'm doing battle with a packet of spinach. Meg again. I hit decline.

I managed to force out some words onto the page today. They're not good words but they're words nonetheless. And, although I already know most of them will be deleted tomorrow, at least it's keeping the story in my head. Not to mention keeping my real/real fake life out of it.

I scan a bottle of vodka and the machine tells me to await age verification. The assistant from before returns and glances at me, the corners of his lips twitching. You'll be my age one day, I feel like shouting. And good to know you can actually smile.

I limp to the bus stop, the plastic bags cutting into my left hand as I clutch an umbrella with my right. Every few seconds, the wind blows the umbrella inside out and I have to stop and right it while wondering if it wouldn't just be easier to give in to getting soaked.

The bus is packed and the windows all steamed up. A baby is screaming at the top of his lungs and I am pressed up against a man who is shovelling fried chicken into his mouth like some kind of zoo animal.

I bet the real Jenna never travels by bus.

The man finishes his meal, wipes his greasy mouth with the back of his hand and belches softly.

The bus disgorges me back into the torrential rain and I resume my fight with the elements and my umbrella.

IDENTITY CRISIS

I can't bear to think of how the kids will feel when they find out Jenna isn't going to be at their show. A lump rises in my throat as I think about Alex picking his little sister's dream holiday as his own. He was so thrilled with himself for managing to get the date of the show moved too.

And of course then there's Sam. Smart, funny, emotionally intelligent Sam who in another lifetime I think I could be happy with. How is he going to feel about yet another undeserved slap in the face?

I turn into Malcolm's road. And remind myself that my mission tonight is supposed to be cheering him up.

Malcolm, the man who I would have sworn sleeps in a sharply-cut suit complete with contrasting pocket square, is wearing sweatpants. He is unshaven and his hair unbrushed.

I think about Meg coming over after the first miscarriage, forcing me into the shower while she changed the sheets. Remember the lemon drizzle cake she'd baked because she knows it's my favourite. A sharp pain stabs at my gut. I've known Meg since we were three years old. We walked hand in hand into 'big school', I gave her her first sanitary towel when her period started unexpectedly in Year 7 and she dried my tears when Tim Broadbent turned out to be the rat I was adamant he wasn't. We've seen each other through highs, lows and too many dodgy haircuts to count. It's hard to imagine my life without her. But then I've learned to live without plenty of other things I thought I couldn't: my babies, my husband, my sense of who I really am.

'How are you doing?'

Malcolm answers with a grunt. 'Did you bring vodka?'

'I did. And dinner.'

'Oof, food. You're reminding me of Jackie. She was here

the other day with her own bodyweight in smoked salmon and bagels.'

I go into the kitchen. It's a glamorous room with deep pink walls and teal units with ornate gold handles, but it's littered with dirty mugs and saucers redeployed as ashtrays and a colony of ants are feasting on some crumbs they've found by the bin.

Malcolm stands behind me watching me unpack the shopping. 'Sorry the place is such a state. But I did tell you not to come.'

'I wanted to come.'

'Hmm.'

'Shall I make us a cup of tea?'

This actually makes Malcolm laugh, albeit somewhat mirthlessly. 'I think we're in need of something stronger than tea, darling. Wine or vodka? I'm out of ice. Oh, and tonic.'

'Wine please.'

We sit down with our drinks and Malcolm lights up a cigarette. I'd like to tell him I'm not keen on passive smoking but if ever there was a man in need of a small thing that brings him pleasure right now, it's Malcolm.

'I'm never going to work again,' he blurts out.

'Don't say that.'

He looks at me, his eyes so full of naked pain I can hardly bear to hold his gaze. 'It's the truth.'

It's funny, I used to hate all Malcolm's talk about Hollywood movies and West End shows and the scores of A-list people he knows; will him to stop showing off and just give it a break, but now I'd love to hear him talk like that. 'Have you thought about taking a normal job? Just something to tide you over?'

'Of course, I've thought about it. I'm not just sitting here waiting for Steven Spielberg to call me, but what could I do?'

Identity Crisis

I hesitate. I want to give Malcolm hope but not false hope. As someone who has been on the receiving end of that (you'll definitely get your baby, just keep trying, don't give up) I know all too well there's nothing crueller.

'I've been in show business, or rather the outer edges of show business, since I did that sausage commercial at the age of four. I'm qualified for absolutely nothing—'

'I'm sure that's not true.'

'It is true. I can't drive so that rules out being a cabbie or a delivery driver and I'd last about thirty minutes working behind a bar or in a shop or a restaurant.' He shudders. 'I prefer to avoid direct contact with the public.'

'I'm sure there's something you could do.'

'Name it.'

'I... I... well, look I need to give it a bit of thought. But there will be a job out there that's perfect for you. I know there will.'

Chapter Forty-Five

Seventeen days until Christmas and I have rarely felt less festive. Even the magnificent glittering angels that hang over Regent Street and are my favourite of the London Christmas lights fail to lift my mood.

I am on my way in to The Leap Agency to take a 'very urgent' new brief on half-fat butter. *I assume I can say you'll be okay to work on this between Christmas and New Year?* Rosamund said in her email. There's so much to unpack in that, from Rosamund's assumption that I'll have nothing better to do, to how urgent it can be to tell the world about half-fat butter.

Smiley happy people spill out of Liberty laden with purple, stuffed carrier bags. Thoughtful gifts for loved ones, no doubt.

The brief from the client is a bit all over the place, Rosamund continued. *But if you pop into the agency, you, me and Hattie can unpick it together.*

Lazy cows. I can't get worked up about them now though, mainly because there are so many more important things to be upset about.

A giant Christmas tree adorns The Leap Agency reception and the normally 'too cool for school' receptionist is wearing a light-up Christmas jumper.

Hattie retrieves me from reception and, as ever, her greeting is as effusive as it is false. It's so great to see me, she and Ros are so grateful to me for coming in at short notice, they really wanted this brief to go to a safe pair of hands.

We go up the spiral staircase, Hattie having to raise her voice to be heard over the sound of music, laughter and chatter. 'The Creative Department are having a bit of a celebration,' Hattie explains. 'The agency was having a bit of a mare on TASK Furniture and the client didn't like any of the work. But then Toby came up with a brilliant idea and completely saved the day.'

My mind whooshes back to that day outside Tottenham Court Road Tube station and how happy I felt when Toby seemed to like my idea of making the furniture your own. He was probably just humouring me though. Still, I'm pleased for him he managed to come up with something the client liked.

'We're in Launchpad,' Hattie says, gesturing towards a meeting room further down on the right.

We pass Toby surrounded by a sea of people. He has a glass of prosecco in one hand and a pool cue in the other. For a second, I think his smile falters but that must be my insecurities talking because, when I look again, not only is the smile full beam but he waves and shouts, 'Hi, Clare.'

Hattie looks visibly shocked that Toby should even acknowledge me, let alone remember my name and I allow myself a little ripple of satisfaction.

And then I look up and see a wall plastered in concept boards.

TASK Furniture.
Make it your own.

*

'Sure you wouldn't like a glass of prosecco?' Toby says, ushering me into a meeting room called Comet.

Not unless you want to be wearing that prosecco.

'Please do sit down,' he says.

'I'll stand.' I clear my throat. 'That was my idea.'

'I'm sorry?'

'The TASK Furniture idea. Make it your own. It was my idea.'

'I'm afraid I don't know what you mean.'

The bastard. I don't know what I expected – an apology, a fudge – but it wasn't flat out denial. 'You and I had a conversation outside Tottenham Court Road Tube station. It was the day you came off your skateboard.'

'Hmm, I remember seeing you that day.' He treats me to a megawatt smile that shows off years of expensive dentistry. 'You were very kind.'

Screw you, thinking you can charm your way out of this. 'We talked about the brief for TASK.'

'Did we? I don't recall.'

'What? You told me you'd presented several creative routes to the client and they didn't like any of them and then I mentioned the hacks you see online—'

'Ahh, yes, the hacks. First thing anyone thinks of, isn't it?'

'Yes,' I say, my voice going up an octave. 'But then I said the idea should be all about expressing your individuality and you could use the tagline: *Make it your own.*'

Toby gives a small, mirthless laugh. 'Oh dear. As I recall, it was me who had a bump to the head that day but it seems you're the one whose memory was affected—'

'NO.' Maybe this is karma? I've stolen Jenna's identity, Toby's stolen my idea. The thought makes me queasy.

Toby rakes his hand through his floppy fringe. 'I know for sure you did not come up with that line. I thought of it in the shower. I was so excited about it, I phoned Al my Deputy Creative Director immediately.'

My brain scrambles for what to say next. If you don't come clean in front of the whole Creative Department right now, I'll tell them the truth, I'll go to the industry press, the idea is my intellectual property and I'll prove that in court.

It's Toby who speaks first though. 'Look, Clare, I understand it can be very hard when you feel as if all your best work is behind you but taking credit for someone's else's creative work is not a good look.'

I'm pretty sure my mouth must literally drop open.

Toby has more though. 'Unless, of course, you can prove your assertion? Perhaps you have the email you sent me where you outlined your thoughts? Or a text message? Some form of written proof?'

'You know I don't. I mentioned the idea to you when we were standing outside the Tube station.'

He shrugs. 'It seems we have rather different memories of that conversation.'

For a second, I doubt myself. Maybe I didn't give him the idea? But I clearly remember how happy I was when he told me it was brilliant.

Toby gives me another full-beam smile. 'You do quite a lot of work for The Leap Agency, don't you?'

'Are you threatening me now?'

He laughs. 'No, of course not. Goodness me, Clare. You have quite the imagination.'

Chapter Forty-Six

I have yet to come up with a solution to all Malcolm's woes or indeed a way to feel okay about the fact that in four days from now I'll have to fake illness and bitterly disappoint a group of kids and a teacher I've genuinely grown to care about.

Right now, all of that has been shoved on the back burner though because I have run out of excuses not to see my parents. I am back in the house I grew up in. It's both familiar and unfamiliar at the same time. The hooks in the hallway still groan under the weight of waxed jackets, the shelves are crammed with the same books, and I know if I open the kitchen cupboard I'll find the novelty mugs bearing messages from 'World's Best Dad', to 'Kiss the Cook', to 'Easily Distracted by Cats'. The sofas sag, the carpets are worn from years of vacuuming and there are whole drawers containing faded birthday cards, swimming and karate certificates and dubious 'art' David and I created as kids. It's a typical family home. The sort I will never have. And, yes, people tell me that I can still have it – that there are women who've had five miscarriages and then gone on to have a baby or indeed that there are all sorts of ways to have a family other than giving birth to children. I honestly can't see it happening for me though.

IDENTITY CRISIS

My parents and I are having lunch. I'm trying to avoid conversational landmines and ignore my mother's glare when I help myself to another spoonful of cottage pie. (My mother was not brought up in an era of body positivity and firmly believes all women, yes primarily women, have a responsibility to 'keep themselves in trim'. She has been known to snack on six raisins.)

'So how's the book going?'

Subtext: Are you ever going to finish it? Maybe you should go back to advertising? Not just scraps of freelance but a proper full-time job. For a second, it crosses my mind to tell my parents that I recently had a great campaign idea for TASK Furniture and someone else has taken the credit but I know the truth. I don't say that though, firstly because my parents wouldn't care and secondly because even I am not quite that tragic. 'The book is going fine.'

My father refills my wine glass. Keep going right to the top, I feel like shouting.

I stare at the framed photographs jostling for position on the mantelpiece. Family holidays and parties and graduations. The biggest category of pictures is my brother's two little girls. There's image after image taking the girls from bean-baggy babies to the four and six years they are today.

My oldest child should be six by now.

'Have you seen much of Meg?' my mother asks, cutting off a delicate sliver of carrot.

My parents like Meg. Everyone likes Meg. Well, apart from me.

'Not for a while. We've both been busy.'

My mother nods. 'Your father and I saw her parents at Fiona and Richard's. Richard has retired now, did you know? I expect he's driving Fiona mad getting under her feet all day. I said to her, you should get him to take up golf. Such a good hobby…'

My mind drifts to *Sunny Side Up* which came out on Thursday and is getting loads of press. Jenna has been quoted in interviews saying she had 'such a ball' writing it and it's made me so crazily, insanely furious because she didn't bloody write it, Nelly did.

I have tried to push this to the back of my mind but it's difficult given the book is everywhere. I walked past my local Waterstones to see it had a huge window display and a spot on the table. I nipped into Asda for bin bags and there was Jenna's smug face grinning back at me from the back cover.

'You should invite Richard next time you play golf,' my mum says to my dad.

'Why? We don't really like each other that much.'

My mother waves away this triviality. 'Right, who's got room for dessert? I know I'm stuffed.'

Having seen my mother's child-sized serving of cottage pie, peas and carrots I highly doubt that. 'Dessert would be lovely.'

My mum shuffles off into the kitchen.

'Have you chatted much to your brother lately?' Dad says.

I shake my head. 'No. You?'

'We usually do a FaceTime with them on a Sunday so I'll see them tomorrow. It's always so lovely to see the kids. They're getting so big.'

I nod. I always get the feeling my parents think that my brother made better life choices than me. The annoying thing is, there was a time when I was the golden child. I was a successful creative director, happily married and about to publish my first book. My brother meanwhile could hold down neither a job nor a relationship. But he was the tortoise who overtook the hare. His real ace card was moving to the other side of the world though. Absence has definitely made the heart grow fonder.

Cinnamon fills the air as my mother returns with an apple

crumble. She puts one extremely modest spoonful into a bowl and hands it to me. My mind flashes back to when I was first pregnant and only family knew. Stephen and I came here for lunch and I was queasy and starving and I watched my mother dish out chicken pie giving her and me a tiny slice each and then cutting huge slabs 'for the men'. I had to stop myself shouting, 'But I'm growing your grandchild,' which would have been unseemly (also inaccurate, their grandchild was already dead).

'Could I have a bit more please?' I'm not even that hungry, it's just the principle.

Wordlessly, my mother spoons some more crumble into the bowl.

I douse it with cream, silently daring her to say something. And, yes, I am being childish but who can blame me?

Jenna's book tour has been documented in breathlessly excited social media posts. *So lovely to meet so many fans in real life!!! Thanks for coming out in the rain Liverpool!!!*

Makes all the hard work worthwhile!!!

I had a sudden panic that she might post something the day she's supposedly puking up her guts, but there is no book tour date listed for Wednesday so I just have to cross my fingers she stays quiet. It's another little bit of jeopardy just in case the situation wasn't stressful enough.

'Stephen's parents sent us a Christmas card,' my mum says.

I freeze, my spoon of crumble hovering mid-air. Because Stephen's mum is well known for the round robin letter she encloses with her Christmas cards. And I know exactly which update will top this year's list.

I choke back tears and put down the spoon. And damn my mother if she hasn't found a way to stop me eating too much after all.

Chapter Forty-Seven

As I left my parents' house, my mother stuffed a large cardboard box into my arms. 'These are some bits of yours I found when I cleared out the loft.'

'What bits?'

My mother shrugged. 'Old schoolwork, keepsakes, that sort of thing.'

'Do I have to take them now?'

My mother nodded. 'Your father and I are death cleaning.'

'How cheery.'

'You and your brother will be grateful when the time comes.'

I place the box down in my living room. I don't like to think about my parents dying. Intellectually I know they're not young but, maybe because they're both in good health, their death isn't something I allow myself to contemplate.

I open the box unleashing a stale musty smell. Right at the top is my treasured baby blanket. I run my fingertips across the frayed pink satin edge and hear my toddler voice calling for 'bubbie'. Years later, my mother confessed to me there were actually two bubbies. 'Otherwise, I'd never have been able to wash it.'

Next out of the box is a 'book' I wrote when I was in Year 6. It's entitled, *Bella Goes to Boarding School*. On the front is a very poor drawing of the eponymous Bella with a large trunk. I skim the story hoping to see signs of precocious talent but what I actually read is wildly derivative of the Malory Towers stories I was hooked on at the time. *Bella was looking forward to pillow fights and midnight feasts and lots of fun.*

I reach back into the box and pull out a bright red folder. Multicoloured bubble writing on the front says: *Clare Palmer, 9K. Creative Writing*. I'd have been thirteen so hopefully would have cottoned on to the fact it's best to aim for originality. I flick through the folder, marvelling at the neatness of my big round handwriting. I rock back on my heels and skim the A4 pages once again trying and failing to find signs of early creative genius.

I come to an essay entitled 'Who Am I?' and am transported back to the classroom. Our English teacher, Mrs Feltham, is standing at the front of the class telling us about this piece of homework. Immediately hands shoot up: What sort of thing should we say? How long does it need to be? Is it going to be read out in class?

Mrs Feltham ignores the signs of dissent. She is wearing a red shirt dress and long black boots. Later, Meg and I will say we think she dresses very well for her age. (Mrs Feltham is all of thirty-two.)

> Hello! My name is Clare Palmer and I am thirteen years old. I live with my mum, my dad and my older brother David who is very annoying. When I grow up I want to be a famous author and have a husband and six children.

A fat tear splashes onto the page.

> I am often described as fun, loyal, honest and kind.

What would I be described as now? Certainly not fun. And honest would be a bit of a stretch given my recent exploits. Loyal and kind are questionable too.

> I am passionate about Take That, the environment and cats.

I snap the folder shut. I have plenty to concern myself with without getting maudlin and mawkish about an essay I wrote thirty years ago.

Instead, I elect to tackle writing an article about how to socialise a puppy. My mind flashes back to Jenna's nauseating crooning of 'Puppy Love' to her brother's poor dog.

I start the article with a short explanation of what puppy socialisation is and why it's so important. I've already done some background reading and interviewed a vet so know what I need to cover. Progress is slow though, not least of all because my mind is still on that silly little essay from Year 9. If I was asked to write an article entitled, 'Who Am I?' today, I'm not sure I'd know where to start. What is my life purpose? What are my core beliefs and values? How would I describe my personality?

Nausea bubbles in my belly. I can't be less sure of who I am at forty-one than I was at thirteen.

I shake the thought from my brain and force myself to keep writing about puppy socialisation.

> As responsible breeders will keep puppies with their mums and litter mates until they are at least eight weeks old, this means they are likely to start socialisation. They will do this by gently exposing your puppy to different environments, people and animals. When you bring your puppy home, it's your job to continue this important process.

Identity Crisis

Who am I?

I think of all the times I've been happy recently. The time I gave Daisy the tote bag, the day Alex decided to MC the talent show, the night I was with Sam. All times when I was Jenna. And, yes, I can tell myself that I was simply borrowing Jenna's 'shell' and the person I was being was myself, but we're not exactly talking about shining examples of authenticity, are we?

Malcolm knows me as Clare and, notwithstanding his current situation, the two of us have fun together. But Malcolm and I only met because of the impersonator work.

Focus on your article.

The Checklist: Ten things to get pooch familiar with

Who am I?

My name is Clare Palmer and I am forty-one years old. I live by myself. I am often described as deceitful, dishonest and miserable.

I wipe away the tears with my sleeve.

1. Other dogs

Your furry friend needs to get used to meeting other dogs of all shapes and sizes.

Who am I?

My name is Clare Palmer and I am forty-one years old. I am passionate about—

Nothing. I am passionate about nothing. When my last baby died, I shut off love as one might a water main in the event of a leak.

1. People

From the postie to small children, it's important your puppy gets used to a wide variety of folk.

A sob escapes from my throat, raw and animalistic.
Who am I?

Chapter Forty-Eight

Malcolm and I are lying side by side on his sitting-room floor looking up at the sage green wallpaper dotted with metallic gold stars that adorns the ceiling. (Wine may have been consumed in some quantity.)

'We're stargazing London style,' I say, giggling as if I've just said the funniest thing in the whole world.

'We are.'

I point upwards. 'I like the way all the little stars catch the light and twinkle.'

'Right? Everyone should have a statement ceiling, I tell you.'

Pretty as the stars are, I'm not sure everyone should have a statement ceiling but I don't bother to correct Malcolm as it's one of the first times I've seen him smile since the Jonny Turner scandal broke. He was in a terrible way when I arrived tonight, barely touched the dinner I made him and is only a little happier now because he's 80 per cent Rioja.

'Where do you think impersonators rate in the celebrity pecking order?' Malcolm says. 'Not that I am one anymore, obviously, but just for the sake of argument? Do you think we come before or after reality TV stars?'

'Hmm, not sure. Maybe before because we're having to act

and stuff but maybe after because at least they got famous for being themselves. Although, is that true? I'm not sure most of them are being what the kids would call authentic. I swear half the people who go on *Married at First Sight* or *Love is Blind* or *Love Island* just want to be influencers.'

'True,' Malcolm slurs. 'I really love my statement ceiling.'

'I thought you were going to say you really love me.' I swat him on the arm. 'Your faithful friend who came over to keep you company in your hour of need.'

Malcolm laughs. 'I asked you not to come. But, okay, I love you and the ceiling.'

'Would you have liked to be a big celebrity?'

Malcolm looks at me as if I'm insane. 'Yeah. Wouldn't everybody?'

I shake my head. 'I don't think I would. People kind of dehumanise them. And it must be awful being scrutinised twenty-four seven. Think about those awful pictures you see in the papers when people don't even know they're being photographed. Them picking their nose or rowing with their partner or looking a bit fat because they've just had a club sandwich on holiday. You're never allowed to have an off day and if a cab driver picks you up from the airport one time and you're not super chatty, you know he's going to spend the rest of his life telling anyone and everyone that you're totally up yourself and nothing like you are on the chat shows.'

'Yeah, I reckon I might be prepared to put up with all that for having thousands and thousands in the bank. I could have statement ceilings in every room of my mansion. Mansions plural.'

I stare at a twinkling star. Think about how I might not generally like the idea of being a celebrity but I'd give pretty much anything to be Jenna next Wednesday so I wouldn't need to let

Sam and the kids down. Faces force their way into my consciousness and I blink back tears.

'Also,' Malcolm says. 'Everyone worships and reveres you.'

'Even that's not great though, is it? You wouldn't know if people genuinely liked you for being you or they were just being nice because you're famous.'

Malcolm snorts. 'I think I could learn to live with it.' He rakes his hand through his hair, which is greasy and sporting a good inch of grey roots.

'I quite like your natural hair colour.'

'Eww. It makes me look so old.'

'No, it doesn't. It makes you look like George Clooney.' This is a bit of a stretch, especially since Malcolm is still sporting baggy sweatpants and a ratty cardigan and smells somewhat less than fresh. Sometimes people need a little boost though.

'Yeah, right.'

I prop myself up on my elbow, immediately feel slightly dizzy and lie back down.

'I'm not sure being a celebrity is as great as you think it is. I read this interview with Kevin Bacon the other day and he was talking about how he gets sick of not being able to do anything normal.'

'What, like queue up in the bank with a stinking head cold or argue with some imbecile about your internet going down? How about getting on the Tube at rush hour? That's always a riot. Especially if you're lucky enough to get the seat that's slightly damp.'

'You're missing the point,' I say, hiccuping softly. 'I wouldn't have wanted paparazzi taking photos of me when I had my miscarriages or during my mental years. I take it for granted that I can go to Sainsbury's with a coat over my pyjamas and no make-up and buy nothing but wine and an enormous chocolate fudge cake.'

'Yeah, living the dream.'

'Shush,' I say, whacking him on the arm again. 'Kevin Bacon said whenever he tries to go incognito and puts on big sunglasses and a baseball cap, he still gets recognised.'

'Well, of course. Big sunglasses and a baseball cap are practically like wearing a sandwich board that screams: Look at me: I'm a celebrity.'

'Again, you're missing the point. Kevin Bacon got so sick of it, he hired a make-up artist to do proper prosthetics on him and make him completely unrecognisable. Just so he could go to a shopping mall and be invisible. He got to wander around and be a normal person for the day.'

'Imagine going to all that trouble just to go to a mall. How American.'

'Again, you're missing the point.'

Malcolm makes a dismissive noise. 'Did he like it?'

'Umm—'

'He didn't, did he?'

'He liked it at first but then, after a while, when he had to stand in endless queues and people weren't that nice to him, the novelty wore off.' I pick a bit of carpet fluff out of my hair. 'I haven't really helped my case, have I? I think I'm drunker than I realised.'

Malcolm laughs.

'I still wouldn't want to be a celebrity though.'

'You so would.'

Chapter Forty-Nine

At four in the morning I had the most brilliant idea. Not about how to get out of the hole I've dug myself into or somehow save my soul – those ships have very much sailed – but the answer to Malcolm's problem.

He would be the perfect drama teacher for Hatfield Academy. Didn't Sam say they didn't need someone with a traditional teaching background and is there anything Malcolm likes better than telling people what to do? He was forever telling me how to improve my Jenna body language or laugh a bit more like her. Then, of course, there was his absolute favourite: 'Tits and teeth, darling.' (I'm hoping he wouldn't say that to a bunch of twelve year olds.)

That's why Monday morning sees me defying my hangover and 'Jenna-ing up'. I've painstakingly blow-dried my hair and am halfway through my Jenna make-up. (No slick of mascara and tinted lip balm for her.) All this is so I, or I suppose to be more accurate, Jenna, can go to talk to Sam about Malcolm and how he'd be perfect for the job.

I know Sam gets into school about an hour before the kids arrive. Nerves swirl around my belly at the thought of seeing him. I'm doing this for Malcolm though. God knows, he needs a job.

I pull on a cashmere sweater, an image rising unbidden of Sam pulling my top over my head, his eyes never leaving mine.

Stop it, this is not helpful! The only way to get through this is to think of it as a work meeting. I will get it out of the way as quickly as I can and then get back here, de glamorise myself and get on with my actual work.

I pull my trainers out of the cupboard. I still can't countenance the idea of wearing 'Jenna shoes' again and, if I did, they would only earn me a lecture from Sam. I think of him putting the bag of frozen peas gently around my ankle and feel tears prick the back of my eyes. Which is no good at all, not only because there's a job to get on with here but also because Jenna eye make-up takes about seventeen and a half years to apply.

When I turned up at the school, Sandra who works in the office asked me if Mr Jackson was expecting me. 'Er, no.'

'No worries,' she chirruped. 'I'm sure he'll be free.'

Not for the first time, it occurred to me that celebrities have a very different experience of daily life than the rest of us. It simply didn't seem to occur to Sandra that Sam would see my unexpected arrival at his workplace on a Monday morning as anything other than a delight.

Looking at his face as Sandra shows me into the classroom though, it's evident that his actual feelings are a bit more complex. If I had to nail down one emotion on his face, it would be wary. Like a bird who has just seen a cat lick its lips.

'You're reading my book,' I blurt out noticing it peeking out of the top of his rucksack. 'Er, the book I gave you.'

Sam looks at me strangely – as well he might. 'Yeah, I'm loving it. The writer has such a wonderful voice. Parts of it are sad but there's this strong undercurrent of optimism. It's also very funny.'

What's left of my heart swells. I barely think of myself as a writer these days, let alone one with a wonderful voice. And coming from Sam too. 'I'm so glad you're enjoying it.'

He smiles but he also looks a bit confused. Surely I haven't pitched up for an impromptu book club? 'Anyway, sorry to just turn up like this but I wanted to ask you about the job you mentioned to me a while back as a drama teacher. Is it still going? I have a friend I think would be perfect for it.'

'Oh.' Sam scratches his head. 'I thought you were going to say you can't come to the talent show.'

'No.' Why does he think that? I mean, I can't obviously, but he's not to know that.

'The job is very much still going so why don't you tell me a little bit more about your friend.'

I nod and launch into a speech about Malcolm. How he's done Hollywood movies and West End shows and how he's a natural born teacher. And even though I'm distracted by the painful realisation that this is the very last time I will see Sam and he smells particularly clean washing-y this morning, I don't let anything distract me from my mission. And, for that, and that alone, I think I can be slightly proud of myself.

Chapter Fifty

That evening, I head over to Malcolm's. I can't lie, his response when I messaged wasn't overly enthusiastic. Perhaps visiting men who don't really want to see me is to be my new trademark move?

Malcolm is wearing sweatpants again. In fact, by the looks of it they're the same sweatpants.

'I brought you ice and tonic,' I say, handing over the bag.

'Thanks.' I am no doubt that the enthusiasm in his voice is down to the gifts rather than my presence. *I'm not really in the mood for company,* he messaged earlier.

There's something I need to talk to you about, I replied. *See you around 6.*

While Malcolm makes us vodka and tonics in glasses the size of fish bowls, I study the huge ornate chandelier that hangs over the glossy black table. Malcolm's maximalist, flamboyant home suits him perfectly (or rather the happier version of him) and, although it's not what I'd pick for myself, it's rather wonderful. It occurs to me suddenly that, while it was very different to this one, my home used to feel like it was a reflection of my tastes and personality but somewhere along the line I stopped caring about all that.

'So,' Malcolm says as we take our seats in the living room. 'To what do I owe the honour?'

'I think I may have found you a job.'

'Excellent. Is it a role in *Succession* or *One Day*? Or am I doing *Uncle Vanya* at the Old Vic?'

'There's a school called Hatfield Academy that's not a million miles away from Herne Hill and they're looking for a drama teacher.'

Malcolm's body sags. 'That's what you came here for? I'm not a teacher.'

'I know but you don't have to be. A frien— Someone I know is a teacher there and he's the one who told me about the job. He said the person doesn't have to be a qualified teacher and that actually they'd prefer to find someone with industry experience.'

Malcolm takes a swig of his drink. 'Really? Is that even legal?'

'Yes, it's fine. You'd have to have DBS checks and everything.'

'Hmm, well, I should pass those.'

I ignore the 'should'. 'I've actually been helping out a bit at the school recently. They're doing a talent show in a couple of days.' My stomach drops at the thought of making the phone call to say Jenna is ill and won't be there. 'They're really lovely kids.' I swallow the lump that has risen in my throat.

'Hmm. I don't think I'd get it.'

'It's worth a shot, no? And it's got to help that my frien—' I hesitate. Sam is most definitely not my friend. 'It's got to help that I've recommended you to the person I know there. I told him how fantastic you'd be at the role. How you've done Hollywood movies and West End shows and there's nothing you like more than teaching people.'

'I'm not sure I do like teaching people.'

''Course you do. When I first worked with you, you couldn't stop giving me notes on how to be a better Jenna. Don't you remember that annoying little thing you used to do where you tapped the corner of your mouth to indicate I should smile?'

He laughs, the first proper laugh I've heard from him since the Jonny Turner scandal broke. 'That was pretty annoying, wasn't it?'

'I'm surprised I didn't punch you right where you were tapping.' I take a sip of my drink, which is about four parts vodka to tonic. 'You will apply, won't you?'

'I don't think I'd interview very well.'

I used to be irritated by all Malcolm's swagger and bravado but now I long for it. 'Of course you will. We'll have to get you out of those sweatpants but, once we've done that, you'll knock their socks off.'

'I'm not sure I like children very much. I once did a tour of *Matilda* and I'm still scarred by the experience. There was always someone pissing their pants or crying.'

'These kids are at secondary school so they'll be no pant pissing and a limited amount of crying. Listen, I'm not asking you to adopt three kids under five or start working in a nursery or a summer camp. You just go into the school, teach a few drama lessons and then come home.'

'True.' He rakes his hands through his hair. 'I suppose the money is dreadful?'

'It won't be great but it's better than nothing, no? And the beauty is that it's part-time so if you get voice-over work or whatever, you'll be able to fit that in too.'

'Okay, thank you. Give me your contact's number and I'll call him first thing tomorrow morning and say I'm the person you recommended.'

'Ah, yes, about that… there's just, er, one small detail I haven't mentioned.'

Chapter Fifty-One

I'm not sure what I was expecting from Malcolm. Maybe for him to fall about laughing and think this was all a huge hoot. Maybe for him to say that of course – of course! – he sometimes lets people in real life think he is the real Jonny. He's pretty sure all lookalikes do it from time to time whether it's to get a better table in a restaurant, confirmation they are playing their part to perfection or simply a feeling of being special.

But Malcolm is slack-jawed and silent.

I listen to the ticking of the grandfather clock coming from the darkened hallway.

'So,' Malcolm says after what feels like an eternity. 'You've been working with these kids for six weeks, going to the rehearsals for their talent show—'

'Yeah, and I think I've actually helped them with the show. Given them some tips and advice.' Even to my own ears, it sounds lame.

'And they all believe you're the real Jenna Cox?'

'Yes,' I say, my voice small.

'And one of the kids has cancer?'

I nod.

'And their teacher – he also believes you're the real Jenna?'

'Ye... yes.' I take a deep breath. I don't want to say the next bit but somehow I feel as if I have to confess everything. 'And I slept with him.'

Malcolm's eyes widen. 'Sorry, what now? You slept with him? While still in character as Jenna?'

'No. Yes. It's complicated. It was definitely the real me who was with him that night. When we were talking and, er, later. In fact, it was a more real version of me than I've been in years. But he thought I was Jenna.'

Malcolm lets out a low whistle.

'I feel awful about all this, if it helps. And I feel awful about the show. It's the day after tomorrow and I know I can't go, but I feel terrible about letting them down.'

'You definitely can't go.'

'Maybe I could get away with it one last time? As long as I refuse to have my photo taken. At least if I go, I'm not letting down the kids or Sam. I've helped them to raise lots of money in ticket sales and I'm going out on a high—'

'Are you actually insane? What you're doing is identity fraud.'

My stomach clenches. 'Well, not really—'

'Yes, really. And even if you could somehow fool this wider group of people into thinking you're the real Jenna, which I very much doubt, do you seriously believe that not one person will blab to the newspapers?'

'You're right.' Tears spill down my cheeks. Sometimes it's not until you say something out loud that you realise how bad it is. And this is bad. Very bad.

Chapter Fifty-Two

I am lying on my bed in a foetal position, my face puffy from crying. Around this time tomorrow, I will be making the call to say that Jenna is unwell and unable to make the show.

I was planning to call the school office but now I have Sam's mobile number (procured so Malcolm can phone him about the drama teacher job) I'll use that. The least I can do is tell him myself.

'Do you think I'm an awful person?' I said to Malcolm late last night.

'I think you've done an awful thing.'

Me too, Malcolm, me too.

I wonder how Sam will deliver the news to the kids? I know he'll try to be upbeat, make out it's not a big deal. He'll tell the kids that of course they're disappointed, but they need to go out there and do their best and the show is going to be awesome.

I listen to the sounds of the people upstairs moving about their flat. I thought they were doctors and, while I know that post-Covid everyone seems to work from home, surely that can't be true for doctors?

I knot the duvet cover between my fingers. Think about how puffed-up Alex was when he told us he'd managed to persuade the Headteacher to change the date of the show. I guess finding out that all that effort was wasted is nothing compared to everything else he is dealing with but that's hardly a consolation.

My phone rings. I reach for it hoping it's Malcolm saying I'm definitely not an awful person. I used to have lots of friends but most of them have either fallen away or been pushed. I see it's Meg and hit decline.

I should be writing but there's no way I can. I can't sleep or eat and even getting myself off the bed and into the kitchen to fetch a glass of water seems beyond me.

A loud mechanical voice comes from the junction outside my window: CAUTION, VEHICLE TURNING LEFT, CAUTION, VEHICLE TURNING LEFT, CAUTION, VEHICLE TURNING LEFT. I squash the urge to scream.

I cannot let Alex, the other kids and Sam down like this. I just can't.

And that's when I have an idea. It's a crazy idea but it's an idea nonetheless.

Chapter Fifty-Three

The walls of the bookshop are covered in posters for *Sunny Side Up* and there are books piled high wherever you look. I pick up one from the table. *Breakfast TV star Sophie Lewis is the queen of the revealing interview,* the shoutline tells me. *But is Sophie hiding secrets of her own?*

Yeah, Sophie is hiding the secret that she wasn't actually created by Jenna.

I flick to the 'author' photo. It's a particularly nice one of Jenna and I should know because I've seen enough of them.

Despite the fact it's a miserable night, the place is packed. The power of celebrity. I am dry-mouthed and nervous. But I have to try this.

An officious looking woman with a clipboard is directing people to buy the books ahead of time. 'There're selling out fast, people,' she says, firing off a false laugh.

A woman in front of me is telling her companion she has always had the feeling that if she and Jenna were ever to meet, she is sure they'd be friends. 'I can't really explain it. It's like we've got so much in common. Like we're the same person.'

More and more people pour into the bookshop. Dripping

umbrellas and soggy coats steam up the windows and create a smell of wet dog.

And then Jenna arrives. Apologises for being a few minutes late. Thanks everyone for coming out on this miserable night. As someone who is never happier than when she doesn't have to get out of her PJs and leave the house, she does not underestimate the sacrifice!

It's weird to be in the same room as this person who I've studied so closely, discombobulating to see in real life the little tics I've practised and practised. I'm sitting quite far back and my view is obstructed by a woman with a mass of hair that resembles wire wool, but the glimpses I get reveal that Jenna looks radiant, lit from within. I feel dull and dowdy by comparison. Still, I guess the two of us can't look too dissimilar.

Jenna reads a passage from the book, her voice clear and confident. 'One of Sophie's first really big interviews was with Joan Collins. The night before Sophie was so nervous, she couldn't sleep. She finally drifted off what seemed like about three minutes before her alarm...'

Titter, titter from the audience.

'Sophie's stomach was in knots as she sat in the make-up chair. "Have you met Joan?" she asked the make-up lady. "I think you mean, have you met Ms Collins," came a booming voice behind her. Sophie winced. What a terrible start...'

I am so nervous I wonder if I can actually go through with this? Whether I can make my gelatinous legs move beneath me or stop myself vomiting or passing out?

I have to.

Jenna finishes her reading to thunderous and frankly mystifying applause before starting the Q&A with the audience. Did she find it hard to write a book, a woman with lots of piercings wants to know.

'Very hard,' Jenna says earnestly.

Eurgh, on a different night, I'm not sure I could stop myself screaming, LIAR!

Jenna beams at the audience. 'But I also found it a total joy. I have always loved writing. I find it like therapy.'

A man in a spotty tie asks who is the nicest celebrity Jenna has ever met.

'Ooh,' Jenna says. 'That's a tough one. I've been lucky enough to meet so many wonderful people.'

'Okay,' the man shoots back, 'who's the least nice?'

Jenna giggles, cupping her hands over her face in the way I have trained myself to do.

She tells the man she couldn't possibly say.

I tune out after that, lost in my own private hell, my stomach somersaulting nervously.

The Q&A comes to an end and I join the snaking queue to get a book signed. I am sweating furiously and light-headed. I deliberately hang back so I can be at the end of the queue and avoid being overhead but am now worried Jenna will leave before signing for everyone, offering some mealy-mouthed apology about how she is so sorry she ran out of time.

The woman at the front tries to get her picture taken with Jenna despite the fact there have been repeated reminders that no photographs are allowed. Clipboard Lady's mouth bunches furiously.

A man approaches Jenna with a stack of what must be about ten books and I feel a flicker of envy. I was pleased when the people who came to my book launch bought one book.

Clipboard Lady glances none too subtly at her watch. The queue isn't moving at the speed she wants it to. I hope I'm going to get enough time to say what I need to say. I'm not keen on the idea of having to do it in public but what are my choices? It's not as if I can ask Jenna if she wants to grab a glass of wine with me afterwards.

A red-faced middle aged man tells Jenna she looks 'nothing like she does on TV'.

Clipboard Lady looks murderous but Jenna laughs graciously and signs his book.

There are still about twenty people in front of me and I am losing my nerve. I have to do this though.

A youngish bloke gets to the front and stands in front of Jenna mute and frozen. Jenna gently prises the book from his hands, the beaming smile never leaving her face as she waits patiently for him to tell her who he wants the dedication made out to.

And then it's my turn. I stand in front of the woman I have spent months impersonating, my legs shaking and my mouth feeling as if someone has wiped all the moisture from it with cotton wool. I am close enough to smell the perfume I know to be Anouk Goutal Eau d'Hadrien and close enough to see that Jenna doesn't seem to have pores.

I could reach out and touch her.

'Hi.'

Chapter Fifty-Four

I have been ushered into a back office and told to wait. (See, I got my private audience with Jenna after all.)

I can't remember exactly what words tumbled out of my mouth in the other room. That I work as a Jenna impersonator and I've got myself involved in a fundraising event at a school, only the thing is they think I'm the real her.

Jenna, pro that she is, didn't let her megawatt smile falter. She beckoned Clipboard Lady towards her and they had a feverish whispered conversation after which I was shown into this room by an anxious-seeming bookshop assistant, who looks young enough for me to have given birth to him.

The room is hot and airless and a headache pulses behind my eyes. I'd like to ask someone for a glass of water but get the feeling nobody will be in the mood to worry about my hydration levels.

The minutes tick past. I guess Jenna must be finishing the book signing. I pick at my cuticle until it bleeds.

Eventually, Jenna enters the room along with Clipboard Lady and a short man with a red, sweaty face. Jenna's megawatt smile is nowhere to be seen. The three of them sit opposite me as if they are about to conduct an interview.

'So,' Jenna says. 'Let me get this straight: you're a lookalike.'

'Yes. Well, an impersonator.'

Jenna's lip curls. 'But you don't look anything like me.'

I'm about to say that clearly I do and I've got plenty of evidence to support that when it occurs to me that this is probably not a great time to argue. I need to keep Jenna sweet and appeal to her better nature.

'You're about ten pounds heavier for a start.'

Ouch. Clipboard Lady smirks.

'Anyway,' Jenna continues. 'Somehow you are a lookalike but, not content with making money out of all my hard work as your…' She creates inverted commas with her fingers. '…career, you decided to start impersonating me in real life.'

'No. Yes. Sort of. Look, I never intended for all this to happen. Just one night I was trying to find a cab after an impersonator gig and a man approached me and thought I was you and, before I could tell him I wasn't, he was telling me about how he was a teacher and his class were organising a fundraising event for a kid in his class who has cancer.'

'*Cancer?*' Jenna says.

'Er, yes. He said they were doing a talent show and asked if I, well you really, would go along to meet this child at one of the rehearsals. He said it would mean the world to him.' All three of them are staring at me and I suddenly realise that neither Clipboard Lady or red sweaty man have said a word since they've come in here. 'And I decided that I should go. As a kindness.'

'A *kindness?*' Jenna's voice drips with disdain.

'Yes. It was a mistake, I realise that now but, at the time, I didn't know how I could say no.'

'I see. But in the other room, you said you've got yourself involved in a fundraising event. If you just met this kid once, pretending to be me, then how are you *involved?*'

'Er, yes, well, the thing is, Alex, that's the kid who has cancer, didn't come to that first rehearsal. He wasn't well enough. So the teacher asked me if I could come the following week to meet him and I did.'

'Pretending to be me?'

'Yes.' Obviously. Wouldn't have been much point in rocking up as myself, would there? I wonder if Jenna is not that bright.

'But that should have been the end of it?'

'Yes, but Alex was telling the other kids that I – well, you – would go to the show itself if you actually cared and they looked so upset that I found myself saying that I – well, you – did care and that even though I couldn't go to the show, I'd go to all the rehearsals and help them get ready. I used to go to youth theatre, you see.'

Jenna ignores the last part, as well she might. 'Wouldn't it be easier to just go to the show now?'

'Yes, but I know I can't pull that off. There are going to be lots of people at the show, not to mention someone might have tipped off a journalist.'

Jenna's eyes widen. 'So what happened to make you come here? Someone realised you're a fake?'

'No, they still believe I'm you. But Alex, that's the kid with cancer, managed to persuade the Headteacher to move the show forward by a day so I could be there.'

Jenna exchanges looks with Clipboard Lady and red sweaty man. 'And why are you telling me all this? Why are you here and what do you want?'

'I want you to go to the show. It's at two o'clock tomorrow afternoon at Hatfield Academy in Battersea.'

Jenna laughs but it's not the soft little chuckle there are so many clips of on YouTube.

This is a hard, mean laugh. 'Are you insane?'

Second time in two days someone has asked me that. 'Look, I get that you're furious with me. I'd be furious with me, but the kids have done nothing wrong. If they don't raise enough money, then Alex and his family won't be able to go to Disneyland. And it's not even just that. The show means everything to them.' My voice cracks.

'So you're expecting me to go along tomorrow and somehow hope the kids won't notice the difference between us?'

'No, of course not. I'll go to the school tomorrow, dressed as myself, and admit everything I've done. But then I'll soften the blow by telling them I've managed to persuade the real you to go along to their show after all.'

Jenna shakes her head. 'Yeah, dream on.'

I look across the table. This is a woman who is famous for welling up on screen whenever she covers a sad story. A woman who cries at the mere mention of an unhappy kid or a suffering donkey. But here I am telling her about a eleven year old with cancer and her face is stony.

'*Please*,' I say. 'I don't want to let the kids down.'

'Well, you should have thought of that, shouldn't you?' She stands and so do her henchmen. 'And, by the way, you'll be hearing from my lawyers.'

Chapter Fifty-Five

The easiest thing to do today is revert to plan A – well, none of this is Plan A, but you get the gist – and phone Sam with my Jenna voice to say I'm sick. But that feels like too much of a cop-out. If I can do nothing else in this ghastly situation I've created, I can be honest and offer Sam, Alex and the other kids a face-to-face apology.

It feels weird going to Hatfield Academy as myself. My hair pulled back into a ponytail, my eyes unadorned by false eyelashes and my face bare except for a slick of mascara and some tinted lip balm.

My first problem is getting past Sandra the receptionist, whose multiple grandchildren I have signed autographs for. Her blank face when I arrive makes it plain she has no idea who I am. I've anticipated this and decided that, although today is a day for honesty, that can start with Sam and the kids. I'm not doing my whole mea culpa routine here. 'Hi, Sandra,' I say in my Jenna voice. 'How are you today? How are the grandkids? Is Richie still teething? Hope Luke is over the disappointment of missing out on that football trial? Is Taylor excited about her birthday party?'

The information that she shared with Jenna on her previous

visit makes a slightly confused smile appear on Sandra's face. 'Richie and Luke are both on the up.' She chuckles.

'And Taylor's beside herself. I'll give Mr Jackson a call to let him know you're here early.'

She makes the call and then the two of us make polite chit-chat. Sandra keeps staring at me, presumably wondering why I look so rough suddenly.

Sam makes his way down the corridor and I feel my stomach drop. Perhaps I should have just feigned illness after all?

'*Jenna?*' Sam says, confusion written all over his face. 'You're, er, earlier than I was expecting you.'

'Yes,' I say, forcing brightness into my tone.

I'm about to follow him down the corridor when Alex appears out of nowhere, a can of Coke in his hands.

'*Jenna?*' he says, his small pale face crumpling.

Jeez, everyone, it's just make-up. 'Hi.'

The three of us make our way down the corridor. My plan was to come clean to Sam while I had him on his own. Let's face it, this has a whole different set of implications for him, so the least I owe him is an adult-to-adult conversation before I repeat my confession to the kids. The appearance of Alex has put the kibosh on all that though, so nobody says very much at all apart from Sam asking how my ankle is and me saying it's a little better thanks. (Unlike my soul which is irreparably damaged.)

'After you,' Sam says, swinging open the double doors to the hall.

Lots of the kids stare. Just make-up, I want to scream.

'Why do you look so different?' Ralph asks.

'*Ralph*,' Sam says reprovingly.

I take a deep breath. 'I look different because I'm not Jenna—'

'You even sound different,' Dylan says.

I nod, staring at at the scuffed parquet because I know if I meet anyone's eye I won't be able to get through this. 'My real name is Clare Palmer. I work as a Jenna lookalike and one night, after doing an event, I was out in the street looking for a taxi and Sa— Mr Jackson saw me and thought I was the real Jenna. I should have told him the truth there and then but it was late and I was tired so I just went along with it. He told me about the show and how you were raising money for Alex and his family to go to Disneyland.' My voice cracks. 'Mr Jackson asked me if I could come to the talent show and then, when I said no, he asked if I'd come along to a rehearsal to meet Alex. I said yes, only intending to come to that one rehearsal. But then I started to get to know you all and care about your show, really care about it, so I kept coming. I told myself I wasn't doing any harm and actually I was doing something good.'

Daisy is staring at me with ill-concealed disgust.

'I told my whole family that Jenna liked some of my jokes,' Joe says.

I nod. 'I'm sorry. What I did was wrong, very wrong.'

'Why are you telling us the truth now?' Joe says.

'Because I couldn't get away with pretending to be Jenna at the show, not with a big audience there, the possibility of someone taking a photo or a journalist turning up. I was going to phone the school to say that I – well, Jenna – was ill but then I decided that the least I could do was come here and tell you the truth.'

'YOU'RE A LIAR AND A FAKE,' Alex shouts, turning on his heel and running out of the hall.

'Alex,' I say, about to go after him.

'Leave him,' Sam says. 'You've done enough.'

Chapter Fifty-Six

Sam escorts me off the premises. 'Listen,' I say, as soon as we're alone. 'I want you to know that what happened between us wasn't me acting. I had genu—'

'Save your breath,' Sam says, stomping down the corridor.

'Please. I know you're angry with me and you have every right to be but I want you to know—'

'I said save your breath.'

I follow him down the corridor, my head hanging low. And good job too because coming the other way is Dylan's dad and I know it doesn't matter now, but *really*? Because I'm not even dressed up as Jenna and maybe he will remember me and how much worse can this day get?

Dylan's dad smiles as he holds the door open for us and for one heart-stopping moment he seems to look at me for a fraction too long. But he doesn't say a thing, which either means he doesn't recognise me (fully clothed) or professional ethics stop him from mentioning it.

Sam stalks towards reception.

'I didn't mean for any of this to happen,' I say. 'It just sort of snowballed.'

Sam shakes his head. 'Pretty big snowball, if you ask me. One that's done a whole lot of damage.'

'I agree but—'

Sam stops in his tracks and turns to look at me. There's none of the usual warmth in his eyes. 'Why would I believe a single word you have to say?'

I open and close my mouth like a fish.

'Exactly,' Sam says, resuming walking.

'Can I say one more thing? My friend Malcolm didn't know about any of this. He's a completely innocent party so I'm hoping you won't let it ruin his chances of getting the drama teacher job. He'd be brilliant at it so please don't let him lose out because of me.'

Sam doesn't dignify this with an answer.

We're just about at the school gate when I notice a familiar figure in a leopard print coat about to press the buzzer. 'Jenna?'

Sam looks from me to her.

'Can someone please open the gate?' Jenna says.

All the colour has drained from poor Sam's face but he does as he is told.

'You came?' I say to Jenna.

She gives me a look that could freeze lava. 'Yes, I came. But not for you, for the kids.'

Chapter Fifty-Seven

Three o'clock. The show will be starting. 'Good luck,' I whisper from my sofa. 'You've got this.'

I picture Alex walking on stage in his role as MC. Four-foot ten-inches of swagger. I know he'll be nervous but I also know as soon as he starts speaking those nerves will fall away, that he'll love every moment of being literally and metaphorically centre stage.

The silence buzzes around me. It won't be silent at Hatfield Academy though. Daisy will be performing 'Rainbow', transformed, at least in her own mind, from gawky pre-teen to pop royalty, her friendship woes temporarily cast aside. I could not be more proud of her. She soaked up every piece of advice I gave her, never got grumpy, never gave up. I close my eyes and hear the applause. You've earned this, Daisy.

The hall will be packed, bursting at the seams. I turn to Sam and the two of us exchange smiles. We did it.

Next up on stage will be Joe. I see his small freckled face and snub nose, tell him in my head that he's going to smash it. Remember, no penguin arms.

Joe delivers his llama joke and laughter bounces all around the hall. Joe's face lights up.

The dance troupe take to the stage and loud discordant music fills my mind, the toes of my good foot tapping in time. I see the dancers clodhopping around, the smiles never leaving their lovely faces. What I wouldn't give for just a fraction of their optimism, their sheer joy in being alive.

The dance troupe leave the stage to thunderous applause. No one cares that they don't know if what they just saw was meant to be gymnastics or dance. No one cares that it was terrible.

I close my eyes and breathe in the smell of sweat, Lynx Africa and excitement. The clean washing smell from Sam who is next to me. We're so close I can feel the warmth of his arm through his dark blue shirt.

The kids are taking their final bows. They are awkward and graceless but they're on a high. The hall erupts. 'More! More! More!'

Tears roll down my cheeks. I am so proud of them. And so alone.

Chapter Fifty-Eight

***She's Got It: Jenna Cox helps kids smash
school fundraising target***

Children putting on a talent show to raise money for classmate battling cancer delighted by appearance of the real-life star of You've Got It.

There's a photograph of Jenna standing on stage surrounded by all the kids. Alex is next to her on one side, Sam on the other. Daisy, Joe, Lucy... all the faces that have become so familiar to me. They all look ecstatic and sweaty. Well, Jenna doesn't look sweaty. I don't imagine she sweats.

I swipe away the tears with the sleeve of my pyjamas. I wish I could have been there.

There's a quote from Sam:

'I could not be more proud of the kids and what they have achieved today. We're also beyond grateful to Jenna Cox. Having her at our Hatfield Academy talent show was an honour and has helped us to smash our fundraising target and raise an incredible £5,459.'

He should be grateful to Jenna. Of course he should.

It must have been some task for him to put things back on track yesterday. Deal with the fallout of my revelations and then the unexpected arrival of the real Jenna. Put whatever feelings he had himself to one side to rally the troops and lift the mood.

I scroll to another newspaper article.

Plucky eleven-year-old Alex Marshall has been undergoing treatment for sarcoma. Alex says, 'It means the world that my classmates did this to raise money to send me and my family to Disneyland. I'm completely bowled over that Jenna Cox was there. I'm a huge fan of *You've Got It*.'

A prickle of something I don't care to name lodges in my chest. I think about all those hours I spent at rehearsals, all the effort I poured into helping the kids hit the right note or tighten a punchline or perfect a step. The latter resulting in my ankle still hurting me now.

Thinking like this makes me a bad person. But then tell me something I don't know.

Chapter Fifty-Nine

For three days I shut out the outside world completely, switching off my phone and avoiding the news and social media. There's the occasional reminder that life is carrying on – the creak of my neighbour's footsteps overhead, the rumble of traffic, a couple giggling in the street as they carry an enormous Christmas tree together (only the absence of heavy snow stopping them from being the full romcom cliché).

This silencing of the outside world doesn't quiet the torment in my mind about everything I've done but, just as when I went mad before, it's a way of coping, or at least surviving.

Then there's a hammering at the door to my flat which I assume must be one of my neighbours who, despite my unwavering unfriendliness, still sometimes want an onion or me to take in a parcel or engage in some conversation about the council's plan for parking permits.

I open the door to Malcolm who is holding a bottle of wine and a mini Christmas tree.

'Don't make that ungracious face, darling. I've been trying to call you for days.'

'I switched my phone off.'

'Hmm. And are you going to invite me in?'

Wordlessly, I move aside to let him past.

'You can't mope around forever, darling. Besides, when I was doing my whole (he adopts his Greta Garbo voice) "I want to be alone" routine you completely ignored that and came over anyway.'

Despite myself, I smile. 'True. But I'm supposed to be writing.'

'And were you writing?'

'No. I suppose you'd like a glass of wine?'

'I thought you'd never ask.' Malcolm surveys the room. 'Where would you like the Christmas tree? I mean, everything is already looking so festive.'

'None of your sarcasm, please. I'm feeling delicate.'

Malcolm puts the tree on the coffee table and stands back to assess whether it's the right spot. 'Any news from Jenna's lawyers?'

'Not yet, but I imagine it's a matter of time.'

'Hmm. Unless she decides you're more mad than bad.'

'She didn't really strike me as the merciful type.' I hand him a glass of wine.

Malcolm moves the Christmas tree to the console table. 'I think here, don't you?'

'Er, yeah.'

Malcolm reaches into his bag and pulls out a selection of small boxes.

'What are those?'

'Baubles and lights, of course. You can't have a naked Christmas tree.' He threads a small string of fairy lights through the branches of the tiny fir tree. I think of the giggling couple I watched from my window. I bet their tree will take two full-sized sets of fairy lights, three even.

Malcolm has taken a step back to assess his handiwork through narrowed eyes. 'I spoke to Sam and we've arranged for me to have an interview on Monday. He sounds like a nice guy.'

'He is.' A nice guy who I treated abysmally. 'And I'm glad you're going for an interview. I'd hate to think all my shenanigans got in the way of you getting the job.'

'By shenanigans do you mean stealing the identity of a national treasure and spending six weeks pretending to be her?'

I groan.

Malcolm hangs a tiny silver bauble on the tree and then takes a sip of his wine. 'It's fantastic the kids have raised so much money.'

'Yeah, over five grand.'

'Nearly forty grand now, darling. Jenna did a post about the talent show on her socials and donations are pouring in from as far afield as Sydney and Florida. And the press are reporting that a generous benefactor has stepped in and promised to pay for Alex to have this exciting new experimental treatment that's only available in the States. Apparently, the clinical trials were extraordinarily positive.'

'Wow. That's amazing.'

Malcolm nods. 'So, while your methods might have been a little… umm… unconventional, you did do some good.'

'Yeah, but not really sure I'll be getting my CBE anytime soon.'

Malcolm puts another bauble on the tree. 'I'm just saying be kind to yourself. Now, I know you're going to your parents on Christmas Day, but what are you doing on Christmas Eve?'

I make a noncommittal sound.

'It's the sixteenth of December, darling, and Christmas is happening whether you want it to or not.'

'It doesn't have to happen for me.'

Malcolm stands back to examine the placement of his latest bauble. 'I shall be making supper for a hideous bunch of old luvvies if you'd like to join us?'

'Well, you sell it well.'

Malcolm moves the bauble. 'You don't have to decide now. You can let me know on the day if you want.'

'Thank you.' Tears spill down my cheeks.

'Hey,' Malcolm says, putting his arms around me. 'I'm supposed to be cheering you up.'

I cry snottily into his chest and he strokes my hair.

'Sorry,' I say when I eventually stop crying. 'I've just made such a bloody mess of everything.'

Malcolm smiles. 'You have.'

'Jenna's going to sue me. And my ex-husband is having a baby with someone else and my agent is expecting forty thousand words and she'll be lucky to get half that and my best friend and I aren't speaking—'

'And now you have to spend Christmas Eve with me and the hideous luvvies.'

'Exactly,' I say, laughing. 'Things just cannot get any worse.'

Chapter Sixty

It can get worse, of course, and almost immediately it does.

'Umm, I think you need to see this,' Malcolm says looking at his phone.

It's the front page of the *Mail Online*:

> Identity Theft: Fake Jenna Cox Exposed.

Underneath it is my Fake Faces profile picture.

A guttural noise emerges from what I presume is my own throat.

Malcolm is scrolling to other news sites. The story is everywhere and so is my photograph, accompanied by increasingly lurid headlines.

> Tragic Lookalike Who Didn't Know When to Stop
> Jenna Cox Feels 'Violated' as Woman Spends Weeks Impersonating Her
> Lookalike Who Scammed Innocent Children

'Shit,' Malcolm says. He was about to leave but now he takes off his coat and puts down his bag.

Why didn't I realise this was inevitable? Of course one or more of the kids would have told their parents the full story and, of course, those parents would immediately pick up the phone to a newspaper.

Malcolm puts his arm around my shaking shoulders. 'It'll be okay,' he says, his tone not matching the words.

'How?' I say through the tears. 'How will it be okay? Everyone I know is going to see this. My parents, my brother, Meg, Stephen and Tamara, the publisher who dumped me, publishers who might have taken future books from me, people I work with. They're all going to see it and think I'm some tragic little freak.'

Malcolm shakes his head. 'Look, people will forget about this – move on to the next story. And the people who know you, properly know you, will never think of you as a "tragic little freak".'

I grab my laptop and start skimming through the articles.

Clare Palmer, forty-one, is childless and divorced. In 2016, she published the novel *Hope Falls* which enjoyed moderate success. There has yet to be a follow-up. Ms Palmer was unavailable for comment.

There are lots of quotes from Jenna about how hard this has been for her, how she has thought about taking legal action but may not pursue it on the basis she imagines I'm mentally ill. 'One of my guiding principles in life is to always be kind and try to be the bigger person.'

'It's good she might not take legal action,' Malcolm says.

'Nothing about this is good.'

'Maybe you should stop reading now?' Malcom suggests.

'I can't.'

Identity Crisis

The mother of plucky Alex Mortimer told the *Mail*. 'How someone could do this to any child is beyond me, let alone to a child battling cancer. Alex believed in this woman, liked her, and she has destroyed his trust.'

Mrs Dana Gray, the Headteacher of Hatfield Academy said; 'The whole school community are shocked by what has happened and we are doing our best to support the children affected. We would like to extend a huge and heartfelt thank you to the real Jenna Cox, who attended the talent show and helped us to smash our fundraising target.'

Mr Sam Jackson, the teacher who organised the talent show, declined to comment.

I snap my laptop shut and put my head in my hands.

'It will be okay,' Malcolm says. 'People have short memories.'

I shake my head. 'I thought I'd been humiliated before. Once at uni, I puked over a guy straight after snogging him. Years later I started to miscarry on a packed commuter train, blood seeping through my jeans and dripping onto the floor, and then there's the time I completely lost it in Pret and started sobbing and screaming. But this? This is next level humiliation.'

Chapter Sixty-One

Malcolm insists on staying the night, no doubt concerned I'm not safe to be alone. At eight o'clock in the morning, he knocks on my bedroom door. 'I brought you a cup of tea.'

'Thanks,' I say, taking it from him with shaking hands.

'Did you sleep?'

'Not really. You? Was the sofa desperately uncomfortable?'

'It was fine.' He sits down on the edge of the bed. 'Jackie called me asking if I know where you are. Obviously I said I haven't spoken to you, but you should probably call her.'

I nod. 'My parents too. They'll be worried.'

'Yeah, I'm going to pop out and get some bits for breakfast so why don't you do that while I'm out?'

Tears prick the back of my eyes and Malcolm squeezes my leg through the duvet.

'It'll be okay.'

He clicks the bedroom door shut behind him and I reach for my phone. As soon as I switch it on, I see I have twenty-eight voicemail messages plus a slew of texts and WhatsApps.

A good deal of the earlier messages are from journalists wanting 'to hear my side of the story'. I delete them and move on.

There are three voicemails from my parents, all trying and failing to sound casual.

'Give us a ring as soon as you can, please.'

Jackie's multiple messages are short and to the point. 'It's Jackie. Call me.'

News has reached my brother in Australia (God bless the internet). 'Sis, sounds like you're in a… er, spot of bother. Hope you're holding up okay.'

Meg says simply she's around if I need her and she hopes I'm doing okay. Lola and Alfie squawk in the background.

Finally, there's a message from Sam. 'Er, hi, I just wanted to say I'm sorry about all the horrible stories in the newspapers. It wasn't me who called them if you're wondering. Anyway, I hope you're okay.'

Tears stream down my cheeks. I call my parents, picturing the phone on the mahogany side table in their too-hot sitting room. My father picks up almost immediately.

Am I okay? Do I want him to come to get me? He can be there in an hour?

This almost undoes me completely but I tell him I'm fine and not to worry. I'm sorry to have embarrassed them like this. Dad tells me not to be silly and that he loves me.

As soon as I end the call, Jackie rings. Where the hell have I been and what was I thinking? I've brought shame to Fake Faces, she has worked for years to build a good reputation. It goes without saying I'm off the books.

Chapter Sixty-Two

On Monday morning, I am woken by a dragging pain in my lower belly. My pyjamas and sheets are soaked with bright red blood.

I swallow down sharp jagged memories of dead babies, and blink back tears. This is just a period. It's so odd that, after years of being a slave to my cycle in the misplaced belief a forensic knowledge of it would confer some kind of control, menstruation can catch me unawares. But things are a lot less regular nowadays and anyway I've been distracted blowing up my life.

I pull a box of tampons from the bathroom cabinet and find it empty. Again, something that would never have happened to 'old' Clare. When Stephen and I were married, I used to moan at him for putting empty boxes back in cupboards. Well, not at the beginning when we were too loved-up to snap at each other about anything and his domestic hopelessness was charming and boyish, but later when it was really bloody irritating to reach for a box of teabags and find it empty.

I pull an old pair of pants from my chest of drawers, stuff a big wodge of loo roll in the gusset, swallow a couple of heavy duty painkillers and head to the chemist.

Identity Crisis

It's horrible outside. Grey and windy with the sort of sideways rain that laughs in the face of your umbrella.

A tuneless lone carol singer wearing a light-up Christmas jumper and battered reindeer antlers is belting out 'Once in Royal David's City' accompanied by a fuzzy backing track. At his feet is a tinsel-wrapped red bucket.

As I pass him, I get the feeling he's staring at me. I suppose he imagines this will guilt trip me into giving him money but he's wildly underestimating the foulness of my mood.

I go into the big chemist on the high street. It's hot and bright and heaving with people. 'Last Christmas' blares from the sound system and I wonder idly how many times a day the people who work here have to listen to it. No wonder they all look so grim-faced.

A young couple with a buggy whisper and giggle as I walk past them and I panic that maybe the wodge of loo roll has given up its fight, but when I glance down at my jeans I'm relieved to see there is no damp dark stain.

I head for what always used to be referred to as the 'feminine care' aisle. I always thought the 'care' a bit of a stretch.

In the perfume aisle, I pass a man with panic in his eyes. I bet he's left buying his wife's Christmas present to the last minute and now she's going to end up with perfume that smells like bluebottle spray. I bet it's the only present he had to buy too, and that his wife, let's call her Marsha, buys all the other presents, including the one for his mother. Leave him, Marsha, screams a voice in my head.

As I move through the shop, I have this peculiar sensation I am attracting attention.

Again, I glance down at my jeans but again there is no sign of a leak.

I keep walking. People are definitely looking at me. It's the sort of looking I became attuned to in the months when I went into the world as Jenna: the double takes, the whispered 'is it her?' conversations, the children told not to stare by hissing parents. But I am not done up as Jenna. In fact, with my hair scraped back into a lank ponytail, my make-up free shiny face and my ill-considered outfit, I have rarely looked less like Jenna.

I must be imagining it.

I grab a large pack of super plus tampons and join the long snaking queue. It's roasting in here and I am starting to feel light-headed.

'It's you isn't it?' comes a voice behind me.

I spin around to see a thickset woman with bleached hair and dark roots.

'We knew it was, didn't we Dec?'

Dec, a man who has an unfeasibly shiny and purple head nods sagely.

How can they possibly mistake me for Jenna today? 'Umm—'

'Terrible what you did. Lying to those poor kids.' She kisses her teeth.

I am so stupid. People weren't recognising 'Jenna' at all, they were recognising me.

The real, horrible me.

Chapter Sixty-Three

Monday has more treats in store for me because it turns out that Jackie isn't the only person who doesn't want to work with me anymore. I return from my joyful outing to Boots to an email from an ad agency who had booked me for tomorrow, cancelling that booking. (They shouldn't really do this at such short notice but I'm not going to humiliate myself any further by fighting with them.) Minutes later, I get a email from Hattie at The Leap Agency saying the half-fat butter project is 'on hold for the time being'.

Neither offer up a reason but it's not difficult to join up the dots.

Panic floods my body as I stare at the dummy pack of butter. With no lookalike work, no prospect of a finished book and two of my regular sources of copywriting income gone, only Russell stands between me and not being able to pay next month's mortgage.

I dry my tears, take a deep breath and call him. 'I just wanted to check in with you about the last couple of articles,' I lie. 'Confirm you'll have them by end of play tomorrow.'

'Excellent.'

Maybe he hasn't seen the news? I feel as if the story has been everywhere but I guess it's possible Russell has somehow missed it?

'We should get a meeting booked in the diary for early January,' Russell says. 'There are a couple more articles I want to brief you on. One on cat urinary tract infections and one on how to stop your puppy chewing.'

'That would be great.' I have never been so unashamedly grateful to cats' bladders and puppies and their sharp little teeth.

'Good. And, Clare?'

'Yes?'

'Chin up.'

'Thanks,' I say, my voice breaking. We wish each other a happy Christmas and say goodbye.

I pace around my flat ignoring my throbbing ankle. It's a huge relief that Russell isn't dropping me but I can't afford to have all my eggs in one basket. It's okay though – in the new year, I'll sign up with some new freelance agencies and surely someone will give me some work? I might have pretended to be Jenna but there's nothing fake about my ability to write copy. And even if I can't get as much advertising work as I'd like, well, at least that frees me up to write my book.

As if on cue, my agent's name flashes up on my phone.

'Hi,' I say, trying to keep my voice light and casual.

'What were you thinking?'

'Umm, it's a long story—'

'I've got time.'

I clear my throat and explain as best as I can. But even to my own ears my words sound lame: I didn't set out to do this, sort of got sucked in, never thought it would get so out of hand.

When I judder to a halt, Kate is silent for what feels like forever. 'I'll be honest with you, Clare, this is not good. If I worked for a bigger literary agency instead of having my own shop, I'd no doubt be under pressure to drop you.'

The breath catches in my throat. This is the woman who has stuck by my side through so, so much.

'I'm not going to drop you but I have to tell you this could hinder our chances of a new publisher making an offer when we send out your new book.'

Tears roll down my cheeks. 'I understand.'

'We might have to think about publishing you under a pseudonym.'

'Okay.'

'But we'll discuss that when the time comes. For now, I want you just to focus on writing the best book you possibly can. Are you still on track to deliver me the first forty thousand words by Christmas?'

'Yes.' I'm so sick of lying. 'No. I don't think so. But I'll spend as much time on it as I possibly can and get it to you by the end of January.'

'I was going to read it between Christmas and New Year.'

'I know. I'm sorry.'

'It'll be with me by the end of January?'

'Yes.'

'Okay, good.'

'There's someone at my door.'

'Okay, go and answer it. I'm looking forward to reading the new book.'

Don't look forward to it too much. Last time I looked, it was shockingly bad.

I open the door to see Malcolm in a particularly sharp navy suit. He's grinning widely and clutching a bottle of champagne. 'I got the job at Hatfield Academy.'

'Fantastic.' I force a smile. At least one of us is going to be employed.

Chapter Sixty-Four

Back in my days of working in an ad agency, by the nineteenth of December everyone would be winding down for Christmas. (And by 'winding down' I mean doing hardly any work and hitting the pub by midday at the latest.)

There is nothing relaxed about the way I've spent today though. I was at my desk by half past seven this morning and it's now nearly six in the evening and I haven't got up except to pee or make a quick cup of tea and a sandwich. There are two reasons for this. Firstly, I want to make sure my latest two pet care articles are on point (within reason – they're hardly my magnum opus) and, secondly, every minute I spend researching or writing about superfoods for dogs or how to deal with a cat who's a fussy eater is a minute I don't spend thinking about my own life.

This means I don't think about Sam, Alex or the other kids at Hatfield Academy and how I deceived them. I don't picture Tamara's smug little baby bump and I don't give any airtime to the fact I'm now a national laughing stock. The papers have yet to lose interest in the story and there was a particularly vicious hatchet job by one columnist this morning who opined on how unhappy I must be to pretend to be an entirely different person (answer: very) and how extraordinary it is that I imagined I could get away with it given I don't have Jenna's 'fine features', 'mesmerising smile' or 'gym bunny body'.

> We all know that green leafy veggies are important to keep us fit and well but did you know they're also vital for your pooch?

Meg is another thing I'm definitely not thinking about, although, every now and again, her face forces her way into my brain and a sharp little jag of pain blooms in my chest. We have been friends for so long and been through so much together.

> Vets recommend that, on a daily basis, dogs have about thirty calories per pound of body weight, but it's important to remember that this is an average…

Maybe Sam refusing to give the newspapers a quote means he knows I didn't plan what happened or have any malign intentions? Maybe he realises I genuinely care about Alex and the other kids and for that matter him?
No, of course he doesn't. Sam is just a nice guy.

> As important as the foods you do give your dogs are the ones you need to make sure they don't get their paws on. These include chocolate, grapes, raisins, sultanas and currants, onions and garlic…

I lean back in my chair and rub the back of my neck. Even though the Christmas tree Malcolm bought me is less than a metre tall, it has filled the room with the resiny scent of fresh pine. I am suddenly back in the living room of the house I shared with Stephen. We are lying on the green velvet sofa, his body curled around mine and his hand on my stomach. His breath is warm against my ear as he tells me that this is our last Christmas just the two of us and that next year we'll have a little person to share it with. We laugh as we say we will definitely be buying a knitted Christmas pudding outfit like the one we saw on the baby in the park the other day.

I force my fingers back onto the keyboard.

> Just like us humans, some dogs need a special diet. This could be because they're overweight, have a health problem or are just getting on a bit in years…

Once I've sent these articles to Russell, I'll be able to turn my attention to writing my book. I think back to my conversation with Kate yesterday and the disappointment and confusion in her voice. The only way I can begin to crawl my way back into her good books (if you'll excuse the pun) is to deliver her a blisteringly good forty thousand words by the end of January. Given I currently have less than twenty thousand and they're not blisteringly good, this is a tall task but it might be achievable if I do nothing else for the next month. (Not impossible given I am persona non grata with pretty much everyone bar my parents and Malcolm.)

Right now, the only words that matter are the ones about superfoods for dogs though. I finish writing the article and then read it back. I don't think I'm in line for a Pulitzer but I'm happy with it. I attach it to an email to Russell along with 'What to do if your cat is a fussy eater'.

I hit send, lean back in my chair and close my eyes, which are gritty from staring at a screen for so long. I hope Russell is happy with the articles. And I hope I don't always feel like this.

Chapter Sixty-Five

The next day, I'm at my desk early again. If there's one silver lining to not wanting to leave the house, having very little copywriting work and refusing to acknowledge the imminent arrival of Christmas, it's that I have plenty of time to write my new book.

I open up my manuscript. For various reasons ranging from having had to deal with the fallout of impersonating a national treasure, to worrying if I'm going to be sued, to writing about pets and their dietary requirements, I haven't looked at it for a while. That's no bad thing though. One of the well-worn pieces of advice given to writers is that you should set aside your work for a while so that when you return to it you come to it with fresh eyes.

I read the first couple of chapters, trying to ignore the gnawing at my stomach that's suggesting that my 'fresh eyes' are telling me this book is utterly shit. That it's bitter and cynical and angry and sad.

No of course it isn't. The first couple of chapters often need rewriting once you've properly uncovered your story. Plus, I'm not in the best of moods.

I carry on reading. This isn't just a bad mood. Panic courses around my body and saliva floods my mouth.

I make myself plough on.

The intention was for this story to be a searing and raw take on a marriage in freefall. It would be honest and unflinching and visceral. But what's on the screen in front of me is miserable and depressing. The story, and I use the word loosely, just sounds like the friend whose conversation loops again and again with how life has disappointed her.

Worse still, there is no honesty. The husband is a cartoon villain instead of a real character, the wife a scorned angry woman with zero accountability. A character who will surely make readers think: well, no wonder he left you.

I think about telling Kate it was going to be a *Heartburn* for our time. Even then, that sounded like hubris and I had to laugh and make it clear that I wasn't comparing myself to Nora Ephron. Despite those disclaimers, I was still sending a message about the book I intended to write being as funny as it was sad.

I look back at the computer screen desperately scanning the page for even a flash of warmth or depth or wit. I think of Sam talking about my first book without even realising it was mine: 'Parts of it are sad but there's this strong undercurrent of optimism.'

I search desperately for a little bit of this optimism as I force myself to keep reading what's on the screen in front of me. It's hard to be upbeat when you're writing about brokenness and vulnerability and loss but I wanted readers to root for my main character Poppy and applaud her courage.

But now I wonder if Poppy is angry and bitter and awful.

No, of course she isn't. And neither is the book.

Chapter Sixty-Six

From: Rosamund Carlton
To: Hattie Kerslake
cc: Clare Palmer
Sent: Wednesday, 20 December 2023 at 11:35
Re: Lumiere Skincare

Hey, babes,

Still lol-ing about Clare going around pretending to be Jenna Cox!!! Still can't believe it but then she always was a bitter, sad old cow!!!

What did you tell her about the half-fat butter campaign? R x

I don't think Rosamund meant to keep me in cc.

Chapter Sixty-Seven

The only wine I have in the flat is a pricey bottle of Chablis I bought to take to my parents for Christmas but I think the circumstances more than justify me opening it. Besides, my mother messaged me this afternoon to say that, of course, she'd give the double room to David and Hannah and, of course, the kids would share the other free bedroom but it was fine for me to have the sofa bed, wasn't it, because it was only a couple of nights. (Sure, whack me in the shed.)

I pour myself a large glass of the Chablis and glug it back, tears rolling down my cheeks. *She always was a bitter, sad cow!!!*

Is that true? Rosamund and Hattie are obviously a pair of cows with hardly a brain cell between them. But that doesn't mean they're wrong.

My glass is empty so I pour myself another.

I think about my book. The nagging feeling that Poppy the main character is angry and bitter and awful. Now I wonder if Poppy is me.

I shove the thought down and glug the wine.

She always was a bitter, sad old cow!!!

I think about something Dr Asen used to do where she made me examine the evidence for something I was 'choosing to believe'.

Many of the newspapers have recently noted I must be a 'very sad individual'. Why else would I have pretended to be Jenna in real life, they reasoned.

I pour myself another glass of wine.

The worst part is I'm not sure I can argue with the assessment. My sadness has taken over my body like a cancer. It's spread to the point I barely notice the things that used to bring me joy: bright sunshine casting dappled light through the trees, a brilliant book or TV programme, laughing with a friend. They're all dulled now – as if I am looking at them through a smeary glass screen.

She always was a bitter, sad old cow!!!

Of course, Rosamund and Hattie didn't just mean 'sad' as in unhappy any more than the newspapers did. It was weighed down by judgement. As if they can see inside my soul. As if they know about the resentment I harbour towards any number of people on a daily basis, or the sharp slap of fury as Stephen told me Tamara was expecting a baby, or my fizzing rage as I discovered Meg already knew.

Bitter? Check.

I go to pour myself more wine and realise the bottle is empty.

I pick up my phone, self-pity engulfing me and bringing on a fresh wave of sobbing. I don't even have someone I can call. Not even Meg. My fingers hover over Sam's number. Perhaps if I admit to being a horrible person, he'll forgive me? There's a certain logic to that, no? Or I could just call to wish him a happy Christmas? Easy-breezy.

The decision is taken out of my hands by Malcolm's number flashing up. 'Malcolm. You're the one I shoulda called. Lovely Malcolm.'

'Are you all right, darling? You sound a bit… erm, worse for wear.'

'Well, actually, I'm ssss… sad.' I go to sit down on the sofa but miss and land heavily on the floor. This makes me giggle until I realise how much it hurt and the laughter morphs into tears.

'Oh dear,' Malcolm says. 'I think someone might have had a little too much of the vino.'

'NO, IT'S NOT THAT!' I rub my stinging coccyx. 'If you must know, I've reread my book and realised it's a pile of shite.'

'Well, it can't be, darling. It got rather good reviews, no?'

'I DON'T MEAN MY BOOK THAT'S ALREADY PUBLISHED.'

'No need to shout, darling.'

'Sssss-orry. But why would I reread that, you ssssss-illy? I mean my book I'm supposed to be writing now.'

'Oh, I see. And are you sure it's as bad as you think?'

'Yes,' I say, hiccuping into his ear. 'But that's not all.'

'Oh?'

'I'm a *terrible person*. Everyone tttttt-thinks so.'

'Right. Darling you need to drink a very large glass of water, take two paracetamol and then put another glass of water and two more paracetamol by your bed.'

'You didn't say I'm not a terrible person.' My voice breaks. 'You think I'm a terrible person.'

'Oh, dear God. I do not think that at all.'

'YES YOU DO. Because I pretended to be Jenna in real life. And I tricked all the kids, even the one with cancer and lovely Sam.' I'm sobbing now. 'I tricked them all.'

'Hmm, not your finest hour for sure. But we all do regrettable things, darling. I once shaved off an ex's eyebrows while he was sleeping. But then he was a lying cheating bastard.'

'You think I'm a terrible person.'

'Clare.'

I carry on wailing.

'Clare.'

'Wha?'

'Stop that now.'

'But I'm ssssss-sad.'

'Yes, and so are my eardrums. But everything will look better in the morning.'

'No, it won't.'

'Okay, well, at least you'll be too hungover to care.'

'I haven't even drunk that much.'

'Sure. Now, darling, go and get yourself that big glass of water. I'll stay on the line while you do it.'

I heave myself up and stumble over to the sink where I fill a glass with water. 'I can't drink all this.'

'Yeah, that's a sentence you should have come out with earlier.'

I drink the water and then follow Malcolm's instructions to refill the glass, get some painkillers and lie down on my bed. 'Am I bitter and angry with the world?'

Malcolm hesitates for a beat too long.

'You think I am.'

'No. Yes. Sometimes. But you're also one of the loveliest people I know.'

Chapter Sixty-Eight

It's been a while since I have called Dr Asen's office. I listen to the ring tone.

Yesterday was a write-off. The combination of a monster hangover and an even more monster dose of self-pity meant I didn't even make it out of my pyjamas. A particularly low point saw me wiping my snot and tears with the edge of the duvet cover because I couldn't get myself to the bathroom to get more tissues.

'Hello, Bridge Lane Psychologists.'

'Hello, I'd like to make an appointment with Dr Asen, please.'

'I'm afraid Dr Asen has retired.'

Sorry, what now?

'Would you like to make an appointment with one of our other psychologists?'

'Dr Asen can't have retired.'

Silence buzzes down the line for a few seconds. 'Would you like to make an appointment with one of our other psychologists?'

'I'd like to know why Dr Asen has retired.'

'Erm… well, I don't—'

'Why?' I say, cutting her off. This is simply not fair. Dr Asen is my doctor and I need her to stop me being angry and bitter and awful. She cannot be off playing golf or looking after her grandchildren or kayaking in Canada or whatever the hell else she's doing.

'Would you like to make an appointment with one of our other psychologists?'

Defeat rushes through my body. This woman isn't going to make Dr Asen come back.

'Yes. Please.'

'I'm afraid I can't fit you in with anyone before Christmas.'

Well, of course you can't. It's Friday 22 December. I'm not insane. Although to be fair, I haven't exactly given this woman any reason to believe that. Also, I guess dealing with crazy comes as something of an occupational hazard. 'January will be fine, thank you.'

'Okay, we have two psychologists with some capacity at the moment. Dr Seamus Feeny and Dr Kerri Harper. Why don't you take a look at both their profiles on our website and then let me know who you'd like to make an appointment with.'

I mumble a lacklustre thank you and happy Christmas and end the call.

I go to the website and click on 'Meet the team'.

Dr Seamus Feely has cold dead eyes and no trace of a smile. He looks more likely to rob you blind than help you to put yourself back together again.

Dr Kerri Harper, on the other hand, is *very* smiley. So smiley I fear she might describe herself as bubbly in a dating profile. My bubbly suspicions are strengthened by the fact she spells Kerri with an 'i'. I bet she dots the 'i' with a heart too.

Not to sound like Goldilocks, but why can't there be a psychologist who is just the right amount of smiley? Like Dr Asen.

Stop it! There is zero evidence that Kerri with an 'i' dots it with a heart. She's probably very nice and an excellent psychologist. And, anyway, there's no way I'm pouring my heart out to Seamus.

Chapter Sixty-Nine

March 2020

My husband has just told me he is leaving me.
'Now, I'll never have a baby.'

Stephen shakes his head, digs the heels of his hands into his eyes. 'Is that all you care about?'

'NO, NO, NO. YOU DO NOT GET TO BE THE PISSY ONE.'

He has the good grace to look embarrassed. 'You're right. I'm sorry. And I'm sorry about… this.'

A thought pops into my head. The colleague he mentions too often. The one who he insists is just a friend. 'Is it Tamara?'

He shakes his head. 'Nothing has happened with Tamara.'

An unspoken 'yet' hangs in the air but I don't press him. What difference does it make why he's leaving?

We are standing either side of the kitchen island we were so excited about when we first moved into this flat. A memory rises of Stephen popping open a bottle of champagne that accompanied a takeaway pizza the night we moved in. We had yet to unpack the glasses and drunk the champagne from mugs.

Now we sit wordless, the drone of the TV providing the only

soundtrack. There have been more deaths in China from this mystery virus. Images of Wuhan flash across the screen.

People there have been told not to leave the house. It's unimaginable.

Tears start to roll down my cheeks. 'What happened to us?'

Stephen shakes his head. He doesn't know.

'Are you taking some time out or is this it?'

Stephen's face tells me the answer and then suddenly he is crying too. 'I'm sorry.'

I go to the fridge and take out a bottle of wine, reflexively holding it up to my husband who shakes his head. 'Where will you go?'

'My parents' house.'

I gulp down the wine, which tastes cold and bitter.

'What will we do about the flat?'

Stephen shrugs. 'Sell it, I guess. But there's no rush. When you're ready.'

I pour myself another glass of wine. Stephen is just saying that. There is a rush because he'll need the money from this place to buy somewhere else. My brain registers how little I care about losing this flat and how odd that is when I once cared so much about it. Perhaps I've lost too many other things that matter more?

Wordlessly, Stephen gets himself a wine glass and reaches for the bottle. 'I really am sorry.'

'I know.'

It's two hours since Stephen's bombshell and the two of us are lying naked and sweaty on our kitchen floor. I have no explanation for what just happened. Why we were suddenly pawing at each other like animals.

The only thing I know with any degree of certainty is that my husband bitterly regrets it.

Chapter Seventy

January 2024

Look, I'm never going to be the sort of person who can stand next to someone on the bus shovelling fried chicken into their mouth and not feel murderous. But I have spent the last four weeks trying very hard to be a better person.

I dragged myself through Christmas keeping a big, fake smile pinned to my face at all times. I didn't let it slip when my brother 'jokingly' ribbed me about impersonating celebrities, or when my sister-in-law told me she envied me being able to have another glass of wine safe in the knowledge no one would be waking me at four in the morning demanding to know if Santa had been, or when my parents treated David like the prodigal son when he's the one who has fucked off to the other side of the world and it's me who'll be visiting them in a care home.

There were even moments over the festive season where my smile was real. I'd never admit it to anyone, and overcompensate wildly, but my six-year-old niece is a dull and unappealing child who tests the limits of blood being thicker than water. Her little sister Anna, by contrast, is an absolute firecracker of a four-year-old who made me laugh every day and whose sticky-fingered hugs made my heart swell even if they also made it ache for the babies I've lost.

If truth be told, Anna is the only one I was truly upset to say goodbye to on 28 December. My sister-in-law and her oldest child are strangers I try to be nice to and, while I love my parents, they also drive me bananas. As for my brother, we have never been close, bound together only by shared memories of fighting in the back of our parents' Volvo as we headed off down to Cornwall. Once there, I'd bury my face in a book and refuse to build sandcastles with him and tell my mum to make him stop bothering me. But Anna's big round doll eyes fixing on mine as she earnestly asked if I'd come to see her in 'Oz-stray-la' made my throat tighten and my chest hurt.

Back in London, I started seeing Kerri with an 'i.' My first session confirmed my worst fears about her bubbliness and it was all I could do not to run out of the hot, airless little room with its eau-de-nil walls and its faux tulips and huge box of peach-coloured tissues (cry, why don't you?). But I didn't run away and I have gone back week in week out.

Kerri asked me to talk about the things that make me angry and didn't smile when I said, 'How long have you got?' I told her about Stephen and Tamara and the baby that's growing inside her. I explained that Meg knew before I did and this feels like the ultimate betrayal and so often I pick up the phone to call her but then I can't make myself do it. I balled my fists and looked at the horrible green carpet as I talked about Rosamund and Hattie and all the other people I used to work with but don't anymore.

And, of course, this led me into talking about pretending to be Jenna. How at first it was for work but then I started to do it in real life. I told Kerri with an 'i' about Sam approaching me in the street and him asking me to meet Alex. I genuinely didn't feel I could say no or realise how it would spiral out of control like that.

I watched Kerri's face as all this unravelled but, of course, she didn't react. They're trained not to show their feelings, aren't they, and presumably she has sat there and listened to people who have done even worse things than me?

When I'm not at Bridge Lane Psychology, I hole up in my flat. I write four more articles for Russell, which will just about cover this month's outgoings. I also work frantically on my new book. I have set aside the story about the marriage in freefall and its awful self-obsessed and bitter heroine, and am now writing about a woman whose life is transformed by a child who isn't hers.

Phoning my agent to tell her I've given up on the marriage story wasn't easy but I'm done with lying.

'Look,' she said. 'It's a shame you've had to dump twenty thousand words but, if something is not working it's not working. And I like the idea for the new one. It's a story that's threaded with hope.'

My hands were shaking when I put down the phone to Kate. I'm grateful she didn't tear a strip off me for flunking yet another deadline, and that she likes the new idea and seems to be sticking by me once again. Kerri has me writing a gratitude journal. Can you imagine? I railed against it at first. Told her I wasn't feeling very grateful at the moment and anyway the last thing I needed was another bloody thing to write. But Kerri just sat there silently until I realised that trying to resist her will is about as useful as trying to hold back the tides.

When I'm not trying to drum up gratitude journal entries or working, I reread my comfort books or watch repeats of TV shows I've seen so many times I hear the actors' lines in my head before they say them.

The only person who lures me out of the house is Malcolm. 'We're going for a walk, darling. Otherwise, your muscles will atrophy.'

He has started the drama teacher job at Hatfield Academy and it's lovely to hear his enthusiasm as he talks about it, even if it does make my heart hurt to hear him casually mention names of people I'll never see again: Sam, Alex, Daisy, Joe…

The other day, I was walking past Comix in Soho and I saw a vintage Spiderman comic in the window that I knew Alex would love. I went inside the dark little shop and tried not to scream as the guy behind the counter with very long black hair went on and on about how it was the first appearance of the gibbon.

'Do you want me to tell Alex it's a present from you?' Malcolm asked when I handed the comic to him the following night. I shook my head.

Maybe it's my way of proving to the likes of Rosamund and Hattie and the newspaper columnists that I'm not a horrible person after all, I told Kerri.

She put her head to one side, twisting a coil of her Brillo pad hair around her finger.

'I'm wondering if it's your way of proving that to yourself?'

Kerri always answers a question with a question. It's infuriating.

Things I am grateful for today:
Hummus.

Chapter Seventy-One

Meg's face falls as she opens her front door.

Anxiety fizzes around my body. 'Hey. Can we talk?'

She shakes her head slightly. 'It's not a good time.'

The comment stings. Meg and I have never had a 'by appointment' friendship. 'It won't take long.'

Wordlessly she steps aside and I follow her into the kitchen. The kitchen where I could lay my hands on a lemon squeezer or a grater or a cake stand. Where I've chopped salads and washed glasses and laughed and cried but now I don't even feel as if I should take off my coat. 'Adam and the kids not here?'

'Adam's taken them to the park.'

'And you're cleaning?' I say, gesturing towards the rubber gloves and assortment of plastic bottles and cloths on the side. 'You should be having a nice soak in the bath or reading a book.'

'What do you want, Clare?'

Her abruptness is like a slap. Meg never talks to anyone like that, least of all me.

'Umm… I… well… I wanted to apologise.'

Meg shakes her head. 'I see.'

I glance down and realise I am still clutching the bunch of

bright yellow tulips I picked up on the way here. 'These are for you,' I say, handing them over.

'Thanks.' Meg puts them on the draining board still shrouded in their cellophane. She spritzes the worktops with a lemony smelling cleaning spray and rubs at the worktops harder than is strictly necessary.

'*Meg.*' I go to put my hand on her arm but she shakes it off.

'What, Clare, what? You cut me out of your life as if I'm a piece of rubbish and for what? Because my husband happened to bump into your ex-husband on a train and then invite him here for a beer—'

'Tha—'

Meg raises her rubber-gloved hand to cut me off. 'I haven't heard so much as a word from you for two months and then you turn up with a bunch of tulips and I'm supposed to pretend nothing ever happened?'

'No. I'm happy to talk about it.'

'Great. Then why don't we start with you telling me why I had no idea you were working as a lookalike?'

'I didn't tell anyone.'

'I'm not anyone.' Meg starts wiping down the front of the fridge.

'I know. I'm sorry. I was embarrassed, okay?'

Meg wheels around to face me, her green eyes flashing. 'No, it's not okay. Any more than it's okay that when it all came out in the newspapers, I was busy trying to defend you to anyone and everyone, saying that I'm sure it all happened by accident and at least you'd helped the kids raise lots of money, but do you know the one person I couldn't speak to?'

'Me,' I say to the floor.

'Yep. Because even though I called you again and again to see if you were okay, you couldn't be bothered to so much as send me a message.'

'It wasn't that I couldn—'

'Just like you couldn't be bothered to answer any of my messages or calls before that. The ones where I was pleading with you to believe that Adam and I don't see Stephen except by chance and that, of course, I wanted to tell you about the baby because I knew how hard it would be for you, but Stephen promised he'd tell you within a few days and I decided the best thing for me to do was just to be here to pick up the pieces.'

'I'm sorry.'

Meg starts wiping down the skirting boards, her mouth a thin line. 'Did you know we had a meningitis scare with Alfie? That it was one of the scariest nights of my life and I thought we might lose him? No, of course you didn't know. Because you weren't talking to me.'

'*Meg.*'

'What? Do you know the worst thing? I realised after that night that, even if you had been talking to me, even if things had been normal, you wouldn't have been the person I called to sit with us in A&E. And do you know why? Because I can't so much as mention "kid problems" to you.'

Tears spill down my cheeks.

'I'm sorry,' Meg says, putting down her e-cloth. 'That was a horrible thing to say.'

'Not if it's true.'

'It's not true.' Meg hesitates. 'It's half true. Of course, you would have been sympathetic if you'd thought Alfie had meningitis. But it's the everyday kid worries that I can't talk to you about.'

I wipe away the tears with the back of my hands. 'I'm sorry.'

Meg is crying too now and I desperately want to pull her into a hug, but my feet stay rooted to the floor and the silence stretches between us. Whether it's the tension or the fact I skipped breakfast, I start to feel lightheaded so I go to sit but, as my bottom makes contact with the sofa, a loud American voice announces 'C is for cat'.

As I leap up Meg starts laughing through the tears and before I know it, I'm laughing too.

Meg takes the offending plastic toy, switches it off and chucks it in a nearby toy basket. 'The kids leave stuff everywhere. I can't believe Adam and I used to have a tidy house. Or that we thought we'd get away with only having tasteful wooden toys.' She pushes a stray blond hair that's escaped her bun behind her ear. 'Shall we have a cup of tea?'

'What about the cleaning?'

She shrugs. 'It's a waste of time anyway. The whole place will be covered in sticky fingerprints within five minutes of them walking through the door.' She flicks on the kettle.

'We don't see Stephen, you know. I've met Tamara once when we bumped into them at a Radiohead concert.'

'Eww, Radiohead. Might have known she'd have terrible taste in music.'

Meg smiles. 'So what have you been up to? Apart from impersonating celebrities?'

'Not much. Work. Trying to be a better person. I'm seeing a therapist. Not Dr Asen because she's retired.'

'Selfish.' Meg pours milk into the tea. I like not having to tell her not to slosh in too much; that she knows milky tea is a beverage of the devil.

She hands me the tea. 'So what's she like – this new therapist?'

'She spells Kerri with an "i".'

'Uh oh.'

'And she wears lots of chunky wooden jewellery and shoes that look like children's school shoes. Oh, and she's making me keep a gratitude journal.'

Meg laughs and makes a vomiting gesture. 'She's never going to be our friend then?'

'No.' I take a sip of my tea. 'We're still friends, right?'

Meg shakes her head. 'We're not friends.'

My heart plummets. I thought she was softening but maybe that's just wishful thinking on my part?

'We're sisters.'

Chapter Seventy-Two

March 2020

The last few weeks have brought about three things I didn't see coming. Stephen leaving (and, yes, I should have obviously have seen that, but denial is a powerful thing), the UK going into lockdown (Coronavirus it seems isn't just a problem far, far away) and me being pregnant.

I knew almost immediately. This, after all, is not my first rodeo. The metallic taste in my mouth, sore boobs and sudden aversion to coffee could only be one thing.

My first instinct was to call Stephen but then I decided I'd wait. I didn't even say anything to Meg or my parents, some primitive superstitious part of my brain telling me that if I kept this as my secret for a bit, then things would be different this time.

My only call was to the Early Pregnancy Unit who said they were very sorry but I would have to attend the scan on my own. No partners were allowed because of the restrictions. I told them this was not a problem.

I sit in the sickly green waiting room, every second feeling like an hour. There is only one other woman here and she is sitting as far away from me as she possibly can. Neither of us wants to take any risks. I have read the official Covid-19 guidance from the Royal College of Obstetricians and Gynaecologists so many times I can recite it by heart:

> There is no evidence to suggest an increased risk of miscarriage. Pregnant women are still no more likely to contract coronavirus than the general population.

I rest my hand on my belly. It's not flat but that's to be attributed to self-medicating with carbs and chocolate rather than a growing child. Maybe there is a growing child in there though? Maybe this time will be different?

For a moment, I allow myself to wallow in that. To picture myself holding my baby in my arms, Stephen by my side. Surely if I manage to keep this baby to term, he will come back to me? We were okay before any of this happened. More than okay.

We have sat in so many rooms like this one, the two of us. I remember how excited we were that first time, how utterly devoid of fear – as if all we had to worry about was getting out enough cash to pay for the scan photos.

I want to weep for those people.

A thought bubbles below the surface, one that's been poking the edges of my consciousness for days: I feel different than I did any of the previous times. More sick and more tired. That's got to be a good thing, right? More pregnant?

I am not just a little girl with a cushion stuffed up her jumper. This is real, this is happening.

'Clare Palmer?' The sonographer is wearing a mask and a visor.

I follow her into the room mumbling about being a little nervous.

This time it *will* be different.

The sonographer says the gel might feel a little cold.

I tell my baby he or she is going to be okay. That I just know it. And I have waited so long for this moment.

'I'm sorry,' the sonographer says.

Chapter Seventy-Three

February 2024

It's been a while since I've stepped inside a nursery store and my chest immediately tightens. I tell myself I will be out of here in no time.

This is made difficult by the sheer volume of different merchandise on offer though. I pick up a Bathtime Bubble Machine. It attaches to the side of the bath with a suction cup and 'surrounds baby with delightful bubbles'. The sort of bubbles one could blow if armed with a pot of bubble mixture, I presume. I put it back on the shelf.

I picture the teddy bear hooded bath towel my mum bought when I was eleven weeks pregnant with my first baby. 'I know I shouldn't have but it was so cute I couldn't resist.'

I walk past an earnest looking couple. She has an almost imperceptible bump which she's stroking protectively. The couple are being talked through 'bathing options' by an intense looking guy of about nineteen, whose badge says: Graham, Baby Expert. Just one look at Graham tells you he is no baby expert. There might be things Graham is an expert on – spot creams maybe – but babies are not one of them. He picks up a bath which resembles a see-through bucket. He explains, in earnest monotone, that this has been designed by child experts in Norway. It allows baby to be bathed in the foetal position, thus easing the transition from womb to world.

I don't want to buy Stephen and Tamara's baby a bath. Or be in this shop.

I reach the healthcare aisles. There are bath thermometers (what's wrong with your hand?) and ear thermometers. There's even a device you can strap to your pregnant belly to monitor your baby's heartbeat.

Maybe if I'd had one of those?

I break into a sweat. I should have got a gift online.

I walk past baby gyms and walkers and on to toiletries.

I need to get out of here.

I walk past an electric swing chair which boasts six different speed settings. ('Just popping the baby in the electric chair, darling!')

What the hell am I going to buy? A mobile maybe. A mobile would be suitably jolly – send the message that, while I am unlikely to ever volunteer myself to babysit, I am grown up about all this. *Not* angry or bitter.

A heavily pregnant woman in bright red dungarees (what cruel misogynist first put forward dungarees as a pregnancy fashion choice?) is having a top of the range stroller demonstrated to her by another Baby Expert, Moira. At least Moira looks old enough to have held the odd baby. Unfortunately though, she's clearly bored and unable to inject enthusiasm into her voice as she outlines the benefits of the 'ergonomic system for a bump-free ride'.

I find the mobiles. Naturally there are several trillion to choose from but I just snatch one that's reasonably attractive and head for the checkout.

Identity Crisis

The woman in front of me in the queue has a very young baby she's carrying in her arms and a little girl of about two, who has suddenly announced she 'needs pee pee'. Her mother asks if there is a loo she can use but is told by Baby Expert, Janice, that there are 'no customer facilities'.

I am so intensely irritated, I can't hold back, 'Excuse me, this is a nursery st—'

Suddenly there is the distinctive sound of liquid hitting lino and we all look down to see that the little girl has used the 'facilities' after all.

Janice huffs. 'I'll get a mop and bucket.'

'Sorry, sorry,' says the woman.

'Don't apologise,' I say.

Janice glares at me and then disappears.

The woman asks me if I'd mind terribly holding the baby while she sorts out her daughter. And, of course, I do mind very much indeed but I can't exactly say that. So I take the baby and jiggle her awkwardly and try not to breathe in her milky new baby smell or think about all the babies of mine who I never got to hold.

Chapter Seventy-Four

Few sights are more depressing than a long, snaking queue out of the door of the post office. And yet here I am. Bloodied and bruised from my visit to Little Scamps and hungry for more punches. Stephen and Tamara's baby is not due until next month so I could easily post this present in the week but, for some reason, it seems important to do it now, maybe so I can't change my mind?

A tuneless lone busker wearing a battered green anorak is belting out 'Back for Good' accompanied by a fuzzy backing track. At his feet is a red bucket but, frankly, I'd pay him to shut up.

Rosamund's words poke at the edge of my consciousness: *She always was a bitter, sad cow!!!*

I should be writing my book now. The trip to Little Scamps and this monster queue is easily a chapter's worth of time.

The busker launches into 'Mr Blue Sky'. Surely he must have some idea that his audience may be captive but they're also considerably less than enchanted?

Slowly, slowly the queue inches forwards until, finally, I am inside the building. It's here that I see two large red self-service machines. Above them is a jaunty poster imploring people to:

Beat the queue! Now, I've mentioned my hatred of self-service machines before, but these ones are a whole new level of fuckery because these ones are OUT OF ORDER. Yes, really. Both of them. So much for the march of progress.

I glance towards the counters to see only two out of six are staffed. TWO. OUT OF SIX. How is that considered acceptable? Where are the other four people? Taking a nice long lunch break, maybe, while the rest of us stand almost faint from hunger and rage.

I force myself to breathe, think about what Kerri with an 'i' would have to say with her eyes. But she should try being here and not feeling angry.

The woman at the front looks as if she is about to cry. She is clutching a battered-looking card and asking the bored-looking man behind the glass if he might be able to take another look to see if they do in fact have her parcel. She explains she was home when they said they tried to deliver it. She didn't leave the house once, not even to walk the dog. The man behind the counter stares at her impassively. Tells her it's not there and, yes, he can see it says it is on the card, but it's not. Maybe it's out for redelivery? She'd better get home quick in case she misses it. It's not clear if the last comment is meant as a joke but the woman does not laugh.

I shift the mobile from under my left arm to under my right. It's not heavy but it's awkward to carry. At least I had the foresight to wrap it in brown paper in Little Scamps though. A young man who smells of cigarettes and BO is trying to package his parcel while he's in the queue. Why couldn't he have done it before he got here?

A teenager in a designer hoody whines at his mother. How much longer? I think about Alex and the other kids at Hatfield

Academy and feel a lump rise in my throat. I hope they realise I didn't mean to hurt them. And that I genuinely got to care about them and the show.

I hope Sam realises that too. Malcolm says he often asks after me but that, every time Malcolm has attempted to talk to him about what happened, Sam has made it clear he doesn't want to go there.

Only three more people ahead of me. I might even get this parcel to Stephen and Tamara before the baby is born. Except the elderly man at the front appears to be doing something incredibly convoluted involving his pension. I dig my fingernails into my palms.

I think about Jenna. She's always banging on in interviews about how normal she is but I bet she never has to queue at the post office. Or scrub her own loo. Or fight with the GP receptionist to get seen before she drops dead. When I went to her that day at the book signing and told her what I'd done, she looked at me as if I was something unpleasant she'd unwittingly sunk her shoe into, but maybe the pair of us aren't so different once you strip away the ease and privilege that surrounds her?

Finally, it's my turn. 'I thought we might be eating our Easter eggs together.'

The man behind the counter doesn't crack a smile. Tells me to put my parcel on the scale.

The rest of the process is conducted in silence.

I step out into the cold. The busker is packing up his things including the bucket that contains a paltry stack of coins. He looks slack-shouldered and sad and I feel a flicker of sympathy. No one grows up dreaming they might stand alone on a chilly street corner singing Take That covers to an audience that's either oblivious or disinterested.

Identity Crisis

He sees me looking at him. 'Y'all right? Did you enjoy the music? Bet it made queuing a little more fun, right?'

'Er, yeah.'

He pokes the red bucket under my nose, gives me what I'm sure he imagines is a cheeky smile and wink.

'Sorry, I don't have any cash.' The nerve of the man. The sheer nerve.

Chapter Seventy-Five

By the end of February, I am not just as poor as the proverbial church mouse but poor as the church mouse who decided to invest all their money in crypto.

Russell's copywriting work, while I'm immensely grateful for it, is not enough to cover my outgoings no matter how many 'meals for a pound' recipes I turn to. My assumption that I'd easily find other sources of freelance work now looks worryingly like hubris and one headhunter asked me, not unkindly, the other day if I'd ever considered a career change. There's hopefully book income on the horizon, of course, but although I'm pleased with how the new book is going, it's conservatively six months away from being finished and even if my agent then loves it and manages to sell it fairly quickly (big ifs), I won't see a sniff of an advance for quite a while yet.

All of which goes to explain why I'm getting dressed to go and meet Hattie and Rosamund. Prostituting myself to email the pair of them was an act of desperation and I wasn't expecting an answer to my email, but answer they did, suggesting the three of us 'grab a coffee'. Like we're mates.

It's unseasonably warm outside and I immediately regret my big padded coat, black jeans and polo neck.

IDENTITY CRISIS

I can't say I'm looking forward to seeing Rosamund and Hattie exactly but Kerri with an 'i' is fond of telling me you 'can't control the situation but you can control your reaction', so I'm trying to be as positive about it as I can. I'm also trying to remind myself that I've seen on LinkedIn that The Leap Agency are 'snowed under with exciting projects' and 'desperately looking for talented freelancers'.

The positivity is not boosted by my Tube journey, first of all because there are long delays on the Northern Line and secondly because, when a train finally does arrive, I am sat between two man spreaders and opposite a nail biter. Tonight's gratitude journal is going to be even more of a challenge than usual.

I assumed Rosamund and Hattie meant a coffee at The Leap Agency but they were insistent we should go 'somewhere nice' and they would expense it. They must have some seriously horrible job they need me to take on, probably with an insanely tight deadline, but honestly I need the money way too much to care.

The pair of them are already in the coffee shop cackling away like the witches they are. *You can't control the situation but you can control your reaction.* I force a smile.

'Hi,' Rosamund says, jumping up. 'So lovely to see you!'

What did she call me in that email? A sad, bitter cow.

Hattie gives me a beaming smile. 'It's been ages.'

Since you dropped me? Yes, it has.

We sit and Rosamund tells me to order whatever I want, which I guess is nice but it's not like we're in the Ritz Carlton.

'I'll have an Americano please,' I say to an unfeasibly young looking waiter.

'So,' Hattie says. 'What have you been up to?'

'Oh, this and that. How are things at The Leap Agency?'

'Great,' Rosamund says. 'Toby is in LA right now shooting some TV commercials for TASK Furniture. Everyone is very excited about the campaign idea.'

My campaign idea. In the scheme of everything that's happened it's nothing though.

'And the whole agency is crazy busy,' Rosamund says.

Hattie nods so hard it's a wonder she doesn't do herself an injury. '*Crazy*.'

'Well, you know I'm always happy to help out.'

Rosamund pats me on the arm as if I'm six. 'Thanks, babes. But let's catch up on the goss before we talk about work.'

Catch up on the goss? We've known each other for nearly three years and we've never spent more than about thirty seconds having a conversation that didn't include the words 'brand values', 'unique selling proposition' or 'laddering up'.

The pre-pubescent waiter delivers my coffee.

'So,' Hattie says. 'Jenna Cox! You dark horse, you!'

And that's when I realise. Rosamund and Hattie never made mention of giving me any work (let's grab a coffee). I'm not here for that, but because they've spent the last couple of months laughing at my expense and picking over every detail of what they read in the newspapers, and now they want to see the poor tragic figure in the flesh and find out what it has to say for itself. Maybe I'll even give them a juicy titbit that will make the whole incident even more hilarious?

I should probably just walk out at that moment. Not stay for the inquisition or humiliate myself further by trying to push the subject of possible freelance work. Because I already know Hattie and Rosamund are going to say it's very quiet at the moment. They'll say this despite having just told me it's 'crazy busy' and despite all the LinkedIn ads pleading for talented freelancers.

But I don't walk out. I sit there while they fire inane questions at me (sample: Are you and Jenna still in contact?) and I keep a smile on my face and answer as politely as I can until finally the vultures have gorged themselves on my misery and have no more to ask. 'So,' I say. 'Tell me what projects I can help you out with?'

'Nothing at the moment, babes,' Rosamund says.

'It's a bit quiet,' Hattie adds.

I dig my nails into my palms and bite the inside of my cheek. Sometimes controlling your reaction is really fucking hard.

Chapter Seventy-Six

Winter gives way to spring and Londoners shed coats and reach for them again sometimes within the space of half an hour.

I write my book, do the little bits of work that come in from Russell and am occasionally lured out of the house by Meg or Malcolm. Stephen and Tamara have their baby and if I don't quite manage to be pleased for them I think I pull off *not* not pleased.

I am still seeing Kerri with an 'i', which I think comes as a surprise to both of us. I can't say I look forward to the sessions exactly but at least Kerri is paid to listen to me, which means I don't feel quite so bad about uncovering the darkest recesses of my mind.

Sam looms large in these recesses. I barely mention him to Meg because, while she may be my best friend, it seems unhinged to admit I spend so much time thinking about a man when we were together for a sum total of one night. And I certainly wouldn't dare to give Malcolm any indication I have feelings for Sam as this would undoubtedly set him off on an absolute mission. Since he has started as a drama teacher at Hatfield Academy, he has been in the grip of a fierce bromance with Sam. The other night over margaritas, he spontaneously announced he could completely understand how I'd 'fallen into bed' with Sam because he is 'kind and funny and downright wonderful'. I nodded and tried to change the subject, but Malcolm was on a roll. 'Not to mention the fact that he's hot, hot, hot, darling.' He fanned himself stagily with a menu. 'Have you noticed he looks like Ryan Reynolds?'

Kerri has made me start regular journaling on top of the gratitude journal. She says writing down our feelings is a great way to process them and, as a writer, it's perfect for me. I don't think Kerri realises that writers get sick of bloody writing and there's a certain point in the day where we have to text in emojis.

Nonetheless, I am doing the journal. Just as when I was trying to keep a baby alive inside my body, I got so desperate I tried all kinds of things I didn't believe in, from Reiki to Chinese medicine to eating industrial quantities of flax seeds, if there's even a 0.1 per cent chance that journaling might help me be happy again, I will give it a go.

I pick up the notebook now and start writing.

I need to put Sam out of my mind. It's ridiculous. I'm a forty-one-year-old woman who has been through stuff. But I keep thinking about the way he is with the kids. How he managed to find something positive to say to each and every one of them. (Except Dylan the body farter but TBH, if he'd found something positive to say about that performance, I'd have lost all respect for him.) It's weird how Sam's puppy dog enthusiasm, which used to grate on me, became so attractive. How I started to see it as something I could learn from rather than scorn, because life is short and maybe we have a duty to try to be happy instead of becoming bitter and desiccated and miserable? And if Sam can do it when he lost his mum, his brother and his dad in separate incidents over a six-month period then maybe so can I?

There are other things about Sam that make him difficult to forget too.

- He made me laugh until my stomach hurt.
- He talks about books like other blokes talk about football.
- He smells of clean skin and washing that's just come off the line.
- He takes responsibility for the end of his marriage and talks about his ex-wife in a respectful way without giving off 'I'm not remotely over her' vibes.
- The way he took care of me when I hurt my ankle.
- The fact he didn't give the newspapers a quote about me and refused to join the pile on when the whole world was gunning for Jonny Turner.
- Because he made dinner from a practically empty fridge and cleared up and didn't then act as if he was waiting for some kind of medal or ticker-tape parade.
- Because Malcolm says he often asks how I'm doing and, even though it's a bit humiliating to think he pities me for turning my life into a train wreck, that still says a lot about him.
- And, yes, also because he looks like Ryan Reynolds. (But doesn't act in that dickbiscuitish way a lot of good-looking men can.)

I throw down the pen and snap the notebook shut. What the hell am I doing? I'm mooning over Sam like a lovestruck teenager who can't get over a holiday romance. The connection between us wasn't real, well, not for Sam at any rate. The woman he felt a pull towards doesn't exist.

Chapter Seventy-Seven

When I open my front door to see Sam standing there, my mind instantly takes me to the worst-case scenario. 'Alex?'

Sam immediately knows what I'm asking and shakes his head. 'No, he's okay. Well not okay, but…'

Not dead. I let out the breath that's caught in my throat. 'Come in.' If Sam is not here to tell me bad news, maybe, just maybe, he's giving me a second chance? Karma from the universe for me trying to be a better person.

And, if that's the case why couldn't I have put on some make-up this morning and not these grubby sweatpants? Also, would it have killed me to wash my hair? It's one thing Sam having to come to terms with me not being Jenna but I'd rather he wasn't seeing *quite* such a real version of me. 'How are you? What have you been up to? I can't believe it's only a couple of weeks until Easter. Where does the time go?'

Sam doesn't answer this admittedly pointless question. His eyes have flickered towards the multicoloured Post-it notes plastered all over the coffee table. I was deep in the throes of writing when he arrived. It's early days but my new book is going well. I sent Kate the first five chapters and she loved them and said I've got my 'voice back'. That doesn't change the fact that the sea of multicoloured notes plastered with half thoughts are a bit embarrassing though. It's like someone seeing the mess inside your head. Still, I suppose in the grand scheme of things, it's one of my less embarrassing moments with Sam.

'Would you like a cup of tea?'

'No thanks.'

We stand there in silence, me having to clamp my lips shut to stop myself blurting out that Kerri with an 'i' says she's very pleased with me and all my 'work', and that I've made things up with Meg and even sent a present for Stephen and Tamara's baby. Because I did a very bad thing and I know that, but I'm not really a bad person. Well, except in the post office when there are only two tills out of six that are staffed and both self-service machines are out of order. But that's enough to make anyone horrible, right?

'Listen,' I blurt out. 'I wasn't pretending with you.'

Sam gives a small mirthless laugh that doesn't sound like him at all. 'Right. Except for the fact, I thought you were a completely different person.'

I swallow hard. 'Yes, but when we talked, it was my thoughts and views I was sharing, not Jenna's. The connection between us was real for me and so were my feelings for you.'

Sam stares at the floor. 'I don't even know what to do with that.'

'I just wanted you to know.'

'Okay, well now I do.'

'And when we were... you know... intimate, I wasn't pretending.' I can feel my cheeks burning but I had to tell him this. It feels like the very least I can do.

'Again, I don't really know what to do with that.'

I nod.

'I am here to talk to you about Alex,' Sam says.

Oh, okay, there are to be no second chances. Of course there aren't.

'He wants to see you.'

'What? Actual me? Not pretend Jenna?'

'Yes.'

'But why?'

'I have no idea.'

Ouch.

'He made me promise to ask you. He's in St Thomas's Hospital.'

'Okay, I'll go there tomorrow.'

Sam shakes his head. 'Look, this is awkward but his mum doesn't want you to be with Alex on your own.' He clears his throat. 'And she doesn't want to… er… she's a bit emotional herself right now, obviously, so she doesn't feel she can be there.'

Sam is staring at the floor. This is hard for him. He may hate what I did but he doesn't relish telling me Alex's mother won't countenance her child being alone with me. Or that she can't stand the thought of having to be in the same room.

'Umm, so she asked me if I'd take you to the hospital. Stick around while you and Alex talk.'

'I see. And that has to be now?'

'No. I can come back. I've obviously interrupted your work.'

'No, let's go now.' I need to get this over with. And stop entertaining stupid little fantasies that Sam will ever forgive me.

Chapter Seventy-Eight

I can't recall a more uncomfortable twenty-five minutes when I haven't had my ankles in stirrups. Sam and I have spent the whole car journey in near silence. I did attempt small talk at first, but I guess that never works when there's so much big stuff hanging unsaid.

I'm relieved when we get to St Thomas's, although the words frying pan and fire rather spring to mind.

'Jen— Clare,' Sam says, alerting me to the fact a hospital porter is trying to get past me with a bed.

The studied cheerfulness of the children's ward brings a lump to my throat: medics in teddy bear scrubs, brightly coloured plastic toys, incongruous amongst the sharps bins and ventilators, a man dressed as a fluffy pink rabbit for no reason I can immediately discern.

Alex is in a bay with three much younger kids. How hard that must be on top of everything else: to be surrounded by 'babies' when you're desperately trying to assert yourself as no longer being a child.

A wave of panic floods my body as we approach Alex's bed. I don't know why he wants to see me but I know I haven't been brought here for a casual catch-up.

Alex's mother looks at me with ill-concealed disgust, grabs the hand of the little girl in a ratty pink princess dress and tells Sam they are going to the coffee shop.

'Hi,' I say to Alex, my voice coming out in a squeak.

'Can you draw the curtains?' Alex says to Sam.

Sam does as he is asked and says he'll wait just outside.

'Why did you do it?' Alex says.

'I… well, it's complicated…'

'I hate it when adults say that. My parents told me it was *complicated* when they decided to get a divorce, the doctors tell me it's *complicated* when I ask them if I'm going to get better, my father says it's *complicated* when I ask him if he left my mum because of Hilary. "It's complicated" just means: I don't want to tell you the truth.'

I take a deep breath. It's oppressively hot in here and I pluck at the neck of my jumper, which suddenly feels tight and itchy. 'Okay, let me start at the beginning. I signed up with the lookalike agency on a whim. I needed the money and I was intrigued to see whether I could actually do it. One day I was going to a gig and someone in real life mistook me for the real Jenna and I was going to correct them but then I didn't—'

'Why?'

I shrug. 'I don't know exactly. Because it was easier than having to explain the truth? Because it made them so happy to think they'd met Jenna? Because it made me happy? All those things probably.'

Alex scratches his arm, which is a patchwork of bruises. My mind flashes back to all the blood tests I had to have when they were investigating the multiple miscarriages. For some reason, there's one particular doctor who stands out in my mind. A very young, very pretty woman who I'd heard shortly beforehand on her mobile trying to get a delivery driver to leave her parcel with a neighbour. There was a quiet desperation in the way she asked me to make a fist and pump my fingers – as if my misbehaving veins were the thing that might very well tip her over the edge that day.

'So after that you started pretending to be Jenna in real life all the time?'

'No. But if I was doing a job where I was dressed up as her and I was recognised before or afterwards, I didn't tell people I wasn't her.'

'My mum says you must have done it to scam people. So you could get free shit or whatever. You should have pretended to have cancer. We get all kinds of stuff.'

I glance at the blue curtains – an illusion of privacy. Sam and anyone else in the vicinity will be hearing every word of this, just as we are hearing every word of the Peppa Pig episode the little girl in the next bed is playing on her iPad. 'I never set out to scam people or profit from it. But if scamming people is lying about who you really are, then I guess your mum is right.'

Alex nods. He looks younger and smaller in his Arsenal pyjamas and I feel a wave of shame at having been one more blow to his faith in the world. 'Go on. Tell me what happened when you met Mr Jackson.'

'I was leaving a gig in Marble Arch and Sa— Mr Jackson saw me. He told me about the talent show and how it was all to raise money for you. He asked me if I'd come along to judge the talent show but I said I was busy. I signed an autograph for you and said goodbye. But then Sa— Mr Jackson chased after me and asked if I would come to a rehearsal and meet you. He said it would mean the world to you—'

'Pah, "mean the world" to me! I bet he said those exact words too. Like I'm a total saddo.'

Despite everything, I can't help but smile at this.

'So you said yes?' Alex says, sitting up a little straighter. 'Because you couldn't say no to the poor saddo cancer kid?'

I nod.

'Weren't you nervous we'd know you were a fake?'

'I was very nervous, but having said yes, I couldn't see a way to get out of it that wouldn't be a huge disappointment to you and the other kids. So I thought I would just come to one rehearsal, meet you and then that would be the end of it.'

The Peppa Pig theme tune plays for what seems like the hundredth time. 'I wish she'd use her bloody headphones,' Alex says. 'So why didn't you do that?'

'You didn't come to that first rehearsal. You weren't well.'

Alex rolls his eyes. 'Fine. But why didn't you just meet me at the second rehearsal and then never come back to Hatfield Academy?'

I pick at the skin around my thumbnail and a little red dot of blood appears. 'Because of what you said to Joe about how I didn't care about you or the other kids or the show.'

Alex's small pale brow furrows. 'What?'

'I did care about the show and raising the money so you and your family would get the trip to Disneyland.' I'm covered in sweat now. I know hospital wards need to be warm but this is ridiculous.

'It wasn't like some game? Let's see how far I can push this?'

'No.'

'I swear to God if I've got one wish right now beyond getting better, it's that Peppa gets turned into bacon.' Alex scratches the skin around his cannula. 'There's another thing I don't get. You seemed to know some stuff. Like always telling people not to have penguin arms or making Daisy do "Rainbow" not the Mariah

Carey song and telling Joe which jokes were okay and which were completely lame. If you're not really a celebrity, how did you know that kind of stuff? Also, how did you sound so much like Jenna?'

'I did a few years in youth theatre when I was a teenager.'

'Are you serious? Youth theatre? That's gay.'

As the only adult present, I'm aware I should probably step in to say we don't use 'gay' as any kind of slur, but the moral high ground does not really seem mine for the taking right now.

'So you must have shit your pants when I told you I'd managed to persuade Mrs Gray to move the date of the show so you could be there? You'd managed to fool us all this time but you knew there was no way you could get away with it in front of a big audience?'

I stare at the green lino wishing its swirls would suck me in. 'Yes.'

'So why didn't you just not turn up on the day? Say you were ill or something? No one would have ever known the truth.'

'I thought about doing that but I couldn't bring myself to. I decided to go to the real Jenna and ask her if she'd go to the show.'

'Right. So you had her phone number?'

I shake my head. 'She was doing a book signing in town. I went along to that.'

'And she said she'd come to the show?'

'No. She was angry.'

'I bet she was.'

I suck a fresh red droplet off my thumb, the ferrous tang of the blood transporting my nostrils back to babies lost.

'So that's when you turned up as yourself and did your big confession?'

I nod.

'And who are you really?'

The sixty-four million dollar question. 'My name is Clare Palmer. I do freelance advertising work and I'm an author.'

'I hate reading.' Alex reaches for his Arsenal water bottle and takes a sip. 'Did you ever actually care about us?'

The question is like a slap. 'Yes.'

Alex slumps against his pillows. This conversation has taken it out of him; depleted his already battered reserves of energy. Another unforgivable action I can add to my long list.

'Do you know what the mad thing is? I liked you because you were one of the few people around me who wasn't fake. You treated me like a normal person, not like the kid with cancer. But you were the biggest fake of all.'

A tear rolls off the end of my nose. 'I'm sorry.'

Alex snorts. 'Well, that's okay then. As long as you're *sorry*. It doesn't matter that you spent weeks lying to us all. That you dressed up like a completely different person and changed your voice and told lie after lie.'

I dig my nails into my palms. He has every right to be angry with me.

'I've got another question: Was it you who got me that vintage Spiderman comic and gave it to Mr Smith for me? I'm pretty sure he has no idea I collect Spiderman comics.'

'Yes.'

Alex shakes his head. 'You're just like my dad.'

'What?'

'I don't see him for weeks and then he turns up with an iPad or a new pair of trainers or tickets to The Emirates. Like that makes up for everything else.'

'That's not fair.'

'*That's not fair,*' Alex parrots in a high-pitched whine.

I have never reacted well to being imitated (and yes, I see the irony). My brother used to do it often when we were kids and once, after he copied every single word I said for nearly an hour, I pulled out a sizeable clump of his hair and ended up in huge trouble. Now, I can feel anger start to bubble in my belly. 'I don't think it makes up for anything.' I fight to keep my voice even. 'I didn't even go looking for the comic – I stumbled upon it and thought it was something you'd enjoy.'

'Yeah, well you thought wrong.'

'The guy in the shop said it's a goo—'

'It's lame.'

'Okay, well, there's no need to be rude.' I paid over fifty quid for that comic and I'm pretty skint right now.

'*There's no need to be rude.*' The high-pitched imitation again.

'Okay.' I force a smile. 'I'm going to go now.'

'Yeah. Course you are. Because you don't care about me. You never did. Just like you never cared about Joe's jokes or Daisy's singing or the rubbish dance troupe. All that "no penguin arms" and "look up when you talk" and "let's play lame old Zip, Zap, Boing" was just part of your act. You never gave a damn about any of us or the show or how much money we raised.'

'DO YOU THINK I WANTED TO SPEND HOURS OF MY TIME AT THOSE REHEARSALS? DO YOU THINK IT WAS FUN FOR ME TO SIT IN THAT SMELLY HALL AND WATCH THE DANCE TROUPE DO THEIR ROUTINE WEEK IN WEEK OUT? WHAT ABOUT THE RAPPERS AND THE BODY FARTER? AND YOU SAID YOURSELF I COULD HAVE MADE SOME EXCUSE AND NOT TURNED UP THE DAY OF THE SHOW. AND HOW ABOUT GOING TO SEE JENNA AND TELLING HER

EVERYTHING I'D DONE – DOES THAT SOUND LIKE SOMETHING YOU WOULD DO IF YOU DIDN'T CARE?'

Alex is staring at my open-mouthed. Which is when I realise I am shouting at a very sick kid in a hospital bed. 'I'm sorry. I shouldn't have raised my voice.'

Alex says nothing.

'Look, Alex, what I've told you is the truth. It's up to you whether or not you decide to believe it.'

Chapter Seventy-Nine

As I pull back the thin blue curtain, all eyes are on me. Doctors, nurses, healthcare assistants, patients, volunteers – everyone needs to see what kind of person yells at a kid with cancer. There's an eerie hush too. Even Peppa Pig seems to have finally gone quiet.

'Don't say a word,' I snap at Sam, my face blazing.

An absurdly young nurse who is cleaning up a child who has just vomited over herself, stops what she's doing to shoot me a look of naked horror. I may not be disgusted by vomit, her stare tells me, but I'm sure as hell disgusted by you.

Her opprobrium is unnecessary though. No one can hate me more than I hate myself. I quicken my pace, desperate to escape this hot airless room.

'Are you okay?' Sam says as he presses the buzzer to release us from the ward.

I choke back tears and nod. Because I can't exactly tell Sam that I'm bitterly disappointed in myself, that I don't know if I'll ever be able to forgive myself for sinking to a new low. Quite an achievement from a woman who recently spent months pretending to be an entirely different person and earning herself the titles 'morally bankrupt', 'shameless' and 'utterly without scruples' from the national press. In the game of moral limbo, it seems I've found a way to go lower still.

Sam and I wait for the lift in silence. For months, I've entertained this crazy fantasy that one day he might want to get to know the real me. But I've just shown him the real me and it's not very pretty.

The lift doors open and out steps Alex's mum and little sister. Brilliant, just when today couldn't get any better.

'I hope you haven't upset him?'

'Umm…'

'Shall Amy and I go and watch telly in the relatives room,' Sam says. 'Give you two a minute.'

Alex's mum says no at exactly the same time as I say yes, but then she looks at Sam and gives an almost imperceptible nod.

The two of us stare at each other and my brain scrabbles around for what to say in this moment I supposedly wanted. I guess it's similar to 'wanting' to throw up.

'I did upset him.' My voice catches in my throat. 'I handled the whole conversation terribly—'

'I should never have let you come here. I knew it was a mistake.'

I nod. 'I'm more sorry than you can possibly imagine.' I use my sleeve to swipe at the tears rolling down my cheeks. 'About today but also about everything.'

She stares at me, disgust written all over her face. Disgust in me. That's not even the worst part though because underneath all that is the raw, naked pain. This is a mother facing the unimaginable.

'Do you have children?' Her voice is almost inaudible.

I shake my head.

'I didn't think you could.'

I should let that go. But somehow the words tumble out of my mouth before I can stop them. 'I've had five miscarriages.'

She rummages in her bag and hands me a tissue. 'I'm sorry.'

This flash of kindness undoes me completely and I start to sob.

'I had two miscarriages. Between Alex and Amy. That's why there's such a big age gap. It was rough.'

We stand facing each other while porters wheeling beds, harassed looking doctors and relatives with pinched, sad faces bustle past us. 'I don't even know your name.'

'Teresa.' She starts to walk away but then turns back. 'I'll never forgive you for what you did to my boy. You know that, right?'

I nod. 'I don't forgive me either.'

The lift stops at every single one of the fourteen floors to ground level. I am pressed up between Sam and a man in scrubs who is jabbing furiously at his phone.

'I'll drive you home,' Sam says.

I shake my head. 'Don't worry, I'll get the Tube.'

'I go practically past your door.'

'I'll get the Tube.'

Sam shrugs.

A woman in a wheelchair is staring at us. She wants to know what the story is here. She knows for sure this isn't just about my transport preferences. Perhaps I should explain to her that I can't stand even one more minute of Sam looking at me the way he is? That I may richly deserve his disappointment in me but that doesn't make it any easier to bear.

The lift spits us out onto the ground floor amongst a teeming mass of people. A man is shouting at a receptionist about parking, a woman in a hijab is crying big hiccuping sobs and a man with a broken leg and the physio alongside him are sharing a joke. For some, being under this roof is everyday. For others, like Teresa, they have almost forgotten what a normal day is.

I remember being in the café in St Mary's with Stephen when I had just lost the second baby and there were two young nurses giggling over a story that involved hiding a pair of spanx behind a radiator, when one of them had unexpectedly 'got lucky' and, in that moment, I hated them. And, of course, just because you're sad, you can't expect the world to be and, of course, if anyone deserves happiness, it's nurses, but the hatred was visceral and real and I had to bite the inside of my cheek so I wouldn't scream at them to just SHUT THE FUCK UP.

'You're sure about getting the Tube?' Sam says.

'I'm sure.'

'Okay, well bye, Clare.'

'Bye.' And then I stand and watch him walk away.

Chapter Eighty

In the days that follow seeing Alex, the shame and pressure build inside me. I cannot believe that, after all this effort trying to be a better person, the real me broke free in all her horrible glory.

I am desperate to talk to Kerri with an i' (something I never imagined myself saying). Desperate to confess. But as luck would have it, my weekly appointment with Kerri fell the day before I went to St Thomas's, which means I have six whole days to sit alone with the magnitude of what I've done and who I am.

I nearly told Meg when I saw her on Tuesday evening, but things aren't quite the same between us. I know Meg isn't the type to hold a grudge but it's as if there's a distance between us that wasn't there before – a slight desire to hold back. And anyway, the kids were buzzing around, inserting themselves into every conversation, their presence so much bigger than their small bodies.

On Wednesday, I walked past a Catholic church and, even though I've never been religious, felt a visceral pull to go inside. I pictured myself sitting in a dark confessional telling all to a stranger behind a screen. Unburdening myself and being cleansed. I didn't go inside though. The newspapers may have described me as 'morally bankrupt' but I'm not morally bankrupt enough to ape religious belief just because I'm desperate.

I kept walking and, by the time I neared Malcolm's house, tears were streaming down my cheeks and I had to stand on the corner of his street taking deep breaths and swiping at the trails of mascara that had run down my cheeks.

'Are you all right, darling?' he said, handing me a glass of wine. 'You look a little… peaky.'

I was tempted to tell him everything then. But, as I'd walked here, I remembered the conversation I had with Malcolm where I first told him about pretending to be Jenna and how I'd got involved with the talent show and with Sam. Malcolm wasn't unkind but nor could he hide his feelings. 'I'm fine,' I said, forcing a smile.

Finally, it's Thursday morning and there are only six hours left until I see Kerri. I wake ridiculously early and am unable to concentrate on either my book or my pet care articles. I am so desperate to get this off my chest. I don't care that Kerri wears stupid red T-bar shoes that shouldn't be seen on anyone over six and big, ugly clattering wooden jewellery. I don't care that her room always smells musty and no one ever dusts the faux tulips. I am beyond worrying about these things because Kerri is a trained professional and it's her job to fix me.

My mother calls as I am putting on my shoes and there's something in hearing her voice that makes me immediately want to tell her everything. It's hardwired to run to your mum, no, even when you're supposed to be beyond that. Also, whether it's nature or nurture that has made me what I am, my mother bears some responsibility. She's left with little choice but to love me no matter what.

I prepare the words in my mind.

Identity Crisis

But then my mother starts waffling on about my father and his maddening habit of stacking the dishwasher like a five year old and the moment is gone.

I end the call and walk to the bus stop. I will be with Kerri in under an hour. I can finally lance this ugly boil.

The bus is crowded and the one available seat is in front of a persistent sniffer. Not now. For Christ's sake not now.

At least the old lady I'm next to is quiet. She has a weathered face, bright eyes and deep laughter lines that speak of hours spent enjoying the company of loved ones.

Sniff, sniff.

For goodness' sake. Blow your nose.

The old lady gives me a tiny smile. A signal that we're on the same page.

I smile back. And notice just how kind she looks.

Chapter Eighty-One

It was such a relief to get everything off my chest. Once I'd started, I couldn't stop myself, the raw words tumbling out of my mouth and tripping over themselves, interrupted only by sobs and the very occasional breath.

Now, I'll admit to being a little disappointed in the reaction. The unmistakeable shock (surely she has heard worse?), the little shake of the head and then the deathly silence.

Where's the wisdom, the answers, the succour?

Finally, she says something. 'This is my stop, love.'

Chapter Eighty-Two

You might have thought that having lost it so completely with bus lady, I'd be relatively calm for round two with Kerri.

Not so. I am a heaving mass of snot and tears. 'I've tried s... s... so hard to be different.'

I pluck one of the peach-coloured tissues from the floral box on the orangey pine table between Kerri and me. Do I imagine it or does a faint glimmer of satisfaction cross her face? Tears to a therapist must be what clean plates are to a chef.

'You must think I'm a t... t... t... terrible person.'

'I'm wondering if you think you're a terrible person?'

Wrong answer, Kerri. You were supposed to say of course you don't think I'm a terrible person. I cry even harder.

Kerri says nothing. Just sits there watching me fall apart. I wish it was Dr Asen and not her in the chair opposite me. She pulled lots of the same kind of annoying stunts — not filling silences, answering questions with a question, repeating what you'd just said back to you as if you were a moron — but she was less annoying somehow. At least she wore normal people's shoes. And there was the occasional flash of humanity. A joke shared before the session properly started. Kerri doesn't do jokes.

Not that I want her to be laughing now. I can't remember the last time I was as bad as this. It reminds me of that day in Pret.

I wipe my eyes with another of the peach-coloured tissues. 'Who sh… shouts at a kid with cancer?'

'You feel guilty?'

'YES I FEEL GUILTY.' Christ, I'm paying ninety-eight quid an hour for this. 'I shouldn't have l… l… lost my temper with him in the hospital. It's un… un… unforgivable. And I never should have deceived him in the first place. Pretended to be J… J… Jenna. I shouldn't have done that to any of the kids, but I feel particularly bad about Alex.'

Kerri cocks her head to the side.

'It's bad enough that I'm healthy. Barren but healthy and he's not.'

'Alex?'

No, SpongeBob Squarepants. 'He hasn't even h… h… had a crack at life.' Fresh tears engulf me.

Kerri watches me. Honestly, she's not much more use than bus lady.

Eventually, I get my breath back. 'And what about what I did to Sam? He's a good man. I'm no better than those romance scammers you read about in the newspapers.'

Kerri makes an indecipherable noise, which I think is supposed to indicate she's listening. It's hard to imagine that I've spent the last six days so desperate to come here, imagining that it would help in some way. If anything I feel worse. 'I feel guilty about my babies too.'

Kerri leans forward. 'Your babies.'

I nod.

'I'm wondering what you would say to them if you could?'

I shake my head. 'That I'm sorry.'

'Maybe you should write them a letter?'

Jesus, what is it with this woman and writing? I had an editor who demanded less words out of me.

'They died before we knew whether they were boys or girls but, every time, I was sure I knew. I remember the first time I was pregnant and my mother laughed when I said I was definitely having a girl. She said of course I couldn't know for sure, that she'd been convinced I was a boy.'

Kerri fiddles with one of the big brightly coloured beads of her necklace.

'They had names, you know. All of them. The first two had names that Stephen and I had come up with together and, then after that, Stephen didn't want to give them names anymore but I did.' I take another tissue out of its floral box and blow my nose. 'I let th… them down. Everyone told me it wasn't my fault but I was s… s… s… supposed to keep them safe.' I let my head drop into my hands. 'I was their mummy. And I was supposed to keep them safe.'

Chapter Eighty-Three

To my babies who I never got to hold,
    Where to start with the things I want to say to you? Words are what I do and yet they seem woefully inadequate when it comes to this.

I'll begin with the obvious. Losing you is the most painful experience of my whole life.

You were so wanted. So loved. I hope you know that.

I know some people question that love. How can you love someone you didn't know? What they don't understand is that, from the moment you started to grow inside me, I talked to you, pictured you, saw your lives play out. I was your mummy.

And then you were ripped away.

There were to be no first smiles, first steps or first days at school. I would never inhale your sweet baby smell, never hear your cry or feel your tiny fingers curl around mine.

I would never get to find out if you looked as I imagined. Did you have my blue eyes and unruly hair, your dad's nose?

I would never see the people you grew into. Never know your hopes and dreams.

What made you smile and laugh.

I lost you first, my darling Chloe. I remember I couldn't bear to shatter your dad's happiness and excitement. Only the day before, we'd bought

Identity Crisis

you a knitted red hat that looked like a strawberry and was no bigger than your dad's palm. The two of us laughed and joked about how 'naughty' we were to buy something before the first scan. (I have never hated an inanimate object as much as I came to hate that hat.) The nurse in A&E asked me if I wanted her to call your dad but I shook my head. I'd give him a little more time thinking the world was okay. I lay on the trolley, bleeding and cramping and crying and told you over and over that I was so, so sorry.

I repeated those same words to all of you.

One of the cruellest things has been not knowing why. People told me it wasn't my fault. But I know they are wrong. My body had failed you. I failed you. I was your mummy and I was supposed to keep you safe.

But I hadn't done that and now the family I had once thought was so certain and so meant-to-be had turned to dust. The school concerts and Christmases and family holidays had all gone. I'd never cheer from the sidelines at a football match or help with homework or wipe away tears after a disastrous date. No one would ever call me Mummy.

People told me I had to move on. Even your dad eventually told me that. He's a good man, your dad, and we loved each other once, but there came a time when all we could see when we looked at each other was the agony and the loss.

I hated him for wanting to be happy. He hated me for not even trying.

But how could I? How can I? The pain never goes away. It's an unending and unbearable ache. As if each of you physically have a piece of my heart.

I need to start mending that heart though. For a long time, I believed that even attempting that was letting you down, but now I see the biggest betrayal of all is living this miserable half life. My anger and bitterness and sadness won't bring you back. I need to look for the joy and live and love for all of us.

That doesn't mean to say I will ever forget you. Or even that I will try to fill the void. I have learned that nothing can do that. So I will embrace the void and see it for what it is: the space in my heart I keep for each and every one of you.

I love you forever,
Mummy xxx

Chapter Eighty-Four

July 2024

I am typing furiously when the phone rings. I'm nearing the end of my book and tempted not to answer but have learned that it's pointless to try to ignore Malcolm, because if you don't pick up his first call, he'll ring again and again until you do.

'Turn on the telly,'

'What?' I say, exasperated. 'I'm deep in the "all is lost" section of my novel, Malcolm. I don't want to break my concentration.'

'ITV.'

I sigh and pick up the remote. As with the phone calls, it's a waste of effort trying to fight Malcolm's will. There's clearly some old luvvie on the telly he needs me to see right now so he can share some bitchy aside about them. 'Er, it's a dog food commercial?'

'*Wait*,' Malcolm says. As if I'm the one being annoying.

I'm so nearly there with this book. And my agent is still pleased with what she's read so far. Yesterday, we chatted on the phone and she told me she's excited about sending it out to publishers.

'We'll probably have to give you a pseudonym,' she said (a polite way of reminding me that I am considered toxic).

'No,' I told her. 'I want to use my real name. And if that stops publishers wanting the book, well then, so be it.'

The *Good Morning* theme tune starts up on the TV and there on screen in front of me is not some Z-list celebrity who has had a botched facelift, but Jenna and Alex.

'Why have you made me put this on? The last time Jenna interviewed Alex, they eviscerated me.'

'Sssshh,' Malcolm says.

'Welcome back,' Jenna says, full-beam smile to camera. 'Before the break, plucky Alex Mortimer was telling us about the pioneering new treatment for sarcoma he's about to undergo in the United States.' She turns to Alex. 'Thank you so much for sharing your story with us, Alex. We've had hundreds and hundreds of people call and message to wish you well.'

Alex squirms on the sofa. 'Thanks.'

'Now, before the break you said there was something you wanted to say about your previous interview with us?'

'Yeah.'

'Great.' Jenna leans forward in her seat. 'Just before you do, let's give our viewers a little reminder of the bizarre events that preceded that interview. A woman dressed up as me had tricked you and your classmates into believing she was me. The deception went on for weeks and this con-woman got deeply involved in a talent show you were doing to raise money.'

'Why are you making me watch this?' I say to Malcolm.

'Sshh,' he replies.

'Yeah,' Alex scratches his head. 'And, at the time, I was angry—'

'Yes,' Jenna says, adopting big puppy dog eyes. 'It was a terrible, terrible thing she did to you.'

Alex shakes his head. 'See, that's the thing, it wasn't. Clare was trying to help us.'

'I knew it!' Malcolm says.

My breath catches in my throat.

Jenna's sympathetic smile falters. This isn't the dirt she was expecting. 'Well, we'll never know what her motivations were—'

'I do know,' Alex says firmly. 'She was trying to help us.'

Malcolm whoops down the phone.

'She came to all of our rehearsals,' Alex says. 'Hours and hours of them.'

I stare at the TV, unable to process what I'm hearing, a lump forming in my throat.

But Alex has more.

'She didn't just sit there at the rehearsals either, she got involved. Helped people sing better or perform better or dance better. Well, actually, she couldn't really help the dancers but that wasn't her fault.'

'Right,' Jenna says. 'But she told a lot of lies. Deceived you and your teacher and the other kids in your class.'

'Only because she was trying to help us. It's because of her that we raised so much money—'

Jenna's eyes flash 'Well—'

Alex sits up straighter. 'And another thing. No one would have ever found out the truth if Clare hadn't owned up to what she'd done and persuaded you to come to the show. She could have made an excuse about not turning up on the day and we'd never have known. All the fuss in the papers and stuff – people having a go at her – that only happened because she told the truth. She cared about us and the show more than she cared about what would happen to her.'

Jenna recovers her smile, although it's noticeably strained. 'You're so *forgiving*, Alex. It's truly inspiring. But I don't think there's a grown-up watching this programme who doesn't think what she did was terribly wrong.'

'Yeah, well they don't know her.'

Jenna cocks her head to one side. 'They know she lied to a child who is bravely battling cancer.'

'That's the other thing I liked so much about Clare. She never talked down to me or treated me as the "child with cancer".'

'Ha ha,' Malcolm says. 'Go Alex!'

Jenna looks as if she might be about to vomit.

'She cared about me and she cared about the other kids and she cared about us raising money'

'Clare?' Malcolm says. 'Clare? Oh my God, you're crying, aren't you?'

Chapter Eighty-Five

November 2024

I stand in the shadow of the huge red-brick building, my legs trembling and my breathing ragged. The last time I was here was that dreadful day I confessed to Sam, Alex and the other kids that I wasn't Jenna. The shock and sadness and disbelief on their faces will be etched on my mind until the day I die.

It's testament to Malcolm's persuasiveness (and that's the polite word for it) that I'm here. He's in charge of another talent show with the same kids and has been nagging me for weeks about how he needs my help. At first I flatly refused.

'Wouldn't you like to see the kids?' Malcolm said.

'Only if I could make myself invisible. I don't need to be reminded of how much they hate me, thanks very much.'

Malcolm tried to tell me it had been a long time and he thought I might be pleasantly surprised. People of that age are way too self-obsessed to stay hung up on someone else's behaviour.

'Yeah, I think it kind of depends on the behaviour.'

Malcolm upped the ante. 'Listen, darling, unfortunately there are thousands of kids like Alex. Thousands of kids who may never live to blow out the candles on the eighteenth birthday cake. Eight H are determined to do their bit to try to help and so am I. We want to raise at least five grand for teenage cancer charities, but that's a big ask. Especially as, despite going all misty-eyed on the telly when she interviewed Alex and saying helping Hatfield Academy had been "one of the greatest privileges" of her life, Jenna has declined to be involved in any way or even give us a shout out on her social media.'

It's a bitterly cold November day, the sort that makes your face sting and I stamp my feet up and down in an effort to keep warm.

I tried to argue with Malcolm, say that of course it was an important cause and of course I'd be making a donation, but I still didn't see why he wanted me to come to the rehearsals. Malcolm let out a bone-shaking sigh as if I was a particularly wearisome toddler asking yet another 'why' question. 'I've had months and months of having to listen to how you managed to help Daisy find the perfect song, and taught Joe to pause before a punchline, and showed Lucy how to keep time to the music. The kids even made me play some ridiculous warm-up activity called zip zap zoing.'

'Zip, Zap, Boing,' I corrected.

Malcolm swiped his hand through the air. 'Whatever. The point is I've had to listen to endless comments from Sam and the kids about the magic you brought. Which is frankly a little irritating when you consider I'm the actual pro. I love you to bits, darling, but it's not like you've appeared in the West End or made Hollywood movies or even had any formal training beyond some provincial youth theatre. However, the consensus seems to be that you made a huge difference to shaping last year's show.'

'Most of the acts were still pretty rubbish, if I'm honest.'

Malcolm nodded. 'That I don't need convincing of. But I also believe they were less rubbish than they would have been without you. Which is why I want your help with this year's show. All hands on deck.'

Of course, I gave in. Although, now I'm actually standing outside the building shivering, despite my big coat, I don't know if I can bring myself to walk in. I stare up at the building which looks forbidding in the pale wintry light.

'I'm sorry,' I whisper under my breath.

Chapter Eighty-Six

I got halfway down the road before I turned back. I might not want to face these kids but I'm going to have to suck it up. If me being here helps in any way at all, well, it feels like the very least I can do.

Sandra on reception is frosty as hell. You wouldn't think I once had to listen to her banging on about how her daughter-in-law drives her bananas because she expects Sandra to look after the kids, but then gives her loads of instructions: Only half an hour's TV, don't give them any sugar, don't let them fall asleep in the buggy. Like Sandra isn't doing her a favour! Like she hasn't raised four kids of her own! Doesn't her daughter-in-law realise how exhausting it is to look after two kids under five when you're pushing sixty and your knees aren't what they were?

Today there is none of that chit-chat. Just sucked-in lips and a curt instruction to take a seat.

Malcolm swoops into reception to collect me. 'Loving the pink faux fur coat, darling. Is it new? Are you channelling your inner celebrity?'

'Actually I've had it years so if I'm channelling anything, I guess it's the old me.'

We walk down the endless corridor, nerves fluttering in my

IDENTITY CRISIS

stomach. We pass posters for options evenings and extra curricular clubs and children's artworks and sports trophies.

'I've got my first gig as a Clooney lookalike this evening,' Malcolm says. 'So it turns out your advice to stop dyeing my hair was sound.'

'That's great. Are you nervous?'

Malcolm does a little shrug. 'A little. I was Jonny for years whereas George is new to me. I've been watching lots of his movies and interviews and stuff to prepare and I must have looked at a thousand photos of the man. It's a tough job!'

I force a laugh, even though all I can think about right now is how we're getting closer and closer to the hall. 'You'll be great.'

'Thanks.' Malcolm stops in the middle of the corridor. 'Wait, I've just had a brilliant idea.' He narrows his eyes and looks me up and down. 'George is promoting a movie he's made with Julia Roberts right now so there's bound to be lots of calls for the two of them together. I reckon if you wore very high heels, you might just about pass as Julia. We could do lookalike work together again. Jackie wouldn't be super keen to have you back on the books of Fake Faces, of course, but I reckon I could sweet talk her, especially if there's lots of commission to be made. What do you think?'

'Absolutely not.'

'Suit yourself, darling.'

We resume walking. The only good thing about Malcom's ludicrous idea is it delayed the moment I'm dreading.

That moment comes as Malcolm flings opens the door to the hall. The room falls immediately silent and all eyes swivel towards me. My stomach knots as I look at the scuffed parquet and will myself not to turn around and run back the way I came.

'Now Eight H, our rehearsal will start in five minutes. In the meantime, I believe you know Clare Palmer. Clare has very kindly offered to help out with the preparations for this year's talent show and I think you're aware we could do with all the help we can get.'

I'm approached by a small mouse-like woman with big round glasses and teeth that look like baby teeth. 'I'm Suzanne Harris, Eight H's class teacher.' She extends a small limp hand. 'I've heard a lot about you.'

Malcolm sniggers at this but I ignore him. 'Nice to meet you.'

We take our seats and I look around the room. Some of the kids look exactly the same but others I could have walked past in the street and not even recognised. Bethany, who was the epitome of peaches and cream, is now a goth, and Dylan the body farter is over six foot and looks as if he might not get ID-ed in a pub. Meanwhile, Mark, one of the rappers, now identifies as female and goes by the name of Mabel.

'It's weird Alex not being here,' I say.

Malcolm nods. 'Yeah, I miss him. He's a right royal pain, of course, but I still wish he was here.'

'Have you heard how the treatment is going?'

'It's going well apparently. It's still early days but the doctors are hopeful. They've even talked about him being able to fly back to the UK for Christmas.'

'That's great news.' My voice catches.

'No blubbing please, darling.'

'I'm not blubbing,' I say, dabbing my eyes with my sleeve.

'Hi,' Joe says, appearing in front of me.

'Hi.' I am pathetically grateful Joe is acknowledging me, even if it's less than helpful in terms of holding back the tears. There were several kids I came to really care about but Joe has a particularly special place in my heart. He's exactly the sort of boy I imagined my third baby growing up into. The goofball who likes nothing more than making people laugh.

'Er, I've got this joke I'm not sure about.' Joe's voice cracks as he speaks. 'It's about cancer and my mum says there's no way I can do it, and I tried to explain to her that cancer isn't the subject of the joke.' His voice seems to change pitch from word to word. 'Anyway, I'm going to try it today, okay?'

I nod, a huge lump in my throat. Joe is talking to me exactly as he did all those months ago and exactly as he did when he thought I was Jenna.

'Not sure I'm ready for the cancer gags,' Malcolm whispers to me as Joe walks away.

Then he claps his hands together. 'Right Eight H, rehearsal time. Who's first up?'

'Me,' Bethany says.

'Are you doing a Lizzo song?' I ask.

Bethany looks at me as if I've just suggested she sing 'Twinkle Twinkle Little Star'.

'I'm doing poetry.'

She takes to the stage and reads a poem she has written about the death of her granddad. It manages to be horribly dark and yet somehow totally devoid of any actual emotion.

I look around the room and am pleased to see Daisy chatting and laughing with Sophie and Olivia. But then she catches my eye and glares at me with naked disgust. It's hardly surprising, of course, and it's unrealistic to hope everyone is going to be as forgiving as Joe.

'Dead. Dead. Dead,' Bethany intones from the stage. 'Gone.'

'Err…' Malcolm says. 'Well done for kicking us off.' He looks to me and I give a slight shake of my head to indicate I have nothing either.

'I told you I wasn't going to be any use,' I whisper to him.

'Don't be silly,' Malcolm hisses. 'Steven Spielberg couldn't have done anything with *that*.'

The next hour brings a variety of different acts, which range from the awful to the borderline bearable. Malcolm and I do our best to offer notes while Suzanne, a limp dishcloth of a woman, barely says a word. My mind flashes back to Sam sitting next to me in the same spot. He always managed to find something positive to say, even to the dance troupe.

In the breaks, I chat to some of the kids and, to my surprise most are reasonably friendly. Daisy shoots me daggers every time I venture within six foot of her, though.

The physical differences I noticed in so many of the kids are underlined by other changes too. Sara the flautist now plays the guitar, Aaron is shooting the longing looks he reserved for Philippa towards Tom and, when I teased Joe about being surprised to see him eating something other than a peperami, he told me earnestly he's vegetarian now. I guess when you're young, you have to try on lots of different versions of yourself before you settle on the one that fits.

I'm washing my hands in the girls' toilets when Daisy emerges from one of the cubicles.

'I don't know how you've got the nerve to come here.'

'Look, Daisy, you've every right to be angry with me bu—'

'You told me to be myself.' She gives a mirthless half-laugh and leans closer to the mirror to scrutinise a spot on her chin.

'I see the irony, Daisy.'

She places her thumb and forefinger either side of the spot and squeezes hard. 'Yeah, because you weren't exactly being yourself, were you? You were lying to all of us – even Alex who has cancer.'

'You shouldn't squeeze spots.'

She spins round to look at me, her eyes blazing. 'And you shouldn't give people advice.'

'It looks as if things are good between you and Sophie and the others now.'

Daisy goes back to squeezing the spot. 'That's none of your business.'

'If you are going to do that, at least wash your hands first. And use a bit of tissue to put some warm water over the spot. It'll help to open up the pores.'

Daisy scowls at me but then washes her hands. 'Why are you here now? Really?'

I ignore the sting of the 'really'. 'Because Mr Smith asked me to help out.'

Daisy runs a wodge of crumpled-up loo roll under the hot tap and applies it to her chin. 'Why would he do that? You're a nobody.'

Ouch. 'It was better for you to sing "Rainbow" than "Without You", wasn't it? And I gave Joe some advice that helped him with his set? And stopped everyone standing around with penguin arms.'

Daisy squeezes the spot. 'Anyone could do those things.'

'Be gentle.'

'Are you going to come to all the rehearsals?'

'Yes.'

Daisy grunts.

'You don't use the tote bag anymore, then?'

Daisy screws up her small freckled face. 'Er, no. They're like over.'

'Right.'

'So it wasn't you who dated Vince Matty, then? That was the real Jenna?'

'That was the real Jenna.'

'Shame. He's hot.'

Not as hot as Sam.

Daisy squeezes the spot harder and pus splats onto the mirror. 'Alex was really nice about you on TV.'

A lump rises in my throat. 'Yeah, he was.'

'Nicer than I'd have been.'

'Nicer than I'd have been too.' I rummage in my bag and pull out a pot of concealer.

'Do you want a bit of this?'

Daisy looks from me to the reflection of her livid red chin. 'Yeah, go on then.'

Chapter Eighty-Seven

I'm less pleased when I walk back into the hall and there on the other side of it, talking to the dishcloth, is Sam.

'You told me he wouldn't be here,' I whisper furiously to Malcolm.

Malcolm affects a look of innocence. 'Did I?'

'You know you did. You said he isn't even their class teacher anymore so why would...' I let the sentence trail off because Sam is walking towards us.

'Hi,' he says.

'Hi.'

'How are you doing?'

My mouth is so dry that my lips seem to be stuck to my gums. 'I'm... er... fine.'

Brilliant, Clare, show the man the kind of wit and charm he has been missing.

'Good. Bet you see a big difference in the kids, right?'

Sam must be as blindsided by this as I am but is handling himself with considerably more aplomb (not hard). I nod.

'Now,' Malcolm says, swooping his arm through the air. 'I need a favour please. The children have been working away on a scenic backdrop for the show. It's been drying in the art room but it should be ready now. I was wondering if someone might go to collect it. It's quite large so probably best if a couple of you do it.'

'I'll go,' Sam says.

'Me too,' Dishcloth says.

Malcolm puts his hand on Dishcloth's arm. 'Oh no, Suzanne, I need you here. Clare will help Sam, I'm sure.'

Oh my God! Does he think he's subtle? Or that anyone including Dishcloth believes he needs her for anything?

'That's okay, isn't it, Clare?'

'Sure,' I say, blushing furiously and hating my Celtic roots.

I follow Sam out of the hall. 'How have you been?' he says. 'Malcolm says you've got a publishing deal for your new book.'

'Yeah.'

'That's great news. I look forward to reading it. I loved your last one.'

It's great Sam is handling all this so coolly (unlike me) but I do wish he wouldn't be kind. God knows, this is hard enough without that. 'Thanks. Look, er, I'm so sorry about all this. I promise you I had no idea you were going to be here.'

'What?'

'I had n— wait, did you know I'd be here?'

Sam stops walking and stares at me, his brow furrowed. 'Yeah. And I specifically asked Malcolm if you would be happy to see me and he said "very happy".'

Bloody Malcolm! The second I get him alone, he's in for a right pasting. Not that he'll be chastened, of course. I can hear him now: Well, darling, are you telling me you weren't very happy?

Sam sighs heavily and starts walking again. 'I'm sorry to have put you in this awkward position. There's no way in the world I'd have made an appearance if I didn't think that was something you were okay with. I feel like a complete idiot. You'd think I'd have got the message when you failed to return my calls. And feigned illness the night of Malcolm's birthday party.' He puffs out his cheeks.

'I... er... umm.' How can I explain to Sam that I couldn't stand his pity? That I know he's a nice guy and wants to make sure I'm okay after all the fallout, but that I couldn't bear that. It's easier sometimes not to have a bite of a chocolate bar if you can't have the whole thing.

'Let's just get this backdrop and then I'll get out of your hair,' Sam says.

I don't want you out of my hair.

We continue along the corridor in awkward silence, my heart thudding so loudly I'm surprised it's not audible.

After what seems like about seventeen miles, Sam swings open the door to a large light-filled white room that smells of paint and wet clay and PVA glue. 'After you.'

The room is full of kids' artwork and there's everything from brightly coloured Picasso-inspired portraits to huge 3D papier mâché sculptures to collages. Some of the work is rudimentary but other pieces wouldn't look out of place on the wall of a gallery.

Less pleasant to look at is the obvious discomfort etched across Sam's face. 'Sam—'

He looks at me and shakes his head. 'Please don't.'

The backdrop is spread out on the floor. It's predominantly black but scattered with yellow splodges that on closer inspection I think are supposed to be stars. 'Is it a night sky?'

'Yeah. Look, there's the moon.'

'Why a night sky? What's that got to do with the talent show?'

'Stars.'

'Oh, right. That's kind of on the nose, no?'

Sam shrugs. He's not interested in my thoughts on artistic interpretation. 'We'd better get this back to the rehearsal.'

Sam is so close I can smell his clean washing smell. We both reach down for the canvas at the same time and my arm brushes his. He pulls back as if he has been scalded.

'Sorry.'

'What would you have said if I'd called you back?'

'Please, Clare. Don't make this worse than it is. I'm already humiliated. I've acted more like one of the kids in my class than a supposedly sane forty-five-year-old man.'

'What would you have said if I'd called you back?'

'I'm not doing this.'

'Okay,' I blurt out. 'Let's try it this way: I didn't call you back because I don't think I can be "just friends" with you.'

Sam looks visibly shocked and I realise I've massively misjudged the situation and made myself look a right tit (hey, no change there). I stare at the night sky backdrop, my cheeks flaming and the deafening silence ringing out all around me.

'I'd have said I'd love a chance to get to know the real you.'

My heart pounds. 'What?'

Sam smiles in the way that makes his eyes crinkle and my tummy flip. 'I'd have said I'd love a chance to get to know the real you.'

Tears fill my eyes. 'Really?'

Sam reaches out and runs his finger along my cheekbone. 'Nice to meet you, Clare Palmer.'

Chapter Eighty-Eight

Lots of things have changed in the last year but the dance troupe are every bit as awful as they've always been. None of them seem to be even attempting to keep time, they have all the gracefulness of a wrecking ball and their dance/gymnastics mash-up is barely on nodding terms with either discipline.

Yet sitting watching them, it's hard to keep the smile off my face. Sam is back with his own class now but the two of us have arranged to meet for a coffee at the weekend. It's early days, of course, and Sam might not like the real me, but at least I get to show it to him and at least I've rediscovered who that real me is. Kerri with an 'i' told me she's proud of all my hard work and, just for a moment, I almost forgave her all her head cocking and wondering and answering a question with a question.

Meanwhile, Alex's treatment is going well, Daisy has friends (even if she definitely doesn't want to be mine) and Joe is still cracking out jokes.

'Dear God,' Malcolm whispers to me. 'There really is no saving this dance troupe.'

'Nope. They may even have got worse than they were last year. Which is saying something.'

'Still,' Malcolm says, grinning. 'It's been a good day. A *very* good day.'

I roll my eyes and give him a mock punch on the arm. 'You can stop being quite so smug.'

Malcolm's eyes widen. '*Moi*?'

His phone pings and he glances at the screen. 'What did I tell you about the need for George and Julia as a pair? That's a message from Jackie now asking me if I know a Julia for a gig next week. Big corporate do with a nice, fat fee. No chance I can change your mind is there, darling?'

I shake my head. 'No. I'm done being anyone else but me.'

Acknowledgements

Thank you to my brilliant agent, Ger Nichol, for good ideas, advice and always being in my corner.

Thank you to my super-talented editor, Carolyn Mays, who always gets right to the heart of what a book needs. Thanks also to the rest of the team at Bedford Square – Laura Fletcher, Jamie Hodder Williams, Polly Halsey, Anastasia Boama Aboagye, Claudia Bullmore, and Rebecca Weigler.

Thank you to Kay Gale for copy editing and Claire Girvan for proof reading and to Henry Steadman for the fantastic cover.

Thank you to my writer friends, especially Frances Quinn who believed in this book even when I didn't, saved me many a time with an emergency plot clinic and never said she couldn't bear to read yet another draft. A shout out too to Olivia Beirne, who taught me all about theatre school, and Louise Fein, Charlotte Levin, Eleni Kyriacou, Nikki Smith and Gillian Harvey who did more than their fair share of cheerleading.'

Thank you to my other friends for their love and support even when I turn down yet another invitation because I'm writing. Hedy-anne Freedman, Debra Davies, Brian Davies, Caroline Donn, Sara Nair, Nicky Peters, John O'Sullivan, Steve Clinton,

Phil Lewis, Georgina Hayward, Carol Deacon, Gemma Champ, Katia Hadidian, Frani Heyns and Cat Collingwood.

Thank you to my big, mad wonderful family who are always there for me. Jenny Crichton-Stuart, Patrick Crichton-Stuart, Kit Crichton-Stuart, Harry Crichton-Stuart, Freddie Crichton-Stuart, Sophie Crichton-Stuart, Toby Green, Lex Green, Saskia Green and Jo Dangerfield.

Thank you to Mum and Dad for making me believe I could do this. It's an enduring sadness you're not here to see it.

Thank you to all the book sellers and reviewers and bloggers who do so much to spread the book love.

Thank you to every reader who picks up one of my books or takes the time to leave a review or send me a message. I've said it before, but it never fails to make my day.

And finally, last but never least, thank you to my wonderful sons Charlie and Max Gill. I may spend my life making up imaginary people but you two will always be by far my proudest creations.

About the Author

Photo credit © Stuart Gill

Nicola Gill lives in London. At the age of five, when all of the other little girls wanted to be ballet dancers, she decided she wanted to be an author. Her ballet teacher was very relieved. When she's not at her desk, you can usually find Nicola reading, cooking up vast vats of food for friends and family or watching box sets. Occasionally she even leaves the house…

www.nicolagill.com

X @Nicola_J_Gill

@NicolaGillAuthor

Bedford Square Publishers is an independent publisher of fiction and non-fiction, founded in 2022 in the historic streets of Bedford Square London and the sea mist shrouded green of Bedford Square Brighton.

Our goal is to discover irresistible stories and voices that illuminate our world.

We are passionate about connecting our authors to readers across the globe and our independence allows us to do this in original and nimble ways.

The team at Bedford Square Publishers has years of experience and we aim to use that knowledge and creative insight, alongside evolving technology, to reach the right readers for our books. From the ones who read a lot, to the ones who don't consider themselves readers, we aim to find those who will love our books and talk about them as much as we do.

We are hunting for vital new voices from all backgrounds – with books that take the reader to new places and transform perceptions of the world we live in.

Follow us on social media for the latest Bedford Square Publishers news.

@bedsqpublishers
facebook.com/bedfordsq.publishers/
@bedfordsq.publishers